The Divine Sedition

The Divine Zetan Trilogy, Volume 2

Martin Lundqvist

Published by Martin Lundqvist, 2018.

THE DIVINE SEDITION

First edition. July 22, 2018.

Written by Martin Lundqvist.

Also by Martin Lundqvist

Watch for more at martinlundqvist.com.

Chapter 1 Prologue.

(This Chapter summarises the events in The Divine Dissimulation. If you have already read The Divine Dissimulation, you can continue to Chapter 1).

The young and beautiful 22-year old Keila Eisenstein, a prominent leader of The Martian Humanist Alliance, is on the run following a defeat against the Terran Council on the asteroid Sylvia. She is pursued by her nemesis, Rear Admiral Bjorn Muller of the Terran Council. The situation looks dire when Keila has a vision of her dead mother Susanna, urging her to take her ship to the Terraformed asteroid world Eden, and free the Edenites from the tyranny of Abraham Goldstein. Keila's righthand man, Sven, is sceptical of going, but he agrees to drop her off on Eden while trying to shake off their pursuers.

Keila reaches Eden, and she uses an emergency pod to reach the surface. As Keila is descending, she watches how her ship and its crew is Bjorn's ship. Keila releases the safety switch on her emergency pod, and crashes down on the Edenite surface. The impact knocks her unconscious

Bjorn Muller wants to send his men to the surface of Eden to apprehend Keila. However, Abraham Goldstein refuses Bjorn's request to land on Eden. Abraham refuses because Eden is used for his megalomaniacal purpose. Abraham has erased the memories of Martian captives to make them believe that he is the god of Eden. In Abraham's religious scripture, the Abrahameon, it's said that the Edenites is all that remains of mankind, and Abraham fears letting the Edenites find out the truth. After an armed standoff, Bjorn withdraws but he gives Abraham the ultimatum to deliver Keila in three days.

An Edenite called Jeshua finds the unconscious Keila on Eden and brings her to the maintenance tunnels where they are safe from Abraham's orbital laser cannons. Eventually, Keila wakes up and she seduces Jeshua to make him an ally. Keila then falls asleep as she is still dazed from the crash. Jeshua is

1

careless and falls asleep next to her, believing that she is an angel sent to bring him joy.

Nuriel and Gabriel, two super-soldiers who are aiding Abraham's tyranny comes across the sleeping Keila and Jeshua. Fortunately, Jeshua's twin sister Adina, hacks the soldiers' minds and hides Jeshua and Keila from their visions. Keila and Jeshua escapes their pursuers.

Abraham is furious with Nuriel and Gabriel and sends them back to finish the job. Meanwhile, Adina manipulates the Edenites to rebel against Abraham's rule as. Amid the confusion, Keila and Jeshua kill Nuriel and Gabriel while the rest of Abraham's men are repressing the Edenites' uprising.

Adina exposes herself as the one orchestrating the uprising against Abraham, to distract him from chasing Keila and Jeshua. Abraham programs his orbital lasers to fire at her when they are in range. Amid a heated telepathic battle between Adina and Abraham, Keila and Jeshua use the dead super soldiers' outfits, and flies up to Abraham's headquarters, which is orbiting Eden.

Once Keila and Jeshua enter the base, Abraham realises that Adina has manipulated him. Abraham sends his personal bodyguard Abaddon, to eliminate Keila and Jeshua. Abaddon injures Keila and Jeshua, and he is about to kill them, when Adina intervenes. Using her mind-control technology, she tries to take control over Abaddon's body and cause him to kill himself. Abraham notices what Adina is trying to do, and they wrestle mentally for control over Abaddon's body. This releases a psionic blast that kills Abaddon and knocks Adina and Abraham unconscious. The psionic blast saves Adina, as it knocks her out of harm's way, when the orbital lasers fire at her. The fight leaves Adina with amnesia and she is trapped in the maintenance tunnels.

Keila and Jeshua drag themselves to the centre of the Divine Control Centre complex, where they find Abraham's unconscious body. Jeshua wants to kill Abraham, but Keila convinces him that he needs to face Abraham in the Divine Dimension.

In the Divine Dimension, Abraham tells Jeshua that Keila deceived him. Jeshua is confused with but tries to kill Abraham. They fight mentally, but this does not harm their physical bodies as their bodies are not in the Divine Dimension. Suddenly, they drop to the ground. They are bleeding from bullet wounds in their heads and everything fades to black.

In the normal dimension, Keila blows the smoke that buzzed out of her pistol, puts down her smoking baby, and smirks a dangerously sexy smile. Her visions and voices told her to kill Jeshua and Abraham while they were both jacked into the Detector machine.

Chapter 2 Keila decides to stay and fight

Keila was overlooking the control room of the Divine Control Centre. There were no other people in the room except for the corpses of Jeshua, and the robot that had enclosed Abraham Goldstein's brain. *"I did it, mum!"* Keila said to herself, and she remembered the vision of her late mum urging her to free Eden from Abraham's tyranny.

Keila looked at a monitor showing the employees of the Divine Control Centre. There had only been 30 employees running the operations with most functions controlled by automated AI and robots. 12 of these employees had died throughout the years, of which three had met their demise at her hand. All the employees had strange ancient names, and Keila recalled the battle suits they had worn. They had looked like angels of war, and they were referred to as angels in the computer systems.

Keila looked at the display. There were no employees at the entire space station. Instead, they were on Eden trying to restore control among the population.

Keila tried to lock down the space station to avoid that the angels came back, and discovered what she had done to their master. Unfortunately, she lacked the biometric codes required to control the base. Keila was uncertain on how to go ahead. She considered escaping and leaving Eden. There was small space shuttle docked that could take her undetected to a nearby smuggler base. But what would escaping achieve? If she left Eden, the people would succumb to the tyranny of another scumbag, or they would perish as the life support systems would shut down if no-one supervised the automated processes.

Keila decided to stay. Eden was the birthplace of her mother, and Keila's return closed the circle. She would lead the Edenites to a brighter future.

Keila needed to come up with a way to lead Eden. The late Abraham had used mind control technology to control everyone on Eden. Would she do the same? It was not her favoured way to go ahead, as Keila believed in liberating people instead of enslaving them, but it was her only realistic choice. She could fight 18 super soldiers on her own and hope to win. Particularly not, since she was already wounded with a bullet in her leg and one in the arm.

Keila searched the system for the secret to Abraham's mind control, and she found it. There was a scheme of everyone with Divine Technology microchips installed in their brains, and Abraham was the only one who had a God chip installed. Keila kept searching, and she found the schematics for the microchip.

Keila knew that Terrans had a particle replicator machine, which could replicate any item that they had a blueprint for. To her great relief, there was a particle replicator in the very room she was in. She instructed the replicator to make a God chip and a timer started. It would take two hours to finish building the God chip. Keila leaned back in her chair. She was drinking from a glass of water in the one hand, and she grasped her pistol with the other. This would be two nervous hours, but she had made her choice. She would stand her ground here; Eden was her destiny.

Chapter 3 A Close Call

Keila woke up with a twist. Exhaustion had put her asleep despite her efforts to stay awake. The computer beeped with a high-pitched warning sound. She had been unable to lock down the space station, but she had set the alarm in case anyone came in from the outside. She looked at the display and she saw a 3D hologram. There was a whole squad of armed men in battle suits advancing on her position. She looked at the remaining time to make god chip. The timer said 10 minutes, and there was no way she would be able to hold out for that long. Keila realised that she needed to divert the angels for long enough to have the god chip done. Once she had the god chip, she would have a mean to deal with angels.

Keila limped out of the control centre, and she took a position in a side corridor that the angels would pass. She needed to distract the angels from the control centre where the replicator was working. Then she needed to find the way back to the control centre and pick up the god chip once it was ready.

Keila spotted an angel running down a parallel corridor heading to the control centre. She lifted her pistol and shot at him. As she had expected, the gun was not powerful enough to penetrate the angel's battle armour, and the bullets ricocheted off him. The shot caught his attention, and he raised his rifle to shoot at her. Keila jumped around the corner, and avoided the bullets in the last second. She heard him calling out his group to follow him. Her plan was working; now she needed to keep them occupied.

Keila turned around the corner and shot at the angel again. Yet again the bullets bounced off his armour, but this time he was joined by his peers. The angels ran towards her. Keila understood she could never outrun the angels in her injured condition. However, she did have one advantage. Keila's small frame made her fit into ventilation shafts. Keila got into a ventilation shaft, when the angels shot at her. One bullet struck her other leg, and she felt the pain

Keila would not let her injuries stop her, and she crawled through the ventilation shaft. One of the angels threw a gas grenade into the ventilation shaft. She looked behind her, and she identified the grenade. It contained a powerful sleep-inducing gas, and one breath would be enough to knock her unconscious. So, she had to hold her breath!

The ventilation shaft was 50 meters ahead of her. It would be tough, crawling 50 meters crawling in a narrow ventilation shaft with her injuries, but it was what she had to do. Keila squirmed and the goal did not seem to get any closer. She was close to passing out, and she closed her eyes. She saw a vision of herself in paradise with her mum, and her ancestors. *"You can do it,"* they said in unison. When Keila looked up, she was at the end of the tunnel. She was back in the Divine Control Centre. Keila got out of the ventilation shaft, and she limped to the particle replicator machine. The display said 20 seconds, and the angels entered the room. In desperation, Keila lifted her pistol and fired off the remaining rounds at the angels.

Upon hearing Keila's pistol clicking, the angel Samael took off his helmet. He walked towards Keila, while screaming obscenities towards her.

Samael:

- Not feeling so tough now, do you? I will rape you and give you a slow painful death for what you did to Grandmaster Abraham.

Keila:

- I am not the one bringing an army to beat one woman. As for raping me, I bet that your dick is too limp!

Samael:

- Oh, we'll see about that.

Keila:

- Alright, I am here, come to get some tough guy.

After saying this, Keila turned around, pulled her pants down and showed her private parts to the group of angels. This was a diversion, and she could see the timer on the replicator ticking down as Samael got out of his battle armour, ready to rape her. As the timer reached 0, the God chip came out of the replicator.

Without hesitation, Keila grabbed the chip and she crammed it straight into her ear. As it merged with her brain, she screamed in pain and released a strong psionic shockwave that knocked herself, the angels and all the people on Eden unconscious.

Chapter 4 Ascended to Godhood.

Keila woke up in the same courtyard in The Divine Dimension, where Abraham and Jeshua had been before her. Was she dead? The last thing Keila could remember was a sharp pain before everything turned black. But if she was in the afterlife, where were her mum and the spirits that she had seen in her visions? The courtyard was empty, and it had a very ominous feel, albeit it was also at the same time a very beautiful place.

Keila made her way to a pond with glittering water. She looked down into the pond and she could see her body attached to the Divine Detector Machine. The angels kneeled in front of her as if they were praying to her. The same people who had tried to rape and kill her was worshipping her. How did this happen?

Keila closed her eyes, and she saw a vision of herself on a golden throne with gemstones shining more beautiful than her senses could understand. She had a gut feeling that the throne was nearby and that providence had brought her to this sacred place. Keila left the pond and she walked through a gate.

Keila reached the inner sanctum of the complex. The golden throne was at the back end of the room, and there was a lifeless body in front of the throne. She approached the body and examined it. The body was of an old bearded man in robes, but it was neither Abraham nor Jeshua. Who was this dead man?

Keila examined the body. It was a strange feeling. Keila had seen a multitude of dead bodies, but none of them had been like this. There was something godlike and majestic about this body, although the death of the person in front of her was dead disproved divinity. She held the hand of the dead divine and closed her eyes. Keila felt a spiritual connection, and she knew who it was. The dead man was Yahweh, a god worshipped on Earth throughout the millennia. Keila opened her eyes and reflected. What did she know about this Yahweh? Evidently, not very much. The significant disconnect between the wealthy minority on Earth and the impoverished majority on Mars had led to a cultural separation, and the Martians did not know much about Earth's history and the gods that they followed.

Meanwhile, the Edenites that were knocked unconscious from the psionic blast started to wake up, and they called out for Abraham, the imposter god of the Edenites. They were filled with fear and their anxiety got stronger when they did not receive any response from their master. Keila, who now had a divine God chip in her brain, got overwhelmed by all the people trying to connect to her. She could feel their fear, and it overcame her senses. Struggling to breathe, she stumbled out of the throne room and walked towards the Lotus tree in the courtyard. Keila sat down next to the tree, and she felt relieved, like the weight of the world was no longer on her shoulders. Keila sank down into a deep meditative state.

Keila spent the next few hours, which felt like eons, learning about the secrets of the universe. Eventually, a white light came in front of her eyes and her consciousness was back in the normal dimension.

Chapter 5: Metatron wakes Keila.

The angel Metatron observed the agitated and fearful Edenites from the Divine Control Centre. The intended paradise governed according to Yahweh's strict but fair rules, had turned into a hellhole. Chaos reigned, and the Edenites were killing and raping each other on an unprecedented scale.

The trouble had started a few days earlier, when a Terran Council starship had arrived, blowing up a rebel ship, at a height only 1.5 kilometres from Eden's surface. The explosion had caused widespread panic on Eden and exposed their great lie about Earth's destruction. From there, things had gone worse. For no reason, the religious militia on Eden had attacked and killed the angel Eremiel. The idiots Hamshal and Haniel had then made things worse when they arrived with guns blazing decimating the militia. Finally, this mysterious woman, Keila, showed up out of nowhere and killed Grandmaster Abraham Goldstein.

But in chaos, there was an opportunity. Metatron did not approve of the way Abraham had governed Eden, and he could not understand the motivations behind his former master's actions. Before they created Eden, Abraham had promised that they would create a new world and that his authority came directly from Yahweh.

Metatron had been enthusiastic about their prospects and being part of such a grand plan. However, his enthusiasm had diminished over the years, and the turning point was when Abraham's physical body had died, leaving only his brain to survive.

The Abraham who came back, as a human brain enclosed inside a machine, was not the same man as he had served his entire life. The new Abraham was a petty, cruel, and narrow-minded abomination who put the Edenites through torment and fear. The Archangel has Lucifer betrayed Abraham, and when they were sent to punish him, Lucifer took Michael with him to the afterlife.

Why had Lucifer betrayed Abraham? Metatron had given the question some thoughts over the years. He had kept the issue for himself and never discussed it with anyone. If Abraham could kill his favourite angel Lucifer, he would have no problems killing Metatron. But now Abraham was gone, and that's where the opportunity lay.

Metatron knew that his standing among the angels was low, in fact, his status was the lowest in the pecking order. He had worked with maintenance of Eden. Although his efforts were crucial for their survival, he did not receive the same recognition as the other angels got. The others expected him to do his job, but they never credited him for doing so.

When Keila seized the God chip, things had changed. When she inserted it into her ear, the system short-circuited and knocked everyone unconscious from the psionic blast. Metatron woke up first and he had felt the opportunity. Keila could be something that he could not; she could be the next leader of Eden. If he played his cards right, he could become her most trusted angel and get the recognition that he deserved.

Metatron had found Keila unconscious and severely wounded. He had placed her on life support and had connected her to the Divine Detector Machine to send her mind to The Divine Dimension. Hopefully, she would regain consciousness and make it possible for the other angels to feel her presence.

Metatron's plan had worked out. The other angels felt her presence, and he had convinced them to elevate her to leadership instead of avenging Abraham's death.

Metatron decided that it was time to talk to Keila. It would help if, he was the first person that she saw. He walked up to Keila's bed and disconnected her from the Divine Detector Machine. This transported her consciousness back to the room she was in. Keila woke up

Keila looked around the room. She could swear that she had been to a extra-terrestrial paradise for several hours, Keila often had intense dreams, but what she had experienced was stronger than any dream. A very handsome man greeted her.

Metatron:

- Welcome back, Mistress Keila. The angel Metatron at your service.

Keila:

- Okay. Am I a prisoner here?

Metatron:

- Absolutely not, quite the contrary. You are the possessor of the God chip, and thus you are the rightful ruler of Eden. At least that's what I told my peers.

Keila:

- But you don't think so?

Metatron:

- I am a humble servant of the divine master. what I think does not matter.

Keila:

- Cut the bullshit. Last thing I remember before the blast I was to be gang-raped, tortured, and killed.

- Now you're talking about elevating me to leadership. What's going on here?

Metatron:

- Okay, if you prefer me to be upfront.

- The psionic blast should have killed you. It probably would have if I did not wake up first and connected you to the life support unit.

- I have argued that you survived the blast to convince the others that Yahweh sent you to replace Abraham, as Abraham had strayed from the righteous path.

- Whether you survived due to divine intervention, or my intervention is irrelevant. If we play our cards right, we can rule Eden together.

Keila:

- What happen if I don't want to take part?

Metatron:

- Well, then I assume that a slow and painful death awaits us when the other angels find out.

Keila:

- That's a good enough motivation for me. I am in on your scheme.

Metatron:

- Good. You'll tell the others that Yahweh sent you to replace Abraham, who strayed from the path.

Keila:

- Got it.

Metatron:

- Just between you and me, did Yahweh send you?

Keila:

- I am unsure. I had visions that told me to come here to Eden after I escaped the Terran fleet at the Asteroid Sylvia.

Keila paused for a bit, she was unsure whether she would tell her new-found ally about seeing the corpse of Yahweh. Keila disclosed everything, as Metatron was the reason, she was still alive.

Keila:

- In my dream, I saw a dead man. I think it was Yahweh.

Metatron studied Keila in silence for a while. Eventually, he spoke up.
Metatron:

- What you experienced was not a dream. It was real. Your mind travelled to the Divine Dimension when I connected you to the Divine Detector Machine.

- If Yahweh is dead, Abraham must have killed him. Yahweh has been looking after our people for over 5000 years. What will become of us now?

- Then again, you could be lying...

Keila:

- It's quite easy for you to find out the truth. Connect yourself to the machine, and go to the throne room. You'll find Yahweh's corpse there.

Metatron:

- But I am just a man, I am not worthy.

Keila:

- Says who?
- If God is dead, who decides who is worthy to enter his domains?

Metatron:

- You are right. I have sent too much time following others. Send my consciousness to the Divine Dimension.

Keila connected Metatron to the Divine Detector Machine. She looked at Metatron's face; he had a masculine and good-looking face, albeit he looked a decade older than her. Metatron slept peacefully.

Seeing Metatron in this helpless state gave Keila terrible flashbacks to her betrayal of Jeshua, whom she had murdered the day before. She had acted on strange voices that told her to murder Jeshua while he was connected to the machine. Her visions were never wrong, and her premonitions was the reason that she had become the beacon of light for the downtrodden masses of the solar system. Keila's regretted killing Jeshua, and she broke down in tears from what she had done.

Eventually, Metatron came back from the Divine Dimension. He was awestricken from what he had seen. Yahweh was dead, and his entire life's purpose to honour Yahweh had come to naught.

Metatron saw Keila sitting in a corner crying. He followed his instinct and went over to her, held her tight and then started crying himself. They sat there for hours, crying silently without saying anything. It was the closest Metatron had ever felt to someone.

Chapter 6 The Zetans Discussing the Events.

The extra-terrestrial species known as the Zetans, gathered in a semi-circle, around an obelisk that they had erected in The Divine Dimension. They remembered the day of Yahweh's betrayal, that took place more than a millennium ago. In the distance, they could see the palace that Yahweh had expelled them from. It was as impressive as it had been when they built it thousands of years ago, but the tear in the space-time that enclosed the palace stopped them from returning.

The Zetans were the most advanced species to ever appear in the universe and the only ones to ever manage to physically travel between the normal dimension and the Divine Dimension.

At the height of their civilisation, they had portals spread across the Milky Way Galaxy that could teleport them between the normal dimension and the Divine Dimension and then back to another location in the normal dimension. This way, they could travel faster than light.

All of this had been lost in the apocalyptic war between the Zetans and the failed product of their own creation, the Xenos. This war wiped out the Zetan civilisation. The war destroyed their home planet Zetani and killed most of their species, except for a few Zetans scattered in the Divine Dimension.

The few Zetans remaining in the universe had led stagnant lives in the Divine Dimension. However, they could activate their portals to Earth, and pose as gods to the simple-minded humans on Earth. This way, they would receive the offerings that they needed to have a good life in the Divine Dimension. All of this was destroyed, when Yahweh had a psychotic breakdown, and destroyed the last active Zetan portal to Earth, and killed himself and his secret lover.

Since Yahweh destroyed the last active portal to Earth, the Zetans had millennia of hell. Being physical beings, they needed food and drinks to sustain themselves, yet nothing of this was available in the Divine Dimension. With the state of timelessness of the Divine Dimension, they couldn't die from natural causes, age, or bear offspring. Yet as physical beings, they could feel thirst and hunger. The result was that they were always hungry and thirsty, while being kept alive by the Divine Dimensions' timelessness

When they had gathered, Zeus spoke:

- Fellow Zetans! For thousands of years, we have been starving in this timeless abyss. But I see hope in the form a human, a promised human that will reactivate the portals and give us back our rightful place as gods on earth.

- The woman's name Keila Eisenstein, and she has something that our former hosts were lacking. She has access to a technology level that is unprecedented in the history of mankind, almost on par with our technology during the peak of our civilisation.

- She has disposed of Abraham who was following the teachings of the traitor Yahweh, and taken control over Eden.

Odin:

- I am questioning your faith in Keila. She is the sworn enemy of the Terran Council that rules Earth and Mars. Having her travel around on Earth to restart our portals to Earth seems impossible. Why are we not influencing a powerful Terran to do our bidding, instead of using a Martian woman?

Zeus:

- Influencing a Terran leader would be better, but unfortunately, the genetic makeup of humans makes a telepathic connection to them implausible. That is why we only get a human that we can influence once every few hundred years. In our time, the destined human is Keila.

- Keila is our future. I have foreseen it, and my premonitions are never wrong.

Brahma felt obliged to join in on the conversation:

- Zeus, if your "premonitions" are so flawless, how come our civilisation got wiped out by the Xenos. Why did you let Yahweh destroy the last active portal to Earth, our only way back to the normal dimension?

Zeus:

- Silence! I never claimed omniscience. I argued that all my premonitions are correct, that is not the same. I never claimed we would not get destroyed by the Xenos, I never claimed Yahweh would not betray us. Whenever I do share a premonition, it comes true.

Brahma:

- Is that so?
- You seemed surprised when Keila murdered Jeshua.

Zeus:

- Yes, that was surprising since we only influenced her to kill Abraham. Then again humans are volatile and prone to violence. They have their own willpower, that's why we used them to fight the Xenos in the multimillennial war.

- However, the killing of Jeshua does not concern us, and everything is going according to plan.

- I would like to thank Odin for his efforts. If he hadn't helped me direct the psionic blast resulting from Keila's incorrect usage of the divine crown, we would not have received a favourable outcome.

- I declare this meeting finished. I urge you to keep observing human activities in the regular universe so we can come up with a
plan on how to continue.

After this, the Zetans dispersed, and each went on their own way. Although they did not have anywhere to go, most of them preferred solitude as
they could meditate deeper in that state.

Most of the Zetan communication occurred telepathically, so they did
not need to be close to each other to talk. Moreover, the presence of too
many peers amassed too much psionic energy in one place. This prevented
the Zetans from reaching deep meditation. Most Zetans preferred to be
in deep meditation, as that was the only state of mind where the Zetans
wouldn't feel the hunger and the thirst that tormented them.

Brahma reached his meditation spot and was tormented by a thought.
What if Rangda had influenced Keila to murder Jeshua? The idea gave him
shivers, and he shrugged it off. Rangda was condemned to stay in a small
prison cell, with a psionic force field that stopped her from contacting anyone. Full of discomfort, Brahma went to sleep to forget about his hunger and
thirst. His sleep was full of nightmares.

Chapter 7 Rear Admiral Bjorn Muller
Becomes Restless

Rear Admiral Bjorn Muller put down the glass of fine Scotch that he was drinking. The alcohol had not helped, and he was reluctant to have another glass. Bjorn was a high-ranking officer in the Terran Council Interplanetary Forces, and it was inappropriate for him to get drunk while on duty.

Bjorn was frustrated that he hadn't heard anything from Nuriel regarding his request to have Keila Eisenstein captured and handed her over to him. He had given them three days and three days had passed. Yet he hadn't heard anything from them, which compelled him to act. Unfortunately, his options were limited. His superior, Admiral Max Wellington, had not sent him any backup and attacking the asteroid B528A, also known as Eden, with a single ship, amounted to suicide.

Bjorn needed a success story, and the capture of a figurehead of the Martian rebellion would gain him a well-deserved promotion. This promotion would take him off active duty in this interplanetary wasteland and give him a cushy lifestyle back on earth. Bjorn wanted a position on the House Muller board as a military advisor. Bjorn felt resigned to his fate. He had been so close to returning to Earth for the last 20 years, but the breakthrough never seemed to come. He damned his younger self for being so ambitious and excelling at the aptitude tests in his youth. If he had been more like his younger brother, his life would be so much better.

Bjorn's brother, Michael, was uninterested in his career, but was, due to his family ties, running one of the House Muller's horse racecourses. Michael was not interested in managing anything, but he served as a figurehead for the racetrack doing what he liked doing, drinking, and mingling. Michael would never be taken seriously, but his life was enjoyable.

Bjorn's other brother, Benjamin, ruled by his father's, Joachim Muller's, side. This led to deep jealousy and between him and Bjorn.

Bjorn's military ambitions led to him being stuck on a gloomy military spaceship with nothing but the darkness of space to look at. Bjorn had no family of his own and would never have if he couldn't get out of active duty. Bjorn was 70 years old, and although he could live to more than double that age without complications due to DNA regeneration technology, Bjorn felt that his life was drawing to the end. Bjorn decided that it was time to act. He went to the hologram generator and he contacted the Divine Control Centre.

Keila woke up with a shocked expression when she saw the lifelike hologram of Bjorn Muller in her room. She reached for her gun and gave out a loud shriek when she couldn't find it. Metatron rushed in to find out what the commotion was about.

Metatron:

- Is everything okay, Mistress Keila?

Keila:

- What is Bjorn Muller doing here?

Metatron:

- That is a hologram machine. He is calling us.

Keila calmed down. She felt silly for panicking at a hologram machine. They had hologram machines on Mars as well, although the devices they had on her home planet made it obvious that is was a hologram, made it almost impossible to tell a hologram apart from a real human.

Keila:

- Are we able to blow up his ship with the weapons on this station?

Metatron

- Yes, but we need to get him in range first.

Keila closed her eyes. A vision came up. It was her mother, and the message was clear. *"Keila, tread carefully. No one needs to die today. This not your destiny."*

Keila:

- No, we should try to avoid violence. I want you speak to him and find out what he wants.

Metatron stepped up on the hologram transmitter and started a communications link with Bjorn.

- This is Metatron from House Goldstein. State your business, commander.

Bjorn:

- This is Rear Admiral Bjorn Muller from the Terran Council Interplanetary Security Forces.

Metatron:

- Okay, state your business, commander.

Bjorn felt how his anger was growing; the arrogant bastard, Metatron, disdained his rank to provoke him. He controlled his temper, and stayed on track.

Bjorn:

- My business as a REAR ADMIRAL for the Terran Council Interplanetary Security Forces is to bring in the fugitive terrorist, Keila Eisenstein. I have already discussed this with your colleague Michael Bernsmith, also known as Nuriel. I do not have the patience to explain myself again. Put Nuriel through!

Metatron:

- There is a slight problem with that request. Nuriel is permanently indisposed, so you'll have to discuss the matter with me.

Bjorn:

- Permanently indisposed?

Metatron:

- I am sure that you understand the term and its implications. Now say what you need.

Bjorn:

- We gave you three days to deliver Keila to us. The time is up, where is she?

Metatron:

- Due to Nuriel's unfortunate passing, that message didn't reach me. I will investigate the matter and see if we can aid you. We'll get back to you in a couple of days.

Bjorn:

- Listen up, you insolent twat! You have failed to carry out your part of the deal, and my men will land on Eden and apprehend Keila ourselves.

Metatron:

- Unfortunately, we would consider that trespassing. That would force us to eliminate you and all your men.

Bjorn:

- This is unacceptable. You are threatening a Terran Council Rear Admiral!

Metatron:

- I am not issuing threats. I am stating a fact.

- If the Terran Council wanted to take something with force, you would show up with a fleet and not a single ship. Stay where you are, commander, I will discuss the matter with my colleagues and get back to you.

- Metatron Out!

As Metatron stepped off the hologram transmitter, he sighed. What a mess they were in. Mistress Keila would never surrender to the Terran Council, and if they did not cooperate, Bjorn would get reinforcements and attack the battle station. He looked at Keila, and she spoke:

- Just as I thought. Bjorn is after me.

Metatron:

- Yes, I assume you are not keen to surrender yourself?

Keila:

- I'll pass. Torture and a public execution don't sound enticing.
- But what if we could give him my corpse?

Metatron:

- Your corpse? You want me to kill you and hand over your body?

Keila:

- Not my real corpse. A decoy.
- How long would it take you to make a clone of me in your medical lab?

Metatron:

- It would take years to make functional clone with memories and well-developed neural patterns.

Keila:

- No not a functional clone. Create a sack of meat and bones that looks like me.

Metatron:

- That would take a couple of days. However, an autopsy would reveal the fraud.

Keila:

- I know about Bjorn Muller. He would swallow the bait sink and hook with no questions.

- Just think about it, he can be the hero of the Terran Council, and finally get his promotion, so he can go back to Earth. If he summons the fleet, his superior will get all the credit.

Metatron:

- You seem sure about this guy.

Keila:

- Yes. Our paths have crossed in the past.

Metatron:

- Okay. Let's do this.

Metatron stepped up on the hologram sender and contacted Bjorn. As Bjorn answered, Metatron stated *"We'll bring her to you in 48 hours".* Then Metatron ended the transmission, without giving Bjorn Muller a chance to get another word in.

Chapter 8 The "Murder" and Delivery of Keila Eisenstein

Keila examined her non-functional clone. It was a dark and surreal experience, like watching a real-life wax doll of herself. The clone was not more alive than the wax doll, and it would never be. The accelerated cloning process didn't create a functioning nerve system. This excluded the possibility of consciousness in the organism.

Metatron stepped into the room. He glanced at the clone and then looked at Keila.

Keila:

- Hey Met! Don't be creepy!

Metatron:

- She looks like the spitting image of you!
- Ready for the last step of the plan?

Keila:

- Yes.

Metatron:

- Okay, here is your pistol. You do the honours.

Metatron gave Keila a pistol and turned a switch, which sent an electric current to the heart of the clone to simulate a beating heart. Keila shot the clone multiple times, destroying its brain and spine. This was to mask that the nervous system of the clone had never been functional. Metatron and a few other angels then wheeled the bed where the clone was strapped onto a shuttle. Metatron set course for Bjorn's command ship ISS Supreme Earth.

Bjorn met them as they docked. He had many armed soldiers by his side. Bjorn walked up to Metatron and spoke:

- Where are Keila? You are supposed to bring Keila Eisenstein, and I cannot see her.

Metatron:

- Look in the body bag.

Bjorn:

- Why did you kill her? From the damages, it seems like she is permanently dead beyond resurrection.

- I told you to bring her, I didn't ask you to kill her! We need her alive for intelligence gathering and a public execution.

Metatron:

- The bitch made a run for it. We had to put her down and make sure that she stayed down.

- We promised to bring her, and we did. We upheld our part of the deal.

Bjorn:

- You idiots. I should arrest you!

Metatron:

- That's a terrible idea since you are still within firing range of our battle station.

- We have gone out of our way to help you. Go home to your masters on Earth.

- Farewell.

Having said this, Metatron and his group went back to the shuttle. The Shuttle took off and flew back to the Divine Control Centre. Bjorn commanded one of his officers to bring Keila's corpse to the science bay while he returned to his private room to reflect.

Chapter 9 Bjorn Muller's Dilemma

Bjorn was lying in the Jacuzzi bathtub installed in his private quarters. Despite having his body in peak condition, he felt phantom pains in a previously lost body part that had been replaced. The phantom pains annoyed Bjorn, there was no reason to have them, and yet he was unable to let them go. He was thinking of Keila. He could not decide whether he was relieved that she was finally dead or angry that he was not the one to kill her. He was mad at Metatron, whose real name was Jack Silver, and Bjorn vowed to get his. Regardless, there was nothing he could do about the idiots on Eden, and there was bigger fish to fry.

Bjorn thought back on his first meeting with Keila, four years earlier. She had caused him immense pain and suffering, but he was to blame for what happened. Keila had been 18 back then and insignificant for the revolution, not one of the poster girls of the Martian revolution that she became later. Keila had tried to travel illegally to Earth when he caught her.

Bjorn was 66 years when he first met Keila, and he was an attractive bachelor back on Earth due to his family wealth and DNA regenerated good looks, which made him look like he was in his 30s. Unfortunately, Keila had attracted a strong urge in him that he did not usually feel. He had felt the urge to subjugate and dominate her.

Bjorn had taken Keila to his private quarters and forced himself on her multiple times. He had kept her there for a long time until he got carried away, and forgot that she was not in bed with him by her free will.

Bjorn had made Keila give him fellatio. This had ended badly with Keila spitting out his severed member on the floor. This left Bjorn in excruciating pain, while Keila headed for an emergency escape pod and escaped back to Mars.

Being ashamed over the incident, Bjorn had not told anyone about Keila. Instead he had been in agonising pain for several days until he could reach a private reconstruction clinic and get restored with DNA repair technology. Although his body had recovered to peak condition, he could still feel the phantom pains, and the last few days had worsened the pains.

To cover up his shameful act, Bjorn had cleared all the records of Keila's capture from the mainframe of the ISS Supreme Earth. He had kept a copy of everything on a private drive, in case he would need it in the future. On this private drive, there was a record of Keila's DNA, and the corpse was a perfect match. Bjorn decided that he would not wait to publicise the news, he would finally get the glory he deserved!

Chapter 10 "Notorious terrorist Keila Eisenstein killed by Bjorn Muller's Troops."

*G**reat news for all the rightful people in the solar system! The notorious terrorist Keila Eisenstein has been eliminated by the brave souls of the Terran Council Interplanetary Security Forces, who are defending our freedom and safety. Miss Eisenstein, who escaped when her brethren fell to the superior might of the Terran Council during the battle of the asteroid Sylvia, was pursued by the valiant troops of Rear Admiral Bjorn Muller, who fought through hordes of rebel scum before reaching Keila's ship Miss Freedom, which was obliterated. Unfortunately, Keila escaped yet again landing on an independent colony, turning the peaceful population on Eden against the just cause of the Terran Council.*

Fortunately, the local people were not deceived by her debauchery and they aided Bjorn team to eliminate the vile terrorist. Unfortunately, they attacked her with such ferocity that her corpse is in such a bad condition that it will be impossible to revive her and trial her for her crimes.

Rear Admiral Bjorn Muller comments, "This is a great day for the families of the victims of Keila's crimes. It's an even greater day for all the good people of Earth who have seen their lives disrupted by the actions of Keila's terrorist group. With the rebels out of the way, trade can resume, and the good people have yet again a chance to make an honest living."

Terran Council Interplanetary Forces press release 20th February 2872

Chapter 11 Chief Scientist Markus Bauer Gets Suspicious

Markus Bauer was lying in a hot bath trying to shake off the cold. He hated waking up from cryogenic sleep, but it was better than wasting his life doing unqualified diminutive tasks for the army. When Markus Bauer enrolled for the ship, Bjorn Muller had told him that he could be cryogenically sleeping for most of his tenure. It had sounded great as it enabled him to get paid for 5 years, being able to afford a beautiful house when he got back to Earth while not aging for most of his tenure. The drawback was missing out on what happened with his parents back on Earth and the disconnect that it caused. The worst drawback, however, was the cold when waking up after a session of cryogenic sleep, and Markus loathed waking up.

Eventually, Markus felt warm enough. He put away his tea, got up from the bath, and got dressed. He had a look at his briefing. His goal was to confirm the identity and the cause of death of Keila Eisenstein. His boss had already publicised that Keila was dead. So, Bjorn expected Markus to fall in line with his boss' expectation and confirm Keila's death. Markus scoffed at the notion that he would be Bjorn's lapdog. He had professional principles and would do a thorough job at examining the case.

Markus entered the scientific lab and he realised that something was amiss. The explanation to the many bullet holes penetrating the body was that Keila was running away from her pursuers and they shot her from behind to make sure she collapsed and died.

Markus dismissed this claim. All the bullets had the same entry angle, and none of the wounds showed any signs of fibre from clothing or body armour. Hence, Markus concluded that Keila must have been shot while lying naked facing down. Why had they acted this way? They should have known that Keila was more valuable to the Terran Council alive. Instead, her brain and nerve system were wrecked by the abundance of bullets penetrating her body. Was the Edenites hiding something?

Another thing bothered Markus, how could he know that this, was the body of Keila and not a random corpse? He had a file on the system that supposedly was the DNA of Keila, and that DNA was matching the body. However, the origin of that file was mysterious. Usually, a record with the DNA of a suspect would come with reports stating how and when the DNA was collected and a detailed dossier on the suspect. Nothing of that was available, just a date stamp for the DNA file, 25 April 2868.

"25 April 2868," Markus thought about the date. He recalled something. That day, an escape pod had disconnected from the ship and crashed on Mars. When he had met with Bjorn to discuss the matter, Bjorn had screamed at him and told him that it was none of his business. This could not be a coincidence.

Markus was thinking a bit longer. Bjorn was hiding something, but he could not be collaborating with the rebels. Bjorn had ordered the destruction of Keila's ship, thus killing its crew only a week earlier. Markus could not contain himself any longer. He walked to Bjorn's quarters to confront him and find out the truth.

Chapter 12: Markus Bauer Confronts Bjorn Muller.

B jorn Muller was enjoying a sensual massage from a limited AI massage robotic drone. The machine looked and felt like a human female, but due to its limited programming, it was only useful at giving massages. Bjorn Muller was happy this way. Although he could afford to bring a female employee from Earth to please his demands, he felt that it was awkward to have one sticking around on a military space vessel. Likewise, a part of him was yearning for a relationship, yet, he felt that his military career was a barrier to such pursuits. Midway through the massage, Bjorn received a message that Markus Bauer requested to see him. Bjorn granted Markus' request; the massage could always wait until after the meeting.

Bjorn got dressed, sat down at his desk, and commanded the AI to let Markus in. Markus walked up to him, but before he had time to say anything, Bjorn spoke.

- Welcome, Markus. Are you here to explain yourself regarding your delay?

Markus:

- I beg your pardon.

Bjorn:

- I have already identified Keila and broadcasted her death. I woke you up seven hours ago to verify her death. Yet you still have not updated our networks with your verification.

Markus:

- Unlike some people, I take my professional integrity seriously. I am here to discuss my findings with you.

Bjorn's gaze blackened; he had not expected this formality to become an issue. *"Go on,"* he said.

Markus:

- "The angels" explanation for what happened does not match reality. I concluded that Keila must have been shot with multiple bullets from the same pistol and the same position, while she was lying face down. Furthermore, as there are no traces of fibre in her wounds, I concluded that she was naked when she was shot.

Bjorn:

- Yes, I thought the same thing, but there was no opportunity to confront those religious fanatics about it when they were threatening us with their battle station.

Markus:

- Did you let them get away with threatening you?

Bjorn:

- Yes. It would be madness for this single ship to fight a battle station. Besides, those religious fanatics would not stand back from a fight.

- Regardless, Keila is dead, and I have already confirmed her identity. Now I am waiting for you to do your part so that we can finalise our report.

Markus:

- About that... I can't identify Ms Eisenstein with enough accuracy. I need to make a thorough examination to conclude the matter.

Bjorn:

- What is there to examine? We have both visual identification and DNA identification.

Markus:

- The visual identification is non-conclusive, due to the wounds of the corpse. Due to the extent of damage to the body, we cannot exclude that they have handed us a non-functional clone of Keila. I also find it unsettling that Keila's DNA profile did not come with a report on how the sample was gathered.

Bjorn:

- The DNA profile of Keila does come with more files, but they are above your clearance level.

Markus:

- Okay. If you give me access to the extra files, that would speed up my work.

Bjorn:

- I do not have the patience for this bullshit! As a Rear Admiral for the Terran Council, I command you to verify my report and go back to sleep.

Markus:

- As a Chief scientist, my primary allegiance lies with the Science Commission. I am expecting your full cooperation in enabling me to make an independent review of this case. If you don't, I will report you to the Science Commission.

Bjorn Muller:

- I will see what I can do to help you, Chief Scientist Bauer.
- Dismissed.

When Markus Bauer had left, Bjorn Muller punched his female massage robot to release his anger. Bjorn heard a fizz as it broke and the massage robot fell lifeless to the floor. That insolent son of a bitch Markus Bauer! This was Bjorn's ship, and a scientist should not dare to oppose him. Bjorn also felt fear. He realised that he had made a crucial mistake and that Keila could still be alive. Worse yet he had deleted her files to cover up his past actions.

After escaping from Bjorn, Keila rose to fame after assassinating Hans Muller, who was the chairman of the Terran Council at the time. The fact that a Martian rebel assassinated the leader of the Terran Council, inspired the downtrodden masses of the solar system to rebel against the Terran Council. This had increased the popular support for The Martian Humanist Alliance, who were the enemies of the Terran Council, and Bjorn had fought this rebellion for the last four years.

To summarise, because Bjorn hadn't contained his sexual desires, the solar system was drawn into a four-year war. He had indirectly caused this war by keeping Keila as a sex slave, as she had killed his grandfather, Hans Muller, after she escaped. The rebellion had caused many fatalities and had halted commerce. The latter had brought Earth to a financial standstill and threatened Terran Council's dominance. Bjorn knew if his peers found out what he had done, his life would be lost. He had to deal with the situation as fast as he could. Bjorn stuck with his idea that Keila was dead, and that she needed to stay that way!

Chapter 13 An Explosion in the Science Bay

M arkus Bauer was eyeing through the files about Keila that Bjorn had given him clearance to view. While they contained interesting information, it was not the files he was after. He was after the DNA collection reports from when Keila's DNA was collected. Markus looked at the corpse one more time. She looked familiar, and he could recall seeing her escorted to a cell some years ago. But he could not recall when he had seen her, and Markus could not be sure of meeting her. However, he did remember whispers about a missing prisoner around the time when Keila's DNA was collected.

Markus opened a file regarding Keila's family history. He could see why this section was classified, as the DNA backtrack analysis revealed that Keila's father was the prominent Terran, Mahmoud Rashid. Mahmoud was disowned by his wealthy family for running off with a non-approved lower caste woman. Markus searched for Mahmoud Rashid. He was born the same year as Bjorn Muller and he died many years ago. Was it possible that Mahmoud and Bjorn had been friends and Bjorn had helped his friend's daughter to escape her imprisonment? This was pure speculation, and Markus realised that he would be better off keeping this thought to himself.

Markus looked at a photo of Keila and the date that her DNA sample was collected. He had a flashback; he was sure that he had seen Keila passing him in the corridor escorted by Bjorn on that day. He also recalled a missing escape pod a few weeks later, and that a prisoner that was deleted from the prisoner checklist. Considering Hans Muller was assassinated by Keila a few weeks later, Keila and Bjorn could be conspiring against the leadership of House Muller and against the Terran Council.

Markus realised that this knowledge posed a severe threat to his life. He needed to find the right people on Earth and make sure that his transmission was encrypted, so Bjorn would not realise that Markus was dobbing him in.

Unfortunately, staff members were not allowed to bring encrypted messaging devices onto the ISS Supreme Earth, except for Bjorn, who had a private encrypted phone. Stealing Bjorn's phone would not be easy, but it was the only way to set things right.

Suddenly, Markus saw a display flashing, *"Contamination detected, Science bay to disconnect in 30 seconds"*. Markus ran to the door, but it was sealed. Acting instinctively, he grabbed the memory unit and an oxygen tank and jumped into an airtight safety-capsule. Seconds later there was a small targeted explosion, and the Science Bay was dislodged from the rest of ISS Supreme Earth.

Chapter 14 Bjorn Muller Orders a Retreat to Repair the Spaceship

B jorn Muller was finishing up his report on the dislodged Science Bay incident. On this occasion, he had been forced to use the keyboard instead of mind-typing which he usually preferred. Mind-typing was a technology where one could put a hat with electrodes on one's head and use that to write documents using one's thoughts. While mind-typing was faster and more convenient, Bjorn used the keyboard on this occasion as he was worried that his mind would betray him and reveal the truth in the report. It had been a couple of stressful hours after the explosion, and one of the crew members, Matt Johnson, was accidentally sucked out into the vacuum of space when they were fixing the damages from the explosion. Bjorn felt sorry for Matt; he had liked the man and felt guilt that his actions that had caused Matt's death.

Bjorn tried to shrug off what happened to Matt; casualties were the fuel of the war machine, and Matt knew what he signed up for. Bjorn checked report that he had written to the council. Its' summary said:

"At 03:00 hours, a collision with a meteor caused a computer malfunction. This caused an explosion that dislodged the science bay from ISS Supreme Earth. Chief Scientist Markus Bauer died in the blast, and Technical Sergeant Matt Johnson died when performing emergency repairs. With the loss of the Science Bay, we lost the following items listed in Appendix 2. Due to the damages to the ship, I ordered the ship to retreat to the closest base without retrieving the lost cargo, as this is a dangerous part of space."

Bjorn looked down on the report. He told himself that he would be alright and that no one would question the validity of the statement. He got interrupted when Captain Adal Schneider requested to see him. Bjorn acknowledged this request and Adal walked into his office. Bjorn studied his 2nd in charge officer, he shared the same idealised North European features as

Bjorn, but Adal looked a lot older than Bjorn despite being 20 years younger. This was because Adal was not wealthy enough to afford top-quality DNA regeneration technology, so he had to settle for cheaper remedies. He walked up to Bjorn's desk.

Adal:

- Sir! We have received an emergency beacon from Chief Scientist Markus Bauer.

Bjorn:

- That must be a mistake, there is no way that he could have survived the explosion and several hours in space.

Adal:

- Nonetheless, I ask that we go back and retrieve the bodies of Matt Johnson and Markus Bauer for their families' sake.

Bjorn:

- Request denied. The ship has sustained damages, and this area of space is not safe. There might still be rebels or pirates in the vicinity.

Adal Schneider:

- Our thermal scanners indicate that there is not a single ship within a 1-million-kilometre radius from us, and the Science Bay is only 90,000 kilometres away. We can retrieve them without any worries.

Bjorn Muller:

- For all we know, the thermal scanners might be damaged as well. We are continuing to outpost 5 for service and repairs.

Adal Schneider:

- Please, Rear Admiral Muller, I am the Captain of this ship. I am in command in your absence, and I want to show my men that I care about them.

Bjorn Muller:

- I do not look absent, do I?
- Proceed to outpost 5 at once.
- Dismissed Captain.

As Adal left the room, Bjorn sighed and leaned back in his chair. What a mess he was in! If only that idiot Markus could have followed orders instead of causing all of this. Bjorn looked for something to punch, but he couldn't find anything, so he took some sedatives and went to sleep.

Chapter 15 Keila Hears About the Explosion and Gets an Idea.

Keila was practising target shooting on a realistic hologram of Bjorn Muller. She was filled with rage and frustration that she hadn't put an end to him when she had the chance. Keila could either have destroyed his ships using the weapon systems on her base, or she could have mind-controlled one of the angels to shoot him when they delivered her *"corpse"* to him. She had chosen to contain her murderous tendencies and instead play the waiting game. Bjorn Muller was a filthy rapist who had violated her, and he would pay for it, but he would pay when it could further her goals. A week ago, she would have given her life to end his. However, since she had found Eden and the Divine Dimension, she had gained a new perspective, and she hoped that hidden Zetan technologies would be the turning point of this centuries-long conflict within humankind. Keila loaded her pistol with another magazine and she unleashed her rage against the hologram. The gun clicked, and Metatron entered the room.

Metatron:

- You are an abysmal shooter, Keila.

Keila:

- No, I am not?

Metatron:

- Yes, you are. You scored only 75 % mortal hits from 15 meters. I have military capabilities nanotechnology chips implanted that give me perfect shooting at that range.

- Hand me the pistol.

She handed him the pistol. Metatron fired 15 shots, with extreme precision.

Metatron:

- That's how you do it, 100 % mortal hits in less than 10 seconds!

Keila:

- Wow! You must have trained a lot!

Metatron:

- Why would I waste time and bullets training? My nanotechnology implant gives me near-perfect marksmanship.

- We have a few spares actually; I can implant one in your brain if you want to?

Keila:

- No, thank you. I promised myself that I would never be a machine, and yet I implanted a God chip in my brain.

- Besides what will you do if your technology malfunctions and you haven't trained? You'd be useless.

Metatron:

- The technology won't fail, so that's a hypothetical scenario.

- Regardless, I didn't come here to discuss the merits of nanotechnology augmentations.

- We have news. There was an explosion on the ISS Supreme Earth, and we have received a distress beacon from one of their crew members.

Keila:

- Yes, I predicted that would happen. As for the beacon, do not respond to it.

Metatron:

- Understood, mistress. Why did you Anticipate an explosion? Did you rig your corpse with a bomb?

Keila:

- Let's just say Bjorn, and I share a less than cordial past. I reckon he would be petrified over the prospect that his scientists would revive and interrogate my corpse. That would expose his secret.

Metatron:

- Understood, Mistress Keila.

- May I suggest that we speed up our efforts to regain control over Eden, now that the Terran Council have left?

Keila:

- Yes, I will prepare my speech and address the people of Eden today. Tell the others to prepare to land on Eden.

Metatron:

- Very well! I will do your bidding. See you later.

After Metatron had left, Keila was left thinking. She hadn't given much thought on how to handle the chaos on Eden. The presence of her nemesis Bjorn Muller had kept her attention. With the Terrans gone, she had time to deal with the Edenites' struggles.

She would tell them the truth. She would tell them that they had been living in a simulation of the Bronze Age governed by the megalomaniac

Abraham Goldstein, and that there were other villains like Abraham that needed to be stopped. Hopefully, they would follow her. Otherwise, she would give them the freedom to leave.

Another thought struck Keila. If all the Terran forces were untrained and reliant on military nanotechnology to perform in battle, blocking that technology would be the key to winning the war. She did not know how to stop the Terran military forces, but could the answer be in the Divine Dimension? Keila plugged herself into the Divine Detector Machine, dedicated to finding the answers that she needed.

Chapter 16 Floating in Space

Markus Bauer was checking the pressure indicator on the oxygen tank. It was down to 50 PSI, so it was a quarter full. This would give him approximately a few hours before he ran out of oxygen, giving him the options of either die from suffocation and a lack of oxygen, or die instantly from the vacuum of space.

Markus realised that the explosion at the Science Bay was not an accident. Instead, Bjorn Muller had caused it to happen to silence him. This was evident as his emergency beacon was activated, and yet they had abandoned him out here, to die in misery. The worst part was that Bjorn would get away with it, as there was no way for him to contact anyone.

Markus felt very nauseous. He realised that the concentration of carbon dioxide in the container was dangerously high. His only choice was to open the tank slightly to let the excess air out while having the risk of the freezing cold vacuum of space pulling him out of his safety-capsule. He exhaled completely to avoid bursting his lungs out and opened the door for a fraction of a second. The stale air was sucked out, just like when one pops a helium-filled air balloon and the freezing coldness of space was let in. Markus quickly closed the hatch and then released enough oxygen from the oxygen tank, to be able to breathe normally. In two hours, the oxygen would run out, and he would die.

Markus made up his mind. He would die from suffocation by staying within the safety-capsule. That way, if they found him, they would potentially be able to revive him. This was unlikely, as his emergency beacon was emitted by a microchip in his body, powered by bioelectricity. When he died, there would be no signal, and it would be almost impossible to find his lifeless body in the vastness of space. On the other hand, if he chose the quick death of letting the vacuum of space kill him, he would burst all his blood vessels including those in his brain, and he would be dead without any means of revival. Having made up his mind, Markus released the remaining oxygen from the oxygen tank into the capsule, and then went to sleep, not expecting to wake up.

Markus did wake up a few hours later. Although he almost hoped that he hadn't, as he was taken prisoner by the notorious space pirate, Mr Morgan Henry...

Chapter 17 Alone in the Dark.

Adina, the twin sister of Jeshua, was wandering around in the dark maintenance tunnels under Eden. She had lost her memory in her psionic blast showdown with Abraham Goldstein a week earlier. She had tried to climb up the ladder that was attached to the wall, but for some reason, the sun had tried to kill her with a laser beam. It had missed and instead hit the ladder's attachment making it melt and drop down to the bottom of the tunnels with her falling as well. It had been a 20-meter fall, but due to the low gravity on Eden, the fall had left her unscathed. With the ladder to the top dislodged, there was no way for Adina to reach the surface from this entrance and regardless, she felt no desire to return there with the sun out to kill her.

Instead, Adina hid in the darkness feeding of the wild mushrooms that grew there. She was alone in the dark, and terror filled her as her angel chip was still connected to her brain and she experienced the Edenites' terrors. Yet her amnesia made her unable to understand what was happening.

The fear from being in total darkness for weeks on end drove Adina insane, and she was sitting in a corner wagging back and forth, mumbling incoherent nonsense. One day, an event up on the surface triggered the return of her memories: Keila's speech to the people on Eden!

Chapter 18 Keila Prepares Her Speech to the Edenites.

Keila was sitting in the Divine Dimension. She felt a bit hesitant on how to address the people of Eden. Being the ruler of a pseudo-Bronze Age tribe was nothing she had ever planned for, and she had been more of a figurehead in the resistance against the Terran Council. Keila was the ultimate figurehead for the Martian Humanist Alliance. She was the beautiful young woman who had assassinated Hans Muller, the ruthless and oppressive leader of the Terran Council. As such, she had given speeches in the past, but those speeches were always written and scripted by others, so she had never needed to make the decisions.

Keila was looking at herself in the mirror. Her auburn hair matched nicely with her light green eyes and symmetrical features with a flawless complexion. She had an athletic body and stood at 170 centimetres; 30 centimetres taller than the average for a Martian female. Overall, she looked a lot more like a human from Earth rather than a human from Mars, which was ironic since she was the poster girl for the resistance against Earth humans.

At the age of 12, Keila's mother Susanna had revealed to her that Keila's father had been a Terran, an exiled grandson of a Terran House ruler, who had fallen in love and eloped with her, a mere Edenite woman who was sold off as a sex slave to a wealthy Terran leader, Ibrahim Rashid. They were cursed for eternity and were deported from Earth to live on Mars in exile for his forbidden relationship with Susanna. Sadly, he had fallen ill and died before Keila was born. Keila had planned to find out more about him, but there had never been the right time, and her mother had kept her silence. In the end, it did not matter; there were more important things in the world than learning about people who died before she was born.

Keila inspected Eden. It was based on 70-year-old technology, and yet it was still a marvel of technology, far surpassing anything she had seen on

Mars. It was also utterly useless to her. It was designed to enable a person living with Bronze Age technology to survive on an asteroid, and while it was impressive, it was a backward technology that was specifically designed to dumb down the population with no military skills whatsoever that would make them strong and win in case of a war.

Since the day Keila had crashed on Eden, the entire fabric of Edenite society had collapsed with mass killings and anarchy because of Adina and Jeshua's insurgence. The sole foundation of Eden's religion and ethics was to follow the commands of the omniscient Grand Master Abraham, which was written in the Abrahameon. When the rebellion and mayhem emerged, morality had collapsed, and society fell into a complete dark frenzy. Out of an original population of 8000 people of Edenites, 1500 of them had died because of the turnover of the religious dictatorship system. However, there were still 6500 individuals left desperately in need of leadership.

Keila decided to deliver the truth to the Edenites. The truth was that they were, living in the future and not living in during the Bronze Age era. Their original forefathers were Martians who were abducted and transported to Eden by the villain Abraham Goldstein, to live in an artificial world created by him. She would tell them that they were free to leave, while she implored them to join her in the fight against the Terran Council.

Keila summoned Metatron to prepare the landing on Eden.
Keila:

- Metatron, have you prepared for our landing on Eden?

Metatron:

- Yes, the others and I are ready and awaiting your command.

Keila:

- Good, I am coming with you.

Metatron:

- Mistress Keila, if you are not transmitting your thoughts from the Divine Dimension, you will not be able to connect to all the Edenites at once. Hence Edenites will not accept your Godhood.

Keila:

- I am not coming down as a Goddess. I am coming as a human aspiring to be their leader. Thus, I will present myself as such, a true Martian leader.

- I will tell them the truth. The time of deception has come to an end!

Metatron:

- I see. But what place would the angels and I have in this new dawn of time? We were deceived too. All I wanted was to serve and do good deeds.

Keila:

- I promise you that there will be opportunities to redeem yourself in the future, should you choose to follow me.

Metatron:

- Thank you, Keila. I will prove myself worthy!

Chapter 19: Keila's Address to the Edenites.

At noontime; Keila, Metatron and the other angels descended from the Divine Control Centre down to Eden. They were floating on a platform above Mount Sinai. Keila had planned to land on Eden to show that she was one of them, but Metatron had talked her out of it. The Edenites were still agitated, and landing in the middle of an upset crowd was very dangerous, both for Keila and for them. Instead, Keila stood on an elevated platform floating above the ground, out of range for the primitive Edenite Bronze Age weapons, but close enough for her to be visible to the people.

For the special occasion, Keila wore a long white dress to signify her innocence and a golden crown with jewels that glittered under Eden's seven suns. She felt a bit strange wearing this religious ancient dress. She was more accustomed to 29th-century skin-tight light battle armour that she usually wore in her public appearances. However, this was how her visions had shown it to her, and Keila trusted her foresight.

The masses waited with anxious anticipation, and when Keila started to speak:

- Dear people of Eden!

- My name is Keila Eisenstein.

- I have good news and bad news.

- The good news is that the Abraham is dead, and his reign of terror is over.

- The bad news is that your entire lives have been based on deceit.

- Your ancestors were not *"saved"* by Abraham *"when Earth was destroyed"*. They were abductees from the planet Mars.

- Earth is still around and the current year is the year 2872, and not year 62.

- You have been living in an artificial replica of mankind's early history, while Earth is a lot more advanced than you can ever imagine.

This message was not well received by the Edenites. The population mistrusted Keila and did not believe her. They were screaming profanities and tried to hit her with arrows and spears, which she was out of range from. Metatron raised his rifle to kill the ones who threw spears at them, but Keila signalled him to stop.

Keila:

- Dear Edenites. I have not come to force myself on you. I have come to offer you a hand and a new path to follow. I will show you images of Earth humans to prove that there are humans just like you outside of Eden.

Keila had planned this move in advance. By showing the Edenites holographic images and visual screen displays about life outside of Eden, she hoped to convince some of them about the validity of her claims. She showed a few television shows from Earth, as Earth was a paradise for Martians and Edenites alike.

The crowd watched the show. While the crowd could not understand most of it, it was clear to them that the people of Earth looked like the Angels that had been guiding them for the last 60 years. One man in the crowd, Elder Gil shouted: *"Is that vision showing the Angels' home planet?"*

Keila:

- No, the paradise you are watching is Earth. It is the rightful home of all humans. If you follow me, one day you might live there yourself.

Elder Gil:

- Tell me, Mistress. What do I need to do be granted that honour?

Keila:

- You'll have to serve our common cause with loyalty to the best of your ability.

- Come with me, I must show you something.

Elder Gil walked up and stood on a ledge on Mount Sinai, and Metatron flew down and picked him up. Keila lifted Elder Gil's arm to show the masses below of his triumph, and she spoke again.

- Elder Gil will come with me and verify what I am saying. When he returns, you should trust in what he says, and together we can start a new golden age for this rock that you call home.

- Until then, be peaceful and enjoy this new hope that you have been given.

After finishing her speech Keila, Elder Gil and the Angels entered a small space shuttle that took them back to the Divine Control Centre.

Chapter 20 Adina Regains Her Memories and Her Psionic Capabilities

Adina heard Keila's speech and witnessed the entire event through a small opening from the dark tunnel down below. In the tunnels, she was safe from the menacing "sun" that was set kill her if she was to come out in the open. Seeing Keila filled Adina with rage. Her head was spinning, and she had to sit down to avoid collapsing as she was weak and injured. Adina's memories all came back to her. She knew who she was, and she remembered her powers.

Adina tried to focus her psionic abilities. She connected telepathically to her foster father, High Priest Markus and concluded that her adoptive parents were still alive. This was a relief for Adina, but it was not her biggest concern. She knew that her real parents were Archangel Lucifer and an Edenite woman by the name of Sara.

Sara had been killed in the crossfire when Lucifer was trying to protect his newborn twins, Adina and Jeshua, from the other angels. Jeshua was taken away and saved by Sara's grandfather, while Adina was kidnapped by the Angels and given to Abraham. Lucifer was captured alive and had received been exposed to a terrible execution. He had been publicly tortured and executed to show the people that no one could defy Abraham, not even his Archangel.

When Adina turned 10, she had learned that she had an unknown twin brother, Jeshua. She had tried to get close to him, but he had been reluctant to get close to her as she was rumoured to be a sorceress due to her psionic abilities. Eventually, at the age of 16, she had saved Jeshua from the Angels and convinced him to form an underground rebellion against Abraham. At the same time, she had pretended to support Abraham's rule. The underground resistance had failed, and all Jeshua's followers got killed, while

Jeshua lost his mind spending years alone in the darkness underground with only wild mushrooms and water to survive on.

The emergence of Keila had changed everything. Realising that there were humans outside of Eden had disproved Abraham's lies about Eden being mankind's last home. Chaos and anarchy had followed. During this chaos, Keila and Jeshua had found each other, fallen in love, killed two angels, stolen their equipment, and had flown to the Divine Control Centre to confront Abraham.

At this time, Abraham had realised the threat that Adina posed to his rule and set his orbital satellites to fire lasers at her. One of the satellites had fired at Adina and missed. This had caused her to fall into one of the tunnels, hitting her head, and losing her memory.

Adina thought about what must have happened since she lost her memory. The emergence of Keila as the new leader of Eden showed that she must have killed Abraham and taken his place. But what about Adina's brother Jeshua? He was not contactable, and Adina had a feeling that her twin brother had died.

What was Keila's future vision for Eden? Adina was the one who was meant to be the Goddess of Eden. Adina and her brother Jeshua were destined to lead, not Keila, who highjacked the rebellion and killed Abraham. There was only one way to find out. Adina closed her eyes to see all the possible divine technology connections on Eden. Keila was the only individual with a god chip implanted and it seemed like Keila was unaware of Adina's presence.

Adina hesitated for a second. She needed to find out about Keila's intentions and what had happened to Jeshua. But what was her best course of action? If she spied on Keila and were detected, she would risk detection, which could be dangerous. If she, on the other hand, tried to communicate with Keila, she exposed her existence and risked being fed lies. Adina made up her mind. She would spy on Keila through the divine technology. This was her only chance to find out the truth. If she chose to communicate with Keila, she would not be able to enter Keila's mind at a later stage, as Keila had a god chip, which was superior to Adina's angel chip.

Adina sat down and focused her mind to penetrate Keila's mind undetected. To her surprise, she entered Keila's mind undetected, no doubt because Keila was not as accustomed to the divine technology as Abraham had been. Adina was not able to enter Keila's deep state of mind, and she was only able to see what she is doing at the time. Accessing what Keila was experiencing at the moment was easy, but it had no relevance to Adina. Adina had more pressing matters at hand than finding out what television shows Keila liked watching before going to bed.

Adina tried to go through Keila's memories and thoughts methodically. It was a challenging job as every human's mind categorised their memories in different layers, so it was difficult for an outsider to find what they were looking for. Adina needed to keep her own mind and emotions under complete control to avoid detection. Eventually, Adina found Keila's vision for Eden.

Keila saw Eden as a base of operations that she could use in her armed conflict with the Terran Council. If Keila's plans were to take place, many Edenites would perish in a pointless battle that they had no part in and the world that Adina knew would be in jeopardy. Adina managed to keep her emotional cool until she saw the memory where Keila shot and killed Jeshua. witnessing her twin brother's murder was too much for Adina, and she screamed her lungs out. This drew Keila attention before Adina severed the connection.

Chapter 21: Keila is Reminded of Adina's Existence.

Keila was in bed watching *"The wealthy wives of Warner"* on the TV screen in her bedroom. It was a vain, materialistic show that reminded Keila of her teenage years when she had lived relative peace and safety in Pamshal city on Mars. Back then she had limited interest in her mum's revolutionary talk against the Terran Council. Instead, Keila had been looking at ways to use her half-Terran heritage to her advantage. She had wanted to secure a Terran citizenship to get off Mars, and start a new life on the pristine Earth.

Those dreams had come to naught though as Keila, was psychologically scarred after being repeatedly raped and tortured by Bjorn Muller. Keila had directed her revenge into killing the leader of the Terran Council, Hans Muller. Killing the leader of the Terran Council ensured that she would be branded a nefarious criminal for the remainder of her life. Keila embraced her fate and became the figurehead of the revolutionary movement, The Martian Humanist Alliance.

Keila's premonitory visions and visual imagery had started appearing at the time when Bjorn Muller kept her as a sex slave. Before that event, she had had weaker premonitions, but from that moment, her visionary gifts intensified. Her visions had told her to injure Bjorn Muller, and they had guided her to safety. The visions had also shown her how to infiltrate the Terran Council and get close enough to Hans Muller to assassinate him. The latest four years they had helped her to perform other near-impossible feats. But what did frustrate her was that she didn't understand how she got all her visions and premonitions and what goal she was serving. Despite having clairvoyance and premonition, she was clueless.

Keila knew that her visions technically speaking, classified her as schizophrenic and that many whispered about it behind her back. It had been hurtful at first, but she had learned to ignore it. A delusional madwoman would not consistently be right, so she knew that her visions were not insanity but something else, something scientifically unexplainable.

Keila's visuals started flicking, and random memories popped up in her mind. Eventually, the memory of Jeshua's murder came up. A woman, similar in age to herself, showed up in the room as a mirage and screamed her lungs out before disappearing again. Startled by the vision, Keila summoned Metatron, to her chamber.

Metatron:

- You called, mistress.

- Pardon me for seeing you in limited clothing. You look very beautiful and alluring.

Keila:

- No apology needed. I experienced something so stressful, so I forgot to dress before summoning you.

Metatron:

- I am listening, Keila.

Keila:

- I'll get to it. But first a technical question. Is it possible for someone with an angel chip, to access my memories and show up as hallucinations?

Metatron:

- I have never heard of it, and it would defeat the purpose of the technology. Then again, the technology is alien in origin, and we still don't fully understand it.

- What happened?

Keila:

- My vision started flickering, and I had random memories pop-
ping up in my mind. Then at one memory, an image of a screaming
woman came up in the room.

- She looked like me but she was less toned, and she was wearing
an Edenite priestess gown.

Metatron pressed a switch, and Adina's photo appeared as a hologram.
Metatron:

- Was it this woman?

Keila

- Yes, that is her. Who is she?

Metatron:

- She is Adina. She was Lucifer's daughter. Abraham ordered her
to have an angel chip implanted, and she was to be raised by high
priest Markus under close supervision from the angels.

Keila:

- Why did he order that?

Metatron:

- I have no idea, but Abraham was not someone you ever questioned.

- Anyways, Adina was rumoured to have special psionic abilities
that no other angel or even Abraham had. Abraham did not realise the threat she posed until it was too late for him, which was
fortunate for you.

Keila:

- Fortunate? What do you mean?

Metatron:

- Do you think Abaddon chose to kill himself when he had maimed you and was about to kill you? It must have been Adina's doing.

Keila:

- Hmm. I did come across this strange woman, Elizabeth, who acted like a remote-controlled zombie. She told me that she brought a message from Adina.

- She helped us back then; does that mean she is a potential ally?

Metatron:

- Considering that you took the position she is yearning for, and you murdered her brother, I would say a non-hostile attitude from her is unlikely.

Keila froze for a moment. She had known Metatron for over a week, and she had never mentioned what she did to Abraham and Jeshua. She had assumed he didn't know what had happened, which was an absurd notion, considering the number of cameras filming everything at the space station. But why hadn't he mentioned it before? Remorse filled Keila, and she was struggling to hold back her tears.

Keila:

- So, you knew all along? I don't know why I killed Jeshua. I was compelled to do it. My visions told me.

Metatron:

- There hasn't been any reason to mention it. Your reason for killing Abraham was apparent, and your reason for killing Jeshua is irrelevant to me.

- Regardless, I mentioned it now to explain the unlikelihood in Adina being friendly towards us.

Keila:

- But if you knew that I murdered my partner, why did you choose to help me?

Metatron:

- I went with my gut feeling!

- After you killed Abraham, I was free from his tyranny. But what would I do?

- I woke up first after the psionic blast. I knew what to do, by elevating you to Godhood, I would also elevate myself and be able to redeem myself for carrying out Abraham's atrocities throughout the years.

Keila:

- Are you not worried that I will do the same to you as I did to Jeshua?

Metatron:

- No, I am not.
- I am an old man in a young man's body. If I am meant to die, so be it.

Keila:

- You are not that old? You don't look much older than 30?

Metatron:

- Quadruple that, and you are closer to the truth.

Keila looked at Metatron with a puzzled expression. It did not make any sense that he would be so old. She was aware of DNA regeneration technology being used among Terrans, but even then, Metatron would bear the scars of aging that the technology could not hide.

Keila:

- How can that be? You don't have the scars of aging that old people always have?

Metatron:

- That is because I have spent most of my years in cryogenic sleep to avoid aging. Abraham envisioned the Eden Project to last for an eternity, and he didn't want his Angels to age.

Keila:

- I see. I would prefer to be alone now. Return to your quarters, Metatron.

As Metatron walked towards the door, Keila failed to control her emotions. Filled with remorse, she let down her barrier, and the feelings overwhelmed her. With tears pouring down from her chin, Keila called out to Metatron: *"Don't go, stay with me, I don't want to be alone"*. The puzzled Metatron turned around, and Keila jumped into his arms. She refused to let go with tears running down her cheeks. They stood there like that for a long time, before Metatron tucked her in.

Chapter 22 Brahma Studies Keila's Mind and is Reminded of Rangda.

Brahma was meditating in his meditation chamber 30 kilometres from the Divine Palace. He was at peace, as deep meditation was the only state where his hunger and thirst weren't tormenting him. Brahma tried to access Keila's mind but he struggled to connect to her. He had struggled to access Keila's mind for the last few weeks.

Brahma thought of reasons why he struggled to connect with Keila. The distance from her could be one reason. He was 30 kilometres away from the heavenly palace, and since distances were compressed in the Divine Dimension, this was the equivalent of being 3 billion kilometres away from Keila in the regular universe. He shrugged off the idea. He had connected with Keila in the past from this location, and before the destruction of Zetani, the planet of Zetans, his predecessors were able to communicate telepathically with each other from light-years away. 3 billion kilometres were only 3 light hours and it wouldn't be a limiting factor.

Brahma thought about Rangda. It was a bittersweet feeling. Being one of the greatest Zetans, he had many concubines, and she had been one of his favourites.

That prominent males had many concubines was one of the great paradoxes of the Zetan civilisation. While Zetans were close to asexual compared to humans and thus had a prolonged reproduction rate, having many beautiful females in his cohort was the best way for a prominent Zetan to show his status to his peers. As the Zetans were governed through a utilitarian mind, facilitated by the Zeto crystals, money and individual ownership were irrelevant to them. Instead, clarity of thoughts and pureness of the genome was their fundamental values. By binding many women to prominent Zetan men, they increased the odds of improving their genome as species.

Brahma had saved Rangda's life, after the fateful day, when the Xenos had penetrated the core of Zetan territory and blew up the star that Zetani was orbiting. The explosion was so powerful that it created the massive supernova in the centre of the Milky Way Galaxy. The explosion obliterated hundreds of star systems and marked the end to the Zetan civilisation. The few Zetans who had survived the blast were the ones that were in the Divine Dimension and the ones on distant, isolated worlds. The ones' stuck in the Divine Dimension were stuck in the timelessness, condemned to immortality suffering from hunger and thirst. The Zetans on the fringe worlds degenerated as species, with Zeto crystals no longer around to unite them.

Zeus and Odin had found Rangda in the Divine Dimension on the same day that most of their civilisation was destroyed by the Xenos. While they had never been able to prove Rangda's betrayal, the circumstantial evidence was strong.

Rangda had been the commander responsible for protecting the Zetani star system, and during her watch, a Xeno crew had stayed close to the Zetani star for long enough to manipulate its energies into the collapse the prompted a colossal supernova explosion. Zeus and Odin had intended to execute Rangda for her crimes, but Brahma, had intervened and requested that she should live and be given a chance to defend herself. The others had no interest in listening to Rangda's defence, but they had allowed her live forever, isolated in an inescapable prison.

Brahma felt Rangda's presence. But he knew that it shouldn't be possible. The prison for Rangda was built of a material that would stop her telepathic abilities. Yet he could sense her stronger than he had for thousands of years. What would he do? He considered contacting the other Zetans, but he decided against it. His relationship with the other Zetan leaders had deteriorated, and they would question his motives for going there.

Brahma made up his mind. He left a note stating that he would be gone for a while. The trip would take a long time. He would have to walk the entire way since the Zetans were out of fuel for their spaceships. Walking 50,000 kilometres would feel like walking for several years, but due to the time divergence between The Divine Dimension and the normal dimension, it would only take a couple of months. Brahma took up a high-powered binocular that had a maximum of 1000x magnification. He faced in the direction of the Rangda's prison and saw a minuscule dot. As the Divine Dimension was a flat, featureless, and endless plane, he could see things that were very far away.

Brahma took a deep breath and he started walking. Hunger and thirst would torment him during the walk, but he kept going. He knew what he needed to do.

Chapter 23: Adina Gives Keila an Ultimatum.

Keila woke up in shock, fell out of her bed, and found herself lying face down on the floor. Blood dripped from her nose and she had an excruciating migraine. She cried out to Metatron, but he was no longer present as he had left when she fell asleep. Keila got up on her knees and looked up. There was an illusion of Adina in front of her.

Without saying anything, Adina launched another psionic blast to strike Keila. But this time, Keila countered Adina's burst, and both Keila and Adina fell backward to the ground. Keila coughed up some blood and spit it out. Adina, in turn, had blood running down from her eyes. Keila screamed out:

- What are you doing, what do you want?!

Adina:

- I came to kill you for killing my brother and stealing my rightful place.

- As it turns out, you're stronger than I thought, and I cannot use my powers to kill you, without risking my own life.

Keila:

- Is that so?
- Crazy bitch! Feel this!

Keila tried directing a psionic blast onto Adina, but it failed as her mental capabilities were also weakened. Adina studied her for a second and spoke.

- Interesting, it seems you are too weak to smite me as well.

Keila:

- What a shame!
- So, what do we do? Duel at dawn?

Adina:

- That is not how we solve problems on Eden.

- My demands are simple.

- You are to remove the god chip and leave Eden under my control. Don't ever think of coming back!

Keila:

- Why would I agree to that?

Adina:

- Because you value your life.
- You are a foreigner here; Eden means nothing to you. Just leave!

Keila:

- You are mistaken.

- Eden is my future. Eden is the future of mankind.

- I didn't come here by accident; providence brought me here.

- With technology and resources on this rock, I will free humanity from the tyranny of the Terran Council.

Adina:

- I don't care about that. You are a murderer and an imposter. Leave, or I will kill you!

Keila:

- Fuck off, bitch!

After screaming out, Keila lashed a second psionic blast at Adina. To her great surprise, Adina simply vanished from her consciousness, and she could no longer detect Adina being a connected node to the Divine Technology. Metatron ran into the room. He looked at her with a worried expression.
Metatron:

- Mistress Keila! You are injured, what happened?

Keila:

- Just take me to the medical bay. I'll tell you later.

Metatron lifted Keila and rushed her to the medical bay for immediate treatment.

Chapter 24: Keila Wakes Up in the Medical Bay.

K eila woke up three days later in the medical bay. Her head was spinning, and she suffered from severe nausea. Keila looked at a display and noticed that she had been unconscious for three full days. *"Three days,"* she thought *"What really happened to me?"* She remembered her psionic fight with Adina, she couldn't tell if it was real or not. Metatron entered the room.
Metatron:

- Mistress Keila. I am relieved to see you awake.

Keila:

- What happened to me?

Metatron:

- We are not sure. The security footage shows you being alone in the room, slamming your head against the floor in a seizure-like way. However, the scarring on your brain tissue was unique and did not match injuries associated with blunt trauma.

- Regardless, you are lucky to be alive, without immediate medical attention, you would be permanently killed.

Keila reflected over what Metatron had told her. She had been lucky, but had Adina died during their altercation? Adina had disappeared from the grid, and she would not have access to advanced medical science in the tunnels under Eden. Keila asked Metatron about Adina.
Keila:

- Adina did this to me. She blasted me with psionic energy. Do you know what happened to her?

Metatron:

- Is that so? I don't see how that would be possible, considering she has a lower-tier chip installed than you do.

Keila:

- That is what happened!

Metatron:

- I believe you.

- She has been gone from the grid for the last few days. Maybe she died in your confrontation?

Keila:

- I am not taking any chances. Send security bots into the tunnels and kill her!

Metatron:

- Hmm, unfortunately, we don't have any security bots to send.

Keila:

- But Eden is vast, and there are lots of robots on the dark side of Eden?

Metatron:

- Well, Abraham's vision for Eden was for it to be a replica of the Promised Land during the Bronze Age. Security bots didn't fit in on that narrative.

Keila:

- I see. We must make sure to get security bots delivered then. We must keep ourselves safe from that crazy bitch.

Metatron:

- Understood. I'll try to get some bots delivered off the black market. It won't be quick or cheap.

Keila:

- Thanks, Metatron.

- One more thing, I want you to be by my side, to protect me in case she strikes again.

Metatron:

- Understood Mistress Keila, I will keep you safe.

Keila closed her eyes again and thought on how to continue. She could not send any Angels or Edenites to confront Adina. If her aptitude with the divine technology were so great so that she almost killed a higher-tier user from afar, it would pose no difficulty for Adina to eliminate any Angels or humans that Keila sent after her. With security bots, it was different. They had no divine technology chips installed, and Keila was convinced that Adina had no other combat skills than those from her superior usage of the divine technology.

But what if Adina was dead, and they wasted precious resources buying robots to chase her down? That could be a tactical mistake. Keila shrugged off that notion as her gut feeling told her that Adina was alive, and Keila always followed her intuition.

Chapter 25 Adina Strikes Again

Three days later, Keila was struggling to fall asleep. The incident with Adina was gnawing in the back of her mind, and she was afraid. They had failed to find any trace of Adina in the Divine Technology neural network, and everyone except for Keila assumed that Adina was dead. Keila had turned down Metatron's offer to use an accelerated sleep pod to get her daily need of sleep in less than two hours. Keila liked natural sleep, as it allowed her to dream and unleash her imagination. The accelerated sleep pod was just two blank hours of her life, and it did not appeal to her.

Keila looked at Metatron, who was watching over her from the corner of the room. He had watched over her for three days straight, and Keila had never known a man that loyal before. She felt how she was yearning for him.

Keila looked away. She tried to control her desire. "This is insanity," she thought to herself. Metatron was a century older than her, but due to extended periods in cryogenic sleep and DNA regeneration technology he was physically in his thirties, or a decade older than Keila.

Despite her attempts to use logic to curb her desire for Metatron, Keila's urge for him kept growing throughout the night. Her desire for Metatron kept her awake. Did he feel the same desire for her? It was easy to find out, all she needed to do was to enter his mind via the divine technology and find out. Keila rejected the notion. The last few weeks, Metatron had grown to be the closest person to her in the world. It would be a betrayal to spy on him instead of trusting him. She called him over.

Keila:

- Metatron, what do you think about me?

Metatron:

- I think you are a capable individual who will provide excellent guidance to the Edenites.

Keila:

- But do you like me, as a person?

Metatron:

- Yes, but my feelings are not what matters. My duty is what matters.

Keila:

- I like you Metatron, and I find you incredibly attractive.

Metatron:

- Thank you, Keila. Is there anything I can help you with?

Keila hesitated. She had hoped that Metatron would be more excited over the conversation. She was in lingerie in bed, and they were the only two people in the room. But maybe he had repressed his sexuality? After all, Metatron had lived in isolated with a group of men for over 60 years. Keila made the leap of faith.
Keila:

- Yes, there is. I desire you! Make love to me!

Metatron:

- Desire... I have buried that feeling so deep inside me, I wouldn't even recognise it anymore.

Keila:

- Well, then it's time to unleash your desire.

Metatron:

- I will if you lead the way. Control my body through the psionic powers of your god chip.

Keila:

- Sure, let's try it.

Keila focused her mind on taking control over Metatron's body. It was an extraordinary feeling, as she was touched by someone else, and yet it felt like she was touching herself. Keila let her worries go and just embrace the orgasmic feeling. They both got undressed, and Keila felt how her desire peaked when she touched Metatron perfectly sculpted physical body. He entered her and was thrusting rhythmically and hitting the spot every stroke. Keila came multiple times and lost track of time and place.

Adina studied Keila through the eyes of Metatron. The plan was working, and in a moment, it would be time for her to strike. Adina touched the scars where her healthy eyes used to be. The eyes were still there, but they had been wounded from the psionic blast during her altercation with Keila that had made her blind. Adina had been clinically dead after her previous fight with Keila, but she had seen the light and felt compelled to go back and face Keila. When she woke up, she was blind, but her psionic powers had improved.

Adina could now stay hidden and manipulate people's inner thoughts undetected. Adina had induced Keila with an irresistible carnal desire towards Metatron. Adina did this because Metatron was easier to control than Keila was. Thus, it would be easier to use him to kill Keila than it would be to face Keila again.

Adina put her plan into motion; she took control of Metatron's body and started strangling Keila with his strong hands.

Keila didn't immediately notice that Metatron was strangling her as she was so aroused. After a few seconds, however, she noticed what he was doing and that she had lost the connection to his mind. She started screaming and punching him to no avail, as the unemotional and remotely controlled angel was too powerful and resilient to pain to notice her resistance at all.

Keila looked into Metatron's eyes, he was out of his mind! Keila's vision faded to black, but before she passed out, she saw Adina for a fraction of a second. Keila managed to gather her remaining powers and blast Adina with a psionic blast. Adina was shocked by getting struck, as she thought she was invisible to the other users, and she passed out. Metatron, also got struck, and he fell unconscious to the floor.

Keila activated the alarm. Samael and a group of angels entered the room. He looked in disgust at Keila and Metatron, both sweaty and naked.

Samael:

  - What is going on in here? This is unacceptable.

Keila:

  - Take Metatron to the medical bay! Connect me to The Divine Dimension. You can whine later.

Samael looked at Keila and obeyed her command. He had strong negative opinions on sex outside of marriage, especially since Metatron had taken vows of celibacy when he became an Angel. However, he was a loyal subject and there to serve.

Chapter 26: Keila Finds a Solution to the Adina Problem.

Keila was back in the Divine Dimension for the first time in a couple of weeks. She hadn't been there for a while, as the Divine Detector Machine there used tremendous amounts of power to operate. Keila had other plans for Eden rather than wasting all the precious fuel on running the Divine Detector Machine.

She studied the ancient Zetan tomes for a way to deal with Adina when Samael contacted her.

- I have some terrible news about your fuck-buddy Metatron.

Keila:

- Show some respect, Samael!
- Metatron is your Archangel and we had sex because I wanted to.

Samael:

- Apologies, Mistress Keila. I should have watched my tongue.

- Anyways. There is irreparable damage on Metatron's brain. If we regenerate tissue to get him back alive, he might be permanently damaged. I suggest that we let him pass away in peace.

Hearing this made Keila upset and she blasted Samael with a light psionic shock for even daring to recommend it.
Keila:

- No, you are wrong! There is hope! I will not let Metatron die!

Samael coughed and brushed off the light blast:

- As you wish, Keila. We'll keep him alive. Don't blame me for the consequences.

Keila:

- I can't guarantee you that. Now get back to work and save Metatron.

Keila severed the connection and she wailed in pain. She couldn't lose Metatron. He was the only one she had left in the world after her mum and her friends in the resistance had fallen. Keila walked around randomly in the Zetan archives room, until she stumbled into a bookcase, causing some of the books to fall on her. As she got up on her knees, she glimpsed at one of the open books on the floor and smiled in relief. The gods had given her the solution to her problems once again!

Chapter 27 Keila Sets Up a Meeting with Adina

Keila was sitting under the Lotus tree in the Divine Palace courtyard. Her mind was at peace, and she knew what she needed to do. She contacted Samael.

- Samael, new directions: Turn off Metatron's life support and let him die; then freeze his body.

Samael:

- That's the opposite to what you ordered before?

Keila:

- I know. Does that bother you, Samael?

Samael:

- Not at all, Keila; I am glad you listened to my advice.

Keila:

- All good. Dismissed, Samael.

Keila leaned back and sensed how Metatron's signal became weaker and weaker until he perished. Keila sighed. It was painful sensing Metatron die, but letting him die now was the best way to save him later. Although Keila felt at peace, she riled herself up for a show. It was time to lure Adina into a trap. She found Adina's signal in the system and contacted her.

Keila:

- Adina, you bitch!
- Metatron is dead because of you!

Adina:

- I know; I sensed it. It hurts to lose someone you love, does it not?

Keila:

- Yes.

- Let's settle this. Let's meet up and determine who is worthy of ruling Eden.

Adina:

- And why would I agree to meet you?

Keila:

- Because you want me dead as much as I want you dead. Besides, what else are you going to do? You are blind and stuck in the tunnels?

Adina considered her options. She was unsure whether grief had driven Keila insane or if she had an ace up her sleeve. Regardless, Adina needed to kill Keila as Keila had all the trump on hand. Keila had an advanced medical bay and unlimited food and resources while Adina had no access to medical treatment and was confined in the tunnels with limited sustenance. Adina made up her mind. She would meet with Keila in the catacombs. From proximity, her psionic powers would be stronger, and she would have no trouble blasting Keila out of existence. With Keila dead, it was an easy task to take control of the Angels, have them turn off the orbital lasers, and elevate her to become the God-queen of Eden.

Adina:

- Agreed. Meet me at the tunnel entrance to the southwest of Mount Sinai. Come alone and unarmed. See you in 12 hours.

Keila:

- See you then. Prepare to die, Adina!

Chapter 28: The Eradication of Adina

Twelve hours later, Keila arrived next to the tunnel entrance southwest of Mount Sinai. She was nervous and knew that there was no help available if things did not play out according to her plan. Before Keila left the Divine Control Centre, she had made sure that the Angels had entered cryogenic sleep to avoid Adina taking control of them. Keila stepped out of her shuttle and walked towards the tunnels. Keila hoped that Adina would to talk to her face to face, instead of taking the shot as soon as she entered within lethal range of the psionic blasts. She didn't dare to take any chances though and she kept her guard up to avoid being taken by surprise. Keila spotted Adina a bit from the entrance. She shone a flashlight at her, and it was a pitiful sight.

Adina had taken severe physical damage from her psionic confrontations with Keila, and the lack of medical attention had not helped her. Her face was bruised, her eyes had been crushed, and they were full of maggots. As Adina's physical senses had weakened, her psionic abilities powered by her Angel chip had strengthened, and she was a formidable enemy.

Keila:

- We meet at last.

Adina:

- Yes.

- You have made a deadly mistake coming here.

- I am wounded, and without help. You could have bided your time waiting for me to perish. Instead, you came here within lethal range for my psionic blasts.

Keila:

- Is that so?
- Then I suggest you try to blast me away with your mind!

During the time she said that Keila used the deactivation code to the divine technology that she had seen in the Zetan book the day before. Adina tried to blast her with a psionic blast, but to no avail, as she fell exhausted to the ground.

Adina:

- Why... Why is it not working?

Keila:

- Because I deactivated the entire system.

- Did you honestly think I would come down here for you when all I needed to do was to wait for you to die?

Adina:

- Do you think your intense emotions and desire for Metatron came from nowhere? I made you fall in love with the tool that I used to try to kill you.

- Your heart is broken because of the death of a man that I made you love. How ironic!

Keila:

- You are lying, bitch. Metatron was always special to me.

Adina:

- Special like all your other men, you filthy whore?!

Keila:

- You have pestered me enough crazy woman! Time to die!

Adina, who was wounded and not much of a fighter to start with tried to fight but she was no match for Keila who was a trained fighter.

As Adina was weakened and coughing blood on the ground, Keila spoke:

- Metatron's death doesn't bother me, since I found a way to revive him!

After that Keila dragged Adina to the tunnel entrance and then she threw her out in the open where the orbital laser cannons incinerated Adina. As she walked past Adina's charred remains, she felt relieved. Her nightmare was over, but her battle had just begun!

Chapter 29 The Revival and Promotion of Metatron

Keila was holding the "God chip MKII", which she had found the schematics for in the Zetan archives. The chip was more potent than the one she had implanted, and it could restore brain tissue. Keila looked at the lifeless body of Metatron in the cryogenic tank. If she was to revive him and implant him with the MKII chip, would he still be loyal to her? or would the reversal of power in their relationship change him? There was no way to know, but she missed him and wanted him back by her side.

Keila made up her mind, she would revive him. He had saved her life, and she had to do everything in her power to protect him. Besides, her intuition told her that he would remain loyal to her, and why question her intuition now, when she never questioned it otherwise? She called in Samael to help her with the procedure. He seemed uneager to help.

Samael:

- This is not right; in our culture, we have never followed more than one deity. Yahweh was our god for thousands of years, Abraham succeeded him, and then you replaced him. Yet, the concept of one god remained. Now you are suggesting elevating Metatron to your level, leaving us with two gods?

Keila:

- We both know that the "Divine Technology" is mind-control technology developed by the alien Zetan race to control humanity.

- Yahweh was an extra-terrestrial being who used technology to manipulate our ancestors. Abraham was a man who used the same technique to manage you and the people in Eden. Through destiny, I am now in control of the technology. This doesn't make any of us divine. I wish to share my power with Metatron, as that is the only way to revive him.

Samael:

- I can't believe that Yahweh was an imposter. His principles guided our people throughout the millennia and gave us hope and comfort.

Keila:

- Yet you have seen his corpse in the Divine Dimension. You have visited the Zetan archives and learned everything about the multi-millennia war and how the Zetans used humans to fight the Xenos.

Samael:

- Yes, I have seen it, but I don't want to believe it. I still want to believe in something higher than myself. Something to look up to.

Keila:

- If it's any comfort to you, I still believe that there is a great maker that created everything. However, the True Maker is too great to focus its attention on detailed rules for how humans should live their lives. The great creator of the universe doesn't need our worship.

Samael:

- I guess that's a comforting thought.

- One more thing bothering me. Metatron was bound by an oath of celibacy and yet he engaged in coitus with you.

Keila:

- Well, his oath was sworn to Abraham, who perished. Once Abraham died, the promise was null and void.

Samael:

- Does that mean that I...?

Keila:

- Yes, you are free to find yourself a suitable partner, Samael. I am sure there are plenty of eligible singles for you on Eden.

Samael:

- Thank you, Mistress Keila. That's a burden that is off my chest.

Keila:

- Yes. Let's focus on reviving Metatron now, shall we?

After saying that, they defrosted Metatron and started the surgical procedure of removing his Angel chip and inserting a god MKII chip instead. The surgery was performed by a medical bot, but as the bot didn't have any file on how to deal with the Zetan technology, they had to control the bot with their minds through an electrode helmet that they had on top of their heads. They had both studied complex reparative surgery in the Zetan archives but to make sure that they avoided mistakes, they acted as each other's fail-safes. After several hours, they had removed Metatron's angel chip and inserted the god MKII chip. They defibrillated Metatron's heart, and he woke up.

Metatron, got a flashback of how he tried to strangle Keila, and was filled with remorse, when he saw Keila's face.

Metatron:

- Mistress Keila. I am... I am so sorry.

Keila:

- It wasn't your fault. All that matters are that you're back with me now.

Samael left the room. Metatron and Keila sat silently, but happy and feeling a mutual connection in each other's embrace.

Chapter 30 Keila's Dilemma

A few weeks later, Keila was sitting in a couch looking at the vastness of space outside, through a sizeable fortified panorama window. When she looked straight ahead, she saw Eden.

Eden seemed vast from her perspective, despite being a small world. Its surface was mostly brownish yellow with some green and blue patches where there were farms and water reservoirs. Eden's atmosphere looked intensely blue from her perspective. This was because the atmosphere was tightly packed with air. The atmosphere on Eden only stretched a kilometre up to the electrified nanotechnology protective layer that kept the atmosphere in, yet the surface air pressure was like that on Earth. To achieve this, the air concentration was a lot higher on Eden than on Earth. Hence its atmosphere was a lot bluer when viewed from space.

Keila looked on a control panel; she saw that all the systems that kept Eden liveable was working like clockwork and now that peace was restored, the people could live safe lives and in abundance.

The potential for good living conditions on Eden was the root of Keila's dilemma. She needed to choose between what was good for the people she was governing and what was good the population in the solar system that was oppressed by the Terran Council's tyranny. She had planned to use Eden as her secret base of operations to make covert strikes on Terran Council ships and mining stations. After getting to know the Edenites better, she felt reluctant to go through with this cruel project. The Edenites had nothing to do with her fight with the Terran Council, and she could not inspire them to fight a battle that wasn't theirs, without deceiving them. Deceiving them would be easy, but if she chose that path, she would not be better than her enemies who had used false promises to dominate the solar system for the past six centuries.

Another issue Keila was wrestling with, was the freedom of her people in Eden. After defeating Adina, Keila had intended to free all her subjects through removing the microchips from their brains. Metatron had opposed this idea which had upset Keila, but she had come around and realised that he was right. Metatron had argued that the people of Eden were happy with being part of something bigger than themselves. To force everyone out of the community was worse than controlling people that wanted to be controlled.

Keila had admitted that forcing atheism was not more freedom than forcing religion, so she had left the people with the choice whether to remain connected. A few weeks later, no one had opted to leave Eden, due to their fear of the great unknown that was beyond Eden.

Keila connected to Metatron to see what he was doing. He was counselling some villagers on Eden after the death of their grandfather. Keila was moved when she watched Metatron counsel the villagers. He treated them with a level of compassion and love that she could not muster. It seemed like Metatron cared for all his subjects and Keila could only imagine how much pain it would have caused him to carry out all of Abraham's atrocities. Keila disconnected from Metatron. She looked forward to seeing him in the Divine Dimension later. The timelessness of that place made their encounters so much more pleasant and blessed. After that, she fell asleep, filled with pleasant dreams for the first time in four years.

Chapter 31 Markus Bauer is Freed

Markus Bauer woke up in his prison cell aboard Morgan Henry's pirate spaceship. For the last month, Markus had felt a sense of optimistic fear for his situation. When he was first picked up by Morgan's crew, he had felt a disappointment that he hadn't perished a peaceful death from suffocation in space. Morgan Henry was notorious for mutilating and torturing prisoners to please his sadistic tendencies. At least this was what media portrayed, and Markus had no reason to question the media portrayal of Morgan Henry, the evil space pirate. But during the first interrogation, he hadn't been tortured. Instead, Morgan Henry had extracted the data from the microchips in Markus' brain and then sent him back to his cell.

After the first interrogation, Markus was left in the cell with little contact with his captors, but they had provided him with enough nutrition and hygiene products to avoid disease.

Markus Bauer heard a pistol discharge. He recognised the sound that he had heard for a few times in the last month. It was Morgan Henry's custommade pistol that used special propellant to accelerate the bullets to ten times the speed of sound, while still being low recoil and easy to carry. The pistol was designed to have enough power to penetrate any armour, even the advanced Terran Council's special operations armour. The door opened, and Morgan Henry entered. He had blood splattered all over his face.

Morgan Henry:

- Aye Lad, you are coming with me.

Markus:

- Are you going to kill me?

Morgan Henry:

- Why would you say that?

- Ah, you mean the blood on my face. I do all the executions on this vessel. The one who gives the sentence should carry out the killing himself, that's our code.

Markus Bauer:

- That's barbaric!

Morgan Henry:

- Nay, what's barbaric is ordering others to kill for you, while rich folks like you are sipping cognac and smoking cigars from the safety of your elegant boardrooms back on Earth!

- But enough of that. Aye, today is your lucky day. Arrrr! Someone posted your ransom; a hefty amount for returning you alive! They will meet you at to the dock, and I will bring you there.

They walked to the docks where they met with Tzi Chen Cheng; the chairman for the Terran Council Science Commission and a high-ranking member of House Cheng. Markus was baffled to see him under these circumstances, and even more baffled to see him alone without any bodyguards. Morgan Henry signalled his men, and the pirates left the docks to the two men.

Markus:

- Tzi Chen! What on Earth are you doing on the ship of the most notorious pirate of the solar system, at the fringe of this solar system?

Tzi Chen:

- We are close to Earth, Mr Bauer.

- Mr Henry and his men work for us as an independent party. By having pirates carry out objectives for us, we have deniability when things go wrong. All Terran houses operate the same way.

Markus:

- But I am not affiliated with House Cheng? I come from House Muller territory, and I work for the Terran Council.

Tzi Chen:

- True, but it would be silly to deny my connection with Morgan Henry when I am on his ship. Besides who would believe your claim, if you made our secretive association public.

- Truth to be told, I came to see the body of Keila Eisenstein, if it even exists.

Markus:

- It exists! I examined it before the explosion at the Science Bay.

Tzi Chen:

- Very well.
- Let's examine it together. It is stored in that crate over there.

Both men walked to the crate where Tzi Chen noticed that this was a phony.
Tzi Chen:

- You fool! You are the chief scientist on a Terran Council vessel, and you cannot identify that this is a forgery!

Markus:

- What do you mean?

- I had a suspicion that it could be a non-functional clone, but it was hard to determine due to bullets destroying the spine and the brain, making it impossible to analyse it.

Tzi Chen:

- You can determine it by studying the bone structure. The bone structure of the corpse matches the body of someone who grew up on Earth. But Keila grew up on Mars. She should have more hollow bones due to the lower gravity on Mars and different colour pigment on the skin tissue, due to the various elements present in Martian food.

Markus:

- I am not sure that I follow you.

Tzi Chen:

- This is a clone, made with Terran equipment emulating a person who lived under the Terran conditions. Whether it was a functional or non-functional clone is still to be examined, but I can guarantee you that it was not Keila Eisenstein.

Markus:

- So, what are you going to do? Will you expose Bjorn's deceit?

Tzi Chen:

- No, that's your job. I am not going to complain about a senior member of another House, based on a corpse I found on a pirate ship. That's not a good look nor a credible claim.

Markus:

- So, what am I going to do?

Tzi Chen:

- You'll figure it out. Let's leave this ship. There are better places to linger than a pirate ship, regardless if the captain is your top-secret agent or not.

After saying that, they entered Tzi Chen's private shuttle and set the course for Earth.

Chapter 32: Bjorn Muller Reacts to the News of Markus Bauer's Rescue.

Bjorn Muller was lying in bed, sipping space Cognac in his private quarters of The Terran Council's army base, on the tiny Martian Phobos Moon. Next to him were two beautiful female twins, named Greta and Magda, who had always been Bjorn's favourite prostitutes. When the conception and birth of Greta and Magda were approved, they had had their genetics DNA modified to suit the taste of Bjorn and other important House Muller members. As such, they were designed to have the perfect DNA for beautiful North European female appearance while also having an elevated sex drive to ensure that they enjoyed their field of work. People on Earth were not slaves and were free to choose whatever job they wanted. However, their preselected genetic abilities and the threat of deportation to Mars made most people accept the path assigned to them by the ruling class.

Bjorn had always enjoyed Greta and Magda's company in the past, but that had changed when he came across the beautiful and mesmerising Keila, four years earlier.

Something about Keila had changed him. His desire to dominate and own her, combined with her seductive rebellious nature, had led to him taking her as a hostage, repeatedly raping her while denying his own immorality. His false sense of righteousness combined with a fake pretence and a high ego had resulted in catastrophic events that followed.

Since Keila assassinated Bjorn's grandfather, Hans Muller a few weeks after her escape from Bjorn, he had never dared to speak to anyone about his disturbing emotions for her. Seeing Keila's corpse had not helped these feelings, and he had constant nightmares of Keila coming after him from the afterlife.

Bjorn sent the sweet and obliging but boring twins, Greta, and Magda back to Earth. He had lost interest in them, and he had consumed large amounts of sexual enhancement drugs, to copulate with them in the past few days. Having sex with them was significant as it would be rude to his father not to accept his birthday gift. More importantly, Bjorn needed to prove to his other relatives that he was still virile.

Bjorn asked his father to send a few concubines from House Rashid territory to replace Greta and Magda. House Rashid's women had Mediterranean/Middle Eastern looks, and this would remind him more of Keila and could satisfy his desire to dominate.

Bjorn realised that his father would not be happy about the request, but he would grant it. While sex between the different races on Earth was not encouraged within House Muller, it was not taboo like it was to have sex with Martians or other extra-terrestrials.

When Bjorn opened his computer, he was met with an email from his superior in the Terran Council Armed Forces, Admiral Max Wellington:

"Good News Bjorn. As it turns out, the chief scientist on your vessel Markus Bauer, was not killed when the science bay dislodged after the explosion. Instead, he survived and was taken hostage by pirates. He has been freed from the pirates and is en route to our Phobos base to debrief after the incident. Best Regards. Admiral Max Wellington"

Reading this Bjorn felt an uncontrollable bout of anger and smashed the monitor with so hard, so he started bleeding. Bjorn bandaged his wounds, and then lined some drugs and headed to the shooting range to blow of some steam.

Chapter 33: Keila Searches for Zetan technology

Keila was getting restless and unsure on how to start her rebellion against the Terran Council. She had a few thousand followers comprising of the population of Eden, but they were mostly illiterate, and living in the past. Furthermore, they had no reason to fight the Terran Council and they seemed happier to live the way they were. Although Keila had started to modernise Edenite culture, they were short of, literally every resource needed to create a modern society with modern armed forces.

The problem for Keila was that Eden could house and equip over 100,000 individuals from Mars with modern advanced farming and technologies, but she could not entice these people to move to Eden and join her cause without getting the attention from the Terran Council. The last thing that she wanted was their attention.

To defeat her enemy, she needed to create an underground movement, and sabotage Earth's economy. Furthermore, she needed to get the Terran factions to start fighting each other. Keila knew that there was a lot of mistrust and scepticism between the great Houses of Earth and that they always fought each other through proxies. So how would she turn them against each other?

Keila realised that the answer might lie in the vast Zetan archives. The Zetans had ruled the galaxy for over 100 millennia, so they would have had superior technology.

After searching for many days, Keila found what she was looking for. She summoned Metatron to join her and to understand the spectacular Zetan technologies that she had discovered. Metatron joined her, and they studied blueprint schematics of the Zetan technologies that could help them win the war against the Terran Council.

The most prominent Zetan technologies were:

The Zetan Spherical Communication Blocker: This technology created a 20,000 cubic kilometre large sphere that blocked all incoming and out-going communications. This would help them to surprise-attack the Terran Council, dominate their fuel-mining colonies and obliterate their military outposts undetected.

The Zetan Advanced Cloaking Device: A highly advanced electromagnetic cloaking device that blocked out 99 % of all the reflected light of a spaceship as well as 95 % of the heat signature, making it almost invisible to the interplanetary military surveillance. While it was not failsafe if someone were looking for them, it would be than enough to approach the Terran Council's military outposts and mining stations undetected.

The Zetan Ballistic Energy Absorber: This device was powered by a high-powered battery that could repel any form of kinetic energy from incoming projectiles. It protected in the form of a 1-metre sphere, and it made all bullets, shrapnel, metal pieces and other projectiles drop to the ground. The battery was the limiting factor, as the design would use up all the battery quickly when the wearer stood out in the open receiving heavy fire.

The Zetan Non-Encrypted Bionic Chip Disruptor: A device that emitted a signal that disrupted the function of all non-encrypted bionic microchips within its range. As the Terran Council forces were reliant on bionic microchips and implants, their soldiers would be useless when their microchips were disrupted by the chip disruptor.

The Zetan External DNA Modifier: The technology the Zetan had used when they came to Earth posing as human gods. The outer layer DNA modifier was an advanced Zetan serum that changed the superficial outer layer of a person to that of another person of choice. This way, a person would look like and smell like the person of choice, but the brain would remain the same as before. This would be very useful for infiltration purposes.

With all these fantastic alien technologies at her disposal, Keila felt a glimmer of hope of challenging and taking on the Terran Council. However, she would still need to rely on espionage and subterfuge for the time being as the difference in numbers was too great to take on the Terran Council at this stage.

Keila realised that she needed to reverse engineer and create these extra-terrestrial devices on a large scale. While she could create all the prototypes with the particle replicator, a future technology equivalent of a 3-D printer, this was a slow process and expensive way to produce equipment on a large scale. Keila needed was to turn Eden into a production plant for these extra-terrestrial technologies. But to achieve that she needed technological know-how as well as obtaining rare compound elements. Keila was low on both. Keila sighed and sat down. She would have to sit back for a while and wait for another sign. The visions would tell her what to do, and it would be silly to risk this excellent opportunity by rushing it.

Chapter 34: Admiral Max Wellington Confronts Bjorn Muller.

Admiral Max Wellington was sitting in his office at the Terran Council base on the Phobos Moon. He had met with Markus Bauer who had returned from the dead to file damning accusations against Bjorn Muller. According to Markus, the corpse of the criminal insurgent Keila Eisenstein was a decoy in the form of a non-functional clone that she had created to fake her own death. Furthermore, Markus claimed that Bjorn had been aware that the body was a decoy and the explosion in the science bay was Bjorn trying to silence Markus and get rid of the evidence at the same time. This was damning accusations, especially since Bjorn's father was the chairman of the Terran Council.

Admiral Max Wellington sighed. He would have preferred to stay uninvolved in this matter as it was a bomb that could blow up in his face. If he accused the son of the Terran Council leader of treason he would be executed if he was proven to be wrong. If he chose to not act on his suspicions it could also lead to his demise. Hence no matter what he did, his life was in danger.

Max evaluated Markus' claims. They seemed far-fetched and unlikely. According to Markus, he had survived for over a day in an airtight capsule with only an oxygen tank and no protective gear. He had passed out, and when he woke up, he had been a captive of the space pirate Morgan Henry. Eventually, Tzi Chen Cheng from the Science Commission, had paid ransom for him, and he was free to go.

This story made little sense to Max. It was unlikely that Markus had survived all this time in space on his own. It was more likely that his corpse was picked up by a House Cheng spaceship, they had revived him, and then told him to make false claims against Bjorn Muller. After being dead for an extended period, Markus would have been a complete mess when he woke up, and thus he was easy to manipulate.

On the other hand, while Markus' claims against Bjorn could be fabrications, Max wasn't ready to write them off. Max saw Bjorn as a spoiled, incompetent brat that had his high position in the Terran Council Interplanetary Forces solely due to his wealth and his family ties. While Admiral Max Wellington came from a poor family and had worked himself up, Bjorn Muller had shown up one day and was appointed as Rear Admiral, without proving himself.

Bjorn had never led soldiers in frontline battle, Bjorn was very distant from the daily lives of the soldiers that he commanded, and he showed very little interest in what was and what wasn't achievable in actual combat and battle missions. When missions didn't go according to plan, Bjorn always passed the blame on someone else, and he got away with it due to his family ties.

Admiral Max Wellington knew that the Terran Council was aware of Bjorn's incompetence. Otherwise, they wouldn't have ordered him to stay in command of their Phobos base. While Max was in command, he could not give orders to his subordinates without Bjorn's approval or get Bjorn to do anything as there was no way to reprimand the rich spoilt bastard. This led to a very dysfunctional command management structure on the military base. Max invited Bjorn Muller to his office, and eventually, Bjorn showed up, lazy and drunk.

Bjorn:

- Hi Max.

- We should really have these meetings in my office instead. It's a bigger room, packed with a nicer couch and a better alcoholic beverage selection.

Max bit his lip in bitterness. He feels a surge of jealousy and rage. Despite being the commander on the base, his office and private quarters were smaller and standard-looking, and it annoyed him every time Bjorn brought it up.

Max:

- As I understand it, your office has a better selection of prostitutes as well. I had to approve your latest requests this morning...

Max showed Bjorn a bunch of brochures and photos with different prostitutes, all posing in their spacesuit bikinis.

Bjorn:

- How delightful. I have been looking forward to these fresh-looking ones.

Max:

- Shut up, Bjorn.
- There are some grave accusations against you.

Bjorn:

- Then, let's be serious.
- What were the accusations?

Max Wellington:

- I met with Markus Bauer the other day, and he claimed several things about you.

Bjorn Muller:

- Wasn't Markus killed during the explosion at the science bay a couple of months ago?

Max Wellington:

- Well, apparently not!

- Markus claimed that the explosion in the science bay was an attempt made by you to silence him and get rid of the corpse of Keila Eisenstein, which he said was a decoy.

Bjorn felt crippling fear, and he had to force himself not to crack under pressure. He took a deep breath, calmed his mind, and nonchalantly answered:

- So, a man of no importance is coming back from the dead to accuse me of treason. How absurd! Does he have any proof of his claims?

Max:

- Yes, it does sound absurd, and there is no proof.
- The question remains: Is he telling the truth?

Bjorn:

- Of course not! The explosion in the Science Bay was an accident. I have several witnesses who saw the body of Miss Eisenstein.

- Tell me, how does Markus claim he survived the explosion?

Max:

- He claims he was taken hostage by the space pirate Morgan Henry, and then freed by a Tzi Chen from House Cheng who paid his ransom.

Bjorn Muller:

- Ahh, I see. This is a political play from House of Cheng.

- As a son of the Terran Council chairman, I command you to stay out of it!

Max:

- Okay, Bjorn. I'm only doing this because of your family ties.

Bjorn:

- Thank you for being sensible, Max.
- Where is Markus Bauer now? I would like to speak to him.

Max:

- I transferred him to another placement.

- As a non-aligned Admiral, I'll keep his location classified, to avoid confrontation between the two of you. He is a worthy scientist of the Terran Council.

Bjorn:

- That's ridiculous! I can call my father, Joachim Muller, and ask for the location.

Max:

- Yes, but then you'll have to tell your father about why you are looking for Markus.

Bjorn stormed out towards the door in anger, and he kicked the door before he left the room. Max interrupted him:

- Rear Admiral, I'm sorry but one more thing...

Bjorn turned around and looked at Max:
Max:

- How come your latest selection of prostitutes are all the spitting images of Miss Keila Eisenstein?

Bjorn lost his temper and yelled back at his superior:

- That's because I like to fantasise about fucking and dominating my enemies, unlike you, you old eunuch!

Having shouted this, Bjorn slammed the door and left Max's office.

Chapter 35: Bjorn Muller Finds Markus Bauer's Location.

Bjorn was seething with anger when he came back to his office after meeting with Max Wellington. How dared that pathetic man reprimand him for his behaviour and refuse to give him the location of Markus Bauer?

Bjorn was fuming, but he realised that he was better off directing his focus towards finding Markus Bauer than he was plotting revenge against Max Wellington. Finding Markus wouldn't be easy, as his location was classified, but Bjorn could find him, using a more laborious way.

As a Rear Admiral, Bjorn had access to all the security cameras from the Terran Council installations throughout the Solar System. There were several thousand of them, and Bjorn would have preferred to just let the computer do the auto-search, but Markus Bauer's location was classified, and Bjorn didn't want to explain to his father why he needed to find Markus' location. Sifting through all the security camera recordings would take months, but if he narrowed the search to only look through the cameras in the science bays of the stations, he was likely to find Markus Bauer's location in a day or two. To Bjorn's relief he had helpers for this task:

Intisar and Kinnette were the latest female assistants that were sent to take care of Bjorn's needs. His father had complained about the expense to hire these exotic-looking women and over their racial genetic makeup. Bjorn had answered that no man could be expected to eat the same meal every day and his father had let go of the topic. The two escorts were surprised when he tasked them with finding Markus Bauer, but they seemed happy to comply.

Bjorn studied Intisar and Kinnette from his fancy expensive armchair, made from the leather of rare animals that only existed in the Alpha Centauri star system. As they were looking for Markus Bauer, Bjorn checked them out from head to toe. Studying them made him aroused. They were the spitting images of Keila. He imagined playing out his fantasies on them. This time without ending up in excruciating pain from the encounter.

Bjorn spent the next few hours drinking expensive Scotch and snorting the synthetic drug Amorphia, which speeded up his thought patterns and made him highly aroused. His sexual satisfaction peaked 5 hours later, when Intisar let him know that she had found Markus Bauer. Bjorn looked on the screen and confirmed that the man was Markus Bauer. Pleased with Intisar's effort, he kissed her cheek and transferred 20,000 Terran Credits to her "diamond bank", a microchip inserted into the user's neck that was the 29th century equivalent of cash as the transaction was untraceable, and discreet.

Having found Markus Bauer's location, Bjorn Muller engaged in a marathon sex session with Intisar and Kinnette before letting them retreat to a sleeping capsule, recovering for their next sexual interaction. After this Bjorn fell asleep drained but fulfilled.

Chapter 36: Markus Bauer Smells a Rat.

A few days later, at the Proxima Thule research and mining station, Markus Bauer was getting paranoid and restless. When he spoke to Admiral Max Wellington about what had happened, the Admiral had seemed sympathetic and had promised him a secret location where he would not be harmed while investigations of the claims occurred. While he trusted the Admiral, Markus was sure that something was amiss.

Since Markus had arrived at Proxima Thule, it seemed like most of the employees on the space station had been granted leave at the same time. It did not make any sense. Proxima Thule required a certain amount of personnel to conduct research, but with everyone on vacation and just a minimal crew left to support the operations, the research had come to a standstill.

Markus worried that he was a sitting duck on Proxima Thule. If someone wanted to hurt him, there was no way to get out of there.

Where would Markus go anyway? If Bjorn Muller wanted him dead, going back to Earth would be suicide. Seeking refuge at Mars was an awful idea, as he was more likely getting robbed and killed by the barbaric Martians than he was securing meaningful employment. But what about joining up with Keila and seeking refuge on Eden? If the body of Keila was a decoy, that meant that the rulers of Eden were collaborating with Keila to rebel against the Terran Council.

Markus felt ashamed. Although his life was at risk, he did not want to betray his brethren on Earth. Although the Terran Council was a brutal plutocratic dictatorship, it brought peace to Earth and stability to the Solar System. The end justified the means and besides it wouldn't make sense to rebel against the organisation he had worked for during the last 20 years.

Markus logged in on a computer to check his work schedule. What he saw overwhelmed him with a wave of paranoia. He was meant to perform maintenance on a set of gravitation turbines on his own at the fringe of the space station. This task was risky and always performed in groups. The only reason someone would have him do it by himself, was that there must be a "planned accident" waiting for him down there.

Seeing this, Markus Bauer changed his mind and he contacted the rebels on Eden. He contacted Metatron via an encrypted message on Spacenet, hoping to obtain some help.

Chapter 37: Keila Receives a Suspicious Signal.

Keila was sitting on the throne in the temple of an Edenite village receiving offerings from the villagers. She was accompanied by several Angels that acted as her bodyguards as a precaution.

Keila deemed it necessary to come down and take part in the daily lives of her Edenite followers. She wanted to utilise a different leadership style than Abraham's, so instead of using commands and threats from afar, she aimed to be a good role model that the people could look up to.

Keila was used to be a role model during her years with the Martin Humanist Alliance, but she wasn't used to being worshipped like a god. She had mixed feelings about her "divinity". While, Keila had pointed out that she was not a divine being, it felt good being revered, loved, and spoiled. In the last few months, Keila had eaten so much tasty food that her previously rock-hard solid body had loosened up and started to get round, something she would have to address.

Despite having a comfortable time as the "goddess" of Eden, Keila got increasingly impatient. The modernisation of Eden was moving at a glacial pace, as she lacked both the personnel and the resources required to make Eden a powerful base of operations in the resistance against the Terran Council.

The city of Pamshal on Mars was one of the Terran Councils recent targets. As Keila grew up there, the entire city was considered hostile, and the military had tested a new dangerous weaponised virus on the Martian settlement. The virus was a synthetic and airborne genetically modified virus, making it the ultimate weapon for chemical warfare. Being synthetic, it would not spread between organisms, so it was easy to contain the target to a specific area. The victims would have Ebola-like symptoms and die a slow and painful death, with blisters and boils appearing from their eyes and bodies. Watching the footage of Pamshal through her holographic television in Eden, Keila recognised several former friends dying slow and painful deaths. The worst part for Keila was that Pamshal was not the collateral damage of war, but an indiscriminate mass murder conducted by an arrogant, and tyrannical government.

Feeling shocked and helpless, Keila lost focus on the Edenite offerings, and she smashed a pot of olive oil in an instance of rage. The crowd turned silent and looked at her in fright. Keila apologised, but did not know how to handle the situation, so she rushed off into the wilderness with the bewildered Edenites staring at her.

Eventually, Keila got out of sight from the crowd, and she calmed down. She sat on a rock near a small pond and stared out at the deep blue sky. Metatron contacted her.

Keila:

- Hi Metatron. I know what you are going to say; I am sorry about smashing the pot. I zoned out and had a rush of anger.

Metatron:

- Don't worry about it, Keila.

- When Abraham lost his temper, he used to have people stoned or set aflame. I am sure that they don't mind a broken pot.

- I'll let them know that you forgive them.

Keila:

- That I forgive them?
- I was the one who broke their olive oil pot for no reason.

Metatron:

- Abraham never apologised for anything. Apologising would only confuse your people. Let's change things for the better but not too quickly.

Keila:

- Okay, fair call.

Metatron:

- Yes. The reason I called you is something far more critical.

- We received an encrypted message from someone called Markus Bauer. He knows that you are alive, and he wants to join our faction. He is on the Terran Council research station Proxima Thule, only a few days travel away. According to Markus, the station is inadequately defended and full of valuable resources and research data.

Keila:

- That sounds like an obvious trap!

Metatron:

- Yes.
- Shall I ignore the transmission?

Keila sat down to think. She didn't trust Markus Bauer, as he was a prominent Terran Council scientist. But if the Terran Council knew that she had faked her own death, they would come with a large fleet to apprehend her on Eden. So why hadn't they? Eden had strong defences, but not strong enough to deter the army from attacking. The resources, equipment, and scientists on Proxima Thule could prove crucial to speed up her efforts to make Eden a base of operations for the resistance. It could be a trap, but it could also be what she needed.

Keila:

- No. Tell him we are coming within a week.

Metatron:

- Is that wise, considering the likelihood for it being a trap?

Keila:

- Yes. My instincts tell me that the Terran Council is not behind this. If they knew about our deception, they would destroy Eden from afar with no regards to collateral damage. They wouldn't send a scientist to plead for our partnership.

- I will take a ship equipped with Zetan technology and surprise him. You stay here and look after Eden.

Metatron:

- But I want to go with you, to keep you safe.

Keila:

- I would feel safer with you by my side, but we must think about the people. If we both die, there is no-one to support Eden. Eventually the civilisation will break, and they will all die. We cannot leave Eden until it's a self-sustaining colony,

Metatron:

- You are right, my love.
- May the light guide you and the True Maker keep you safe!

Chapter 38: The Attack on Proxima Thule.

The officer in charge of Proxima Thule, Captain Berndt Messerschmitt was looking at a screen. He felt that the research station he oversaw was threatened. For some reason, the spoilt, arrogant brat Bjorn Muller had authorised everyone to leave the station. This left the Proxima Thule station with only 10 per cent staffing. This amounted to only a dozen security officers and around 50 scientists and engineers.

Considering the amount of valuable resources and technology on the station, Berndt worried that the station would get attacked and looted. Bjorn had dismissed the concerns and said that they had enough automated defences to deal with any enemy before they entered the station.

A display started beeping saying that a ship had docked with the station. Berndt looked out and to his shock, he saw that an old House Goldstein transport vessel had docked with the station.

House Goldstein! They were no longer part of the Terran Council, and had no business being there. How had the ship snuck up on him unnoticed? Berndt activated the emergency beacon, and he tried to contact other stations close by for backup. But the communications were down, all that he heard was eerie static.

Berndt grabbed his gun and ordered the other security officers come with him to the docks. What he saw. At the docks was the infamous terrorist Keila Eisenstein flanked by a group of soldiers with wings-like space suits. As he approached her, she called out:

"Captain, I require that you surrender this station to me. Do this and you'll live. Do not, and you will die"

Berndt noticed that Keila and her soldiers were standing out in the open, with no defensive armour. It didn't make sense, but they were easy targets and killing her would bring him a promotion. *"Fire at will!"* he commanded his men, and they all started shooting at Keila's group.

To Berndt's shock and awe, the bullets stopped mid-air and they fell to the ground as the bullets came close to Keila and her troops. Keila ran up to Berndt and shot all the other soldiers in their heads with her pistol. Keila said, *"You should have surrendered Captain"*. It was the last thing Berndt heard before everything turned black.

Chapter 39 The Looting of Proxima Thule

Keila looked at the battery indicator on her Zetan Ballistic Energy Absorber, which strapped nicely on her arm. It was down to 1 %. A few more bullets and she would have been dead, if her battery had run out and her Zetan technology no longer stopping the bullets. She had been careless, but lucky, and she reminded herself that she needed to be more careful in the future.

She needed to act quickly. The Zetan Spherical Communication Blocker would stop anyone from communicating with the outside, but the complete absence of communications would arouse suspicions. The Terran Council would send people to investigate what had happened.

Keila gathered the scientists and engineers in one room and sprayed in sleep-inducing gas to put them all to sleep. After that, she and her group removed any bionic microchip that could give away a person's location from the sleeping scientists. After that, they inserted Divine Technology "Human" chips into the scientists' brains so she could force their loyalty once they woke up.

After placing the unconscious scientists aboard their vessel, they looted all the rare elements and equipment that they could find, and they also downloaded all the data available unto memory units. Finally, they blew up a small EMP grenade inside the mainframe of Proxima Thule. This would delete all the security footage of the attack and turn off the station's air supply, suffocating any survivor that might be in hiding.

After doing all of this, they returned to their transport ship, activated their cloaking device, and travelled back to Eden.

Chapter 40 Reconnaissance Report to the Terran Council

Wednesday 17*th* October 2872:

We arrived at Proxima Thule, three days after communications with the space station ended. What we found indicates an organised attack by an unknown assailant. We found all the members of the station's security team shot in the heads with a pistol from a close distance. Initial findings indicate that they are all permanently dead, but we will freeze their bodies and bring them back to Earth for a thorough examination. The attack must have come as a surprise for the security team as they were all just wearing standard-issue jumpsuits and not combat armour.

Despite the security team being shot point-blank execution-style, there are still indications of them firing their weapons at the assailants. The corridor is littered with empty shells next to their bodies and their hands are filled with traces of gunpowder. Strangely, we found a lot of undamaged bullets lying around between the corridor and the docks of the station. We do not know how these bullets ended up there with undamaged tips, as it defies the laws of physics. We have attached pictures of the scene.

As for the scientists and engineers on the vessel, we have not found any trace of them and we must assume that they were taken as hostages by the assailants.

I recommend that you send a specialist forensic team to investigate the occurrence. We will set up a perimeter and secure the area for further investigations.

Captain Michael Meyer

5*th* reconnaissance squadron

Chapter 41 Markus Bauer Meets Keila.

Markus Bauer was in a holding facility on the dark side of Eden with his fellow scientist abductees from Proxima Thule. He was regretted what he had done and felt a deep shame for causing the death of the security staff due to Keila Eisenstein's violent raid.

What was he thinking? Alerting the enemy about a weakly-defended research base could only lead bloodshed. While the loss of life was regrettable, Markus Bauer's biggest concern was his own wellbeing and he worried about it. He had hoped to be introduced to Keila in high regard when they attacked Proxima Thule. Instead, she and her cronies had grouped him together with the rest of the science staff and put him to sleep with gas. He had woken up in this holding facility with no idea where he was or what day it was.

Markus felt someone's presence, and Keila appeared out of nowhere in the centre of the room. Was he losing his mind? Markus concluded that he wasn't, as the rest of the room also stared at the woman in the middle of the room.

Keila:

- Greetings, Scientists from Proxima Thule. You are my prisoners of war and will be treated as such. While you were asleep, you were implanted with Divine Technology human chips, an experimental technology that allows me to see your every thought as well as communicating to you.

- I am going to give you a choice. Either you can defect, join my faction, and thus eventually win your freedom. Or you can stay loyal to the Terran Council and remain here as prisoners. Choose carefully, because if you join me and betray me, I will know about it and you'll die a terrible death.

Markus answered Keila's message. Not knowing how the implanted chip worked, he opted to scream out his words instead of just relaying it telepathically.

Markus:

- I am Markus Bauer, and I am the one who informed you about the weak defences on Proxima Thule. I pledge myself to your cause, and I require that you treat the captured scientists well.

Hearing about Markus Bauer's betrayal, and it prompted some of the other prisoners to attack him. Keila intervened and sent psionic blasts against some of the attackers to keep Markus safe.

Keila:

- Prisoners! I wish to speak to this prisoner in private. Do not harm him or you'll pay the ultimate price. Markus, go through that the door I just opened, the rest of you stay where you are.

Markus walked through the blast door and entered a waiting area. As he came in the door closed behind him. He was waiting there for a long time, until one of the Angels escorted him to a shuttle. The shuttle flew to the Divine Control Centre. The Angel escorted him to the meeting room where Keila was sitting in an armchair overlooking Eden through a large panorama window. The Angel left, and Markus was left alone with Keila in the room. She turned the chair around and looked at him.

Keila:

- So, Markus. Why are you here?

Markus:

- Because I am your prisoner and you summoned me.

Keila:

- While technically correct, that doesn't answer my real question. How did you know I was alive and why do you want to join me?

Markus:

- I knew you were alive, because I was the one who carried out your autopsy. I want to join you because Bjorn tried to kill me to cover up that you are not dead.

Keila:

- Fair enough. Did you ever wonder why Bjorn Muller was so afraid of the truth coming out?

Markus:

- I suppose it would be embarrassing to admit that you are alive after announcing your death.

Keila:

- No. That's not it. I will tell you the truth.

- When I was 18 years old, Bjorn took me as a prisoner. He never took down my details as he wanted me as his unregistered sex slave. I escaped and mutilated him in the process.

- After that I infiltrated the Terran Council Martian Headquarters, and I assassinated Hans Muller, who was the chairman of the Terran Council at the time. That's how the latest rebellion started.

- Because of Bjorn's sexual depravity, Hans died, and House Muller got weaker.

- Bjorn is terrified that my corpse would reach the Terran Council. If they found a way to revive me, the world would know about his failure.

- That's why he never questioned why my men delivered him a non-functional clone. Because Bjorn never intended for me to be revived and interrogated.

Markus:

- So, all of this is because Bjorn raped you?

Keila:

- No. All of this is because I want justice and freedom for my fellow Martians. If my only goal were to kill Bjorn, I would have blown up his ship with Eden's weapon systems when I had the chance. That would have exposed me and destroyed my opportunity to reignite the insurrection against the Terran Council.

Markus:

- Reignite the Rebellion? Are you kidding me? We wiped out your entire leadership, and we killed tens of thousands when we destroyed your rebel base on the asteroid Sylvia. Eden is nothing compared to what you had on asteroid Sylvia. You were no match back then, so what's different this time?

Keila:

- I have something that you lack: faith.

- And do not refer to the Terran Council as "we". You are working for us now.

Markus:

- Understood. What do you want me to do?

Keila:

- I have acquired advanced alien technology. I need you to assemble a group of scientists, and reverse engineer this technology so we can mass-produce it here on Eden.

Markus:

- Interesting. I will get on it at once.

Keila:

- Good. Build a good team, Metatron will show you to your site on Eden.
- Dismissed.

As Markus left the meeting room, he was filled with disbelief. What on Earth had he got himself into? For over 800 years of space, exploration humanity had never come across any advanced alien civilisations. The probability that Keila accessed technology that the rest of mankind hadn't was minuscule. Then again, she seemed very sure of herself, and the mind control probe she had inserted into his, and the other scientist's brains were new technology. Markus decided to keep an open mind as he set up a list of scientists who were likely to be willing to become Keila's followers.

Chapter 42: Joachim Muller Summons Bjorn Muller to Earth.

Bjorn Muller exited his shuttle at the landing site in Hansstadt in the European Alps. Hansstadt was the location for the House Muller headquarters, Europeum Tower, which was the tallest building in the world. Although the tower was not as magnificent as when it was constructed a century prior, it was still a marvel of technology displaying the wealth and power of House Muller.

Bjorn Muller was happy to be home and able to live a life of comfort and luxury. It had been over a year since his last visit to his home city, and although his position in the space force comfortable, there was only so much one could do to make a military ship comfortable. Although he was offered a ride from the landing site to Europeum Tower, Bjorn Muller opted to walk. He wanted to inhale the fresh air and experience all the smells he could not experience in space.

Although Bjorn's head was energised, his body was not. Even though both his command ship ISS Supreme Earth and the Terran Council military headquarters on Phobos had artificial gravity, this gravity was not enough to simulate the gravity on Earth and as such Bjorn felt very weak and unfit once he had to move on Earth with full gravity.

After walking for two hours, Bjorn reached Europeum towers and entered the lift to his father's penthouse level. The elevator scanned his DNA and gave him access to his father's penthouse. As it was 3000 meters up, he would spend a couple of minutes in the elevator, so he had a rest on the bench inside the lift.

He looked at himself in the mirror, and much to his dismay his Rear Admiral uniform was drenched in sweat from the exerting walk from the space port. As Bjorn was used to working in conditions with 20 % gravity, the 100 % gravity on Earth felt very heavy for him.

Bjorn wondered why his father had summoned him and he concluded that his father had summoned him to Earth to be closer to him. Had his father organised a suitable bride for him? Bjorn would agree to any bride. He was sick of space and if he had to spend his days with some stupid swamp monkey to please his father, so be it; he could always have fun on the side.

The lift reached its destination. Bjorn exited the elevator and walked to his father's dining room. Much too Bjorn's dismay, his father was the only one at the dinner table, which was set for three persons. Apparently, his father had not organised a welcome party. Joachim Muller gave Bjorn a sour look.

Joachim Muller:

- I haven't seen you in over a year, and here you are, a slob bringing disgrace to your uniform!

Bjorn:

- Nice to see you too, dad...

Joachim:

- The pleasure is all yours...

Bjorn lost his patience. His relationship with his father had been strained for many years, but he could not accept being treated like dirt after travelling this far.

Bjorn:

- Fucking hell, dad. I came all the way from Phobos, and you treat me like this.

- Why did you summon me?

Joachim:

- Sit down!!

Bjorn Muller sat down, and Joachim continued speaking:

- Our medical team managed to temporarily revive Captain Berndt Messerschmitt before he succumbed to his injuries...

Bjorn Muller:

- Who is that?

Joachim Muller got up, slapped his son, and got seated again.
Joachim:

- You fucking degenerate. Stop obsessing with your hookers. You should know.

- Captain Berndt Messerschmitt oversaw Proxima Thule, our science and mining station that was hit by unknown assailants, a month ago.

Bjorn bit his lip and said nothing. He was angry at his dad for slapping him, but even more irritated at himself for his embarrassing mistake. Bjorn had plenty of implants to help his memory and reasoning skills, yet too often his stupidity took over.
Bjorn:

- Okay.
- Did he say anything worthwhile during his short return to life?

Joachim:

- He claimed that Keila Eisenstein and a group of men with peculiar armour arrived out of nowhere. Apparently Keila had mind-blowing technology that stopped bullets mid-air. She killed him and the other defenders.

Bjorn:

- That's absurd. His brain must have been beyond repair. That's why he died shortly after.

Joachim:

- Yes. But the days before the attack, you sent 90 % of the staff on leave.

Bjorn:

- That's coincidental. The rebellion forced me to keep bases fully staffed for years on end. I just saw the opportunity to sort out all the leaves at once, especially since no vital research takes place there.

- Besides Captain Messerschmitt should have done his job instead of being taken by surprise. How easy is it to sneak into an asteroid base undetected? It is unheard of!

Joachim:

- Blaming the dead won't teach us anything worthwhile.

- I don't like your connection with this Keila woman. I don't like it one bit!

Bjorn Muller:

- Connection?

- You mean risking my life chasing her down, while you sit in your cushy boardroom? You're welcome!

Joachim thought of hitting Bjorn again, but he controlled himself. Instead, he spoke in a cold and distant voice barely hiding his contempt.
Joachim:

- No. I am talking about the fact that you asked me to send you whores looking like her at a great expense.

- I am talking about the fact that you lost her corpse in space and instead of retrieving it, ran back to Phobos with your tail behind the back.

- I am talking about the rumours that you were seen with her on ISS Supreme Earth, just weeks before she accessed to our Martian headquarters and killed your grandfather Hans Muller.

Bjorn sat silent. He didn't know how to defend himself, and his father's fierce attack made him feel both heartbroken and afraid. Bjorn felt deep shame and sense of guilt, for indirectly causing the death of his grandfather. Joachim continued his tirade.

- If you weren't my son, I would have you assassinated by now. Unfortunately, you are my son, so I can't use those options. This leaves me with a third option.

- As Admiral Max Wellington cannot keep you in line, I am putting you under the command of Alicia White.

Bjorn was flabbergasted and couldn't believe what he was hearing. Working under the freak Alicia White?! His father was surely joking about this. Bjorn:

- I hope you are joking.

Joachim:

- I certainly am not.

Bjorn:

- But she is a freak?! She is a failed genetic mutation experiment, a by-product of DNA modification error?!

Joachim:

- I suggest that you share your emotions with her. She is joining us
for dinner.

Alicia White was the daughter of House White CEO's John White. She
was his favourite child, but to everyone else, she was a freak; a fearsome re-
minder of the dangers of excessive genetic modification of embryos.

John White had always wanted a warrior-princess type of human as his
successor, and when the genetic modification of Alicia's embryo took place,
he took it too far outside of the box.

By mixing in the human embryo with DNA from other predator species,
Alicia was born fearless and dangerous, with predatory super senses, but lacking human empathy and any regard for social standards. She had the sense
of smell of a wolf, the night vision and sharp retractable claws of a tiger, the
courage and temper of a bull and the explosiveness of an ambushing croco-
dile. Unfortunately, her explosive feats came with a drawback, as she was de-
formed with fangs hanging outside of her lips, the tongue of a serpent, glowing yellow eyes, and a tiny tail that formed a round lump at the end of her
back. She also had the unfortunate tendency to scratch people with her claws
and lick them in the face.

As Alicia could not be seen on the board of House White, her father
had to hide her away in the Black Operations department of House White.
Alicia was happy to work there as it provided her with the opportunity to
take part in her favourite activities: torturing and killing other humans in the
most brutal sadistic way possible.

When Joachim complained to John about his problems with putting
Bjorn in place, John had suggested that Bjorn was assigned to serve under
Alicia, as her fearsomeness had put others in place throughout the years. To-
gether they had tasked Alicia's group to find with the people that attacked
Proxima Thule the prior month.

Alicia entered the dining room. Bjorn and Hans stood up to greet her.
Without a word, she walked up to Bjorn, grabbed him by the balls and licked
him in the face. *"Bjorn Muller: we meet again"*, she hissed. Bjorn Muller was
stunned by shock, and his father felt compelled to act.

Joachim:

- That's enough Alicia! Let him go.

Alicia:

- As you wish, Chairman Muller.

Alicia let go of Bjorn, who took a deep breath of relief. After that, she walked up to Joachim, shook his hand, and bowed to him, before taking her place at the table. The butler came in and served the meal. Bjorn looked in disgust at Alicia, as her meal was a kilo of raw meat and nothing else. She declined the offered wine and instead drank a glass filled with animal blood. Bjorn felt compelled to comment on her choice of drink:

- Alicia! House Muller is famous for making the best wine in the world, and we are also known for making the best wine glasses in the world. Glasses that are not meant for the filth that you are drinking.

Alicia hissed back at him:

- Alcohol is a deadly poison; animal blood is good for you!

Alicia drank the glass of animal blood, and then she licked her lips, while looking at Bjorn. Joachim Muller added in:

- Due to Alicia's unique genetics, her liver cannot break down alcohol. Thus, her refusal to drink our most excellent vintage wines isn't rude

Bjorn:

- So, a drink is all it takes for her to go down? Good to know!

Joachim:

- Anyways. The reason that you are here is that John and I have decided to put Bjorn under Alicia's command. You are to use unsanctioned methods to find the assailants of Proxima Thule and to determine whether Keila Eisenstein is alive is true or not.

Alicia White:

- With pleasure, sir.
- I have waited five years to mix business and pleasure with your son.

Bjorn Muller:

- Never going to happen, freak!

Alicia White:

- We shall see.
- I must take my leave.
- I'll see you tomorrow sexy boy...

Alicia purred and winked with a wicked and predatory look in her eyes. After Alicia had left, Bjorn stared at his father with terror in his eyes, close to tears:

Bjorn:

- You cannot send me on a mission with that hideous monster??

Joachim:

- Yes, I can, and I will.

- Your whoring and substance abuse have annoyed me for decades, but the breaking point is your failure with this Keila Eisenstein. If she were to resurface after we declared her dead, we would lose face, and everyone will laugh at us. This is your mess, and you'll have to sort it out.

Bjorn:

- But Alicia is a monster. She infected the city Pamshal with a deadly synthetic virus killing tens of thousands.

Joachim shrugged his shoulders:

- Casualties are the fuel of war.

Bjorn:

- But this was after the war had ended.

Joachim Muller:

- Oh really. I better discuss this with John White. One faction cannot unilaterally destroy Martian cities without first consulting the Council.

- Anyway, this changes nothing for you, Bjorn. You better fix your mess or not come back at all.

- Those were the options that my father gave me back in 2785, and I did redeem myself in the end.

Bjorn was looking for words, but he came up with nothing. His father was right; except for his family name he had not achieved anything.

Instead, he was in trouble if Keila had tricked him and faked her death. He would be ridiculed throughout the solar system after his triumphant display of her body a few months prior, and he would be barred from holding a position of power. Dealing with the Proxima Thule situation and finding out the truth about Keila's death was the way to go, and it was his own responsibility to do so.

Bjorn was against his father's decision in one regard. He should have overseen the operation leading House Muller operatives, instead of being a subordinate of the vicious half-beast Alicia White.

Chapter 43 Alicia White Requests an Audience with Metatron.

Bjorn Muller was trying to catch some sleep in his room on Alicia White's unregistered black operations shuttle "SS Shady Business". He had been on the shuttle for a couple of weeks, and he hated every minute of it. His room was cramped, and a lot of it seemed to be used for storage. The food was basic and not close to the standard he was used to. But the worst part was that the shuttle was so small so that it lacked artificial gravitation. This meant that he had to sleep strapped to a bed, vastly different from the comfort he was used to.

Bjorn's former command ship ISS Supreme Earth was large, about 100 meters long and 60 meters wide and 60 meters high. Being of that size, it had double hulls. The outer shell had the thrusters that propelled the craft forward as well as armaments. The inner hull contained the living quarters and the command centre of the ship. The inner hull accelerated around its own axle to create gravity while being attached to the outer shell that propelled the craft forward. While the gravity on board a large vessel was still a lot weaker than on earth, it was still enough to be able to walk around, eat, drink, and sleep regularly.

Even more than the comfort of his command ship, Bjorn missed the feeling of being in command. While Bjorn was technically second in command for the mission, Alicia and her staff disrespected and ridiculed him, since they knew that he had no real power on this vessel.

Bjorn was interrupted in his thoughts when Alicia knocked on his door. Alicia:

- Rise and shine, pretty boy.

Bjorn:

- I am awake, you freak!

Alicia:

- Good. We are at the B528B asteroid. Time to sniff out your girl-friend, Keila.

Bjorn:

- I doubt that they will give us free access to search their base. Besides we have no official business being here.

Alicia:

- You'll find that I can be very persuasive.

They docked with B528B and Metatron with a group of angels met them at the docking station. Without a word, Alicia walked up to Metatron, grabbed him by the balls and hissed in his ear.

- Where is Keila?!
- I can smell her on you!

The other angels lifted their weapons and so did Alicia's entourage, so an armed standoff ensued. Alicia let go of Metatron. After gasping for air, he spoke.

- She is dead; we delivered her body to your friend over there, Bjorn Muller.

Alicia:

- Liar!

- I can smell her on you. She is here. I require access to search the station.

Meanwhile, Keila saw what was happening through the divine technology chips installed in the angels. She realised that fighting the Terrans was her last resort and she made her way to an emergency pod that took her down to the surface of Eden. She instructed Metatron to stall the intruders.

After a long wait, Metatron broke the silence:

- Okay, you can have a look around. But I can assure you that we will complain with the Terran Council about this.

Alicia:

- Complain as much as you want, you'll have a lot to answer for when we catch Keila!

Alicia and Bjorn walked around in the space station with Metatron as their hostage. After a few hours, they had seen everything, and they walked back to the docking station.

Alicia:

- Thank you for the tour. What a lovely station. We will meet again shortly.

Metatron:

- No, we will not. You are not welcome here anymore. Try anything funny, and we will shoot you on sight.

Alicia disregarded the threat. The man in front of her was gutless and had already been a pushover once. The people on the space station were scared of the Terran Council so there was no way they would ever try anything against them.

Alicia:

- Are you inviting me to dinner on Friday?! I don't know if I can fit it in, but I'll see you soon handsome!

Hearing her response, Metatron stared at her dumbfounded as she entered the shuttle and took off with her crew.

Once they were back in space Alicia spoke to Bjorn:

Alicia:

- Keila is there. Did you notice there was a room with female clothing in it and that one of the emergency pods was missing?

Bjorn:

- That doesn't prove anything. I doubt the Council will give us the permission to strike and the attack ships needed, based on circumstantial evidence.

Alicia:

- Oh, but I have proper evidence.

Alicia pulled out a pair of female underwear that she stole from the visit and smelled them. She growled.

Alicia:

- That is the smell of Keila!

Bjorn:

- Very well. Let's match the underwear with her DNA.
- If they match, we will get reinforcements and attack the station.

Alicia dumped the underwear into a garbage collector and propelled them out into space.

Alicia:

- No! Keila is my prey. Now that I know what she smells like, I know that she will be delicious!

Bjorn Muller:

- You are a fucking psycho. How do you think we'll reach Keila now?

Alicia White:

- I will find a way.

- But first, let's head to Proxima Thule. We have captured a spy, and I am hungry.

Chapter 44 Keila Receives a Disturbing Video Message

A few days later, Keila sat on a couch in the reception area of the Divine Control Centre overlooking space through the panorama window. She was angry and felt violated. The freak that the Terran Council had sent to look for her had intruded her residence and violated the integrity of her lover, Metatron. Worst of all, Keila had opted to hide on Eden instead of confronting her foe. While it had been a strategically correct decision as she couldn't fight the Terran Council at this time, it had still stung her. Keila was filled with anger and frustration over the intrusion.

What angered her the most was to see the disgusting slimeball and rapist Bjorn Muller among the intruders. Keila could not understand why he came down to lead a strike team instead of leading from the back of his command ship like he would However there he was, commanded by the beastly abomination that had driven the intruders.

Filled with anger, Keila punched a boxing sack in the gym with her bare fists until her knuckles bled and then she had a round of very rough sex with Metatron. Afterwards they lay in bed exhausted and satisfied, when they received a holographic video message with the following text, *"Keila! I found a survivor from the unfortunate Ebola outbreak in your hometown Pamshal. Hope to meet you soon!"*

The video was of Alicia White and a prisoner. Keila recognised the prisoner. He was her teenage crush from nine years earlier. In the video, the prisoner was chained to a wall, and Alicia was viciously tearing pieces of flesh from his body with her teeth. With blood all over her face, she turned towards the camera and smirked at it. She licked her lips and showed her sharp nasty fangs.

Keila had seen enough! She turned off the TV and rushed towards the shooting range for some more anger management as her knuckles were sore from before. *"Find out more about that woman! I want to kill her myself she screamed at Metatron!"* and then she left the bedroom.

Chapter 45 A Frenzied Alicia White Rapes and Almost Kills Bjorn Muller.

Alicia White was feeling ecstatic as she was resting after a violent and gruesome meal. There was nothing better to her than blood, violence and fresh human meat and she had it all. There was no better taste to Alicia than eating a human alive, and it was a pleasure Alicia seldom came across. She knew that her father was against her cannibalistic behaviour, but her men were loyal and would not tell him anything.

Besides, her father, John White never asked for the details about her secret operations as he preferred plausible deniability if things went south.

Alicia White felt that her blood was boiling with intense sexual desire. The object of her desire was Bjorn Muller. Alicia was craving for Bjorn for several reasons. Firstly, his genetics were optimised for good looks while the other men of her crew lacked that optimisation. Secondly, his prominent position in another faction made him attractive compared to the low-level grunts she usually slept around with. Thirdly, his disdain and revulsion towards her made him the ultimate object of sexual desire as Alicia thrived on dominating others against their will.

For the last month, she had contained her desires out of respect for her father's will and business interests. Giving in to her desire and sodomising Bjorn would lead to severe diplomatic tensions and problems between House White and House Muller. Her father could not afford that as he needed to keep House Muller close as he had hostile relations with other factions on the Terran Council. But Alicia felt a desire that was she couldn't resist any more.

Unbeknownst to Alicia, the man she devoured was a heavy user of synthetic Martian drugs. Combined with Alicia's hyper-sensitivity to recreational drugs, the drug residues she ingested from her victim's blood was enough to send her into a complete frenzy.

She tore off her tight-fitted snake-skin clothes and grabbed a syringe with a potent male aphrodisiac and made her way into Bjorn's quarters. Baffled, he couldn't get a word out before she jumped him, grabbed him with one arm and jabbed him in the neck with the syringe. *"I want you to fuck my slimy and horny pussy"* she hissed at him with the sounds of a deadly snake.

Bjorn regained his composure and pushed her away. Then he screamed at Alicia:

- What the fuck are you doing?!
- Get out of my room, you crazy freak!!

Alicia:

- I have waited long enough for you to come around. Fuck me now!

Bjorn:

- Over my dead body, freak!

Alicia gave Bjorn a psychotic smile and replied:

- As you wish, perfect human specimen. As you wish.

After that, Alicia jumped towards Bjorn and started strangling him. He punched her several times to get free, but in her frenzied state the impact from his fists made her even more aroused, and she grabbed his throat even stronger. As Bjorn passed out, she growled and let go of his neck so that she could tear apart his military pants and ride him as he had an involuntary erection from the drug that she had injected him with.

Having regained his breath, Bjorn screamed for help, and Alicia grabbed his throat again while she also bit deep into Bjorn's arm and drank the blood as it pumped from his artery.

Bjorn passed out and was close to dying. He was saved in the last minute when Alicia's operatives, rushed in to restrain Alicia White. She put up with a good fight but eventually the six of them managed to control her. They put

Bjorn on emergency iceblock and rushed him to the Phobos base for imme-diate medical treatment.

After dropping off Bjorn at the Phobos base, they took off, as the group was not inclined to explain how Bjorn had sustained his injuries.

Chapter 46: A Diplomatic Crisis.

Joachim Muller was lying restless in his bed in the penthouse level of Europeum tower. Bjorn had got him in trouble this time, and it was because of Joachim's incorrect decision to put Bjorn Alicia White's command. A few days earlier, Bjorn had arrived unconscious at the Phobos base, and when he woke up, he had made grave accusations against Alicia who was nowhere to be found. The medical examination supported Bjorn's allegations, and it was likely that Alicia had raped him and bit him.

Bjorn being sodomised was not the issue for Joachim. Bjorn was a sexual degenerate, and there were a lot of rumours stating that consent wasn't his primary concern when choosing his sexual partners. The fundamental issue was that Bjorn had aired his story in the media, and issued an arrest order for Alicia over what had happened.

Bjorn's accusations against Alicia had caused Joachim a lot of issues on the Terran Council, and it threatened his position as chairman. House White was his closest ally in the Terran Council, and they were both hostile towards House Rashid. Joachim was unsure whether House Cheng was with him or against him, as they were shifty and unpredictable. The fifth member on the Terran Council, House of Bolivar was too weak and unaligned to be a matter of interest.

Joachim's problem was that he needed to prove himself strong and loyal to his family. So, he needed to require that Alicia came back to Earth for a trial, while also trying to keep his ally John White.

John White had claimed that Alicia and her crew had gone rogue and that he was unable to command them back to Earth. This had forced Joachim to issue and arrest order against Alicia. Joachim hoped that John understood his predicament and avoided escalating the issue.

Realising that he wouldn't be able to sleep naturally, Joachim entered a sleep pod to rest and let go of his worries.

Chapter 47: A Challenge to a Duel.

Alicia White was sitting on the abandoned Moreno outpost in the asteroid belt. The Moreno outpost had served as a hotel, bar, and brothel for workers on the nearby asteroid mining facilities, but as they were mined out of minerals, the outpost had shut down. She was in a pickle and there was only one way to redeem herself, was to bring Keila Eisenstein's dead body to the Terran Council. That would shift focus from Bjorn's allegations against her to Bjorn's failure.

Alicia was shocked that Bjorn had acted the way he did. In hindsight, her actions were unacceptable but the conventional method of solving issues within the Terran Council was to settle them behind closed doors, away the public's knowledge. Bjorn had done the opposite. By accusing Alicia of rape, and issuing a warrant for her arrest, he had created the most significant crisis since the death of Hans Muller, five years earlier. The alliance between House White and House Muller was dissolved, and it was only a matter of time before skirmishes would take place, as the balance of power had shifted.

Alicia considered her options. She could come back to Earth to stand trial, but that was a considerable risk. Even if she got away with what she had done to Bjorn, a hearing risked spreading light on the atrocities Alicia had committed throughout the years. Another way would be to convince Bjorn to drop the charges. This option was unlikely as he already had made his accusations public. The third option was the best: To find and kill Keila Eisenstein and bring back her body to Earth. That would make Alicia a hero and humiliate Bjorn. The only problem with that was that Keila was hiding on a well-armed battle station with her advanced technology and soldiers.

Alicia realised that she needed to provoke Keila to come out from her base and face her on this outpost. Alicia recorded a provocative message and sent it to Eden. It was a risky move, because if Keila was smart, she could send the message anonymously to the Terran Council and let them deal with Alicia.

However, Alicia counted on Keila coming after her. Alicia was the one who had used synthetic viruses to kill everyone in Keila's hometown on Mars, the City of Pamshal. Alicia sent the message and she anticipated for the upcoming battle.

Alicia dragged a rat out of a cage, crushed it with her bare hands. Blood splattered all over her face, and then she licked the blood off her face and slurped it up ravishingly.

Chapter 48 Challenge Accepted.

Keila was heading towards Alicia's position in a shuttle, accompanied by a strike team. The strike team was Edenites that she had trained in modern combat. She had left Metatron and the Angels back on Eden for two reasons:

- If she was to walk into a trap and die, she wanted Metatron and his Angels to rule and modernise the Edenites. She cared about the people of Eden, and they were not ready to govern themselves yet.

- She wanted to test the ***Zetan non-encrypted bionic chip disruptor*** in action. Keila assumed that Alicia and her squad had unprotected microchips that would be affected. The angels had a lot of implanted microchips that would be affected by the device and make them perform poorly in combat. If Alicia's group were incapacitated when their bionic chips was disrupted, Keila and her inexperienced team would to kill their foes with ease.

Keila recalled the conversation she had had with Metatron before she left. He had wanted to relay the information to the Terran Council and let them deal with Alicia. It was common knowledge that Alicia had gone rogue and the Council had a warrant out for Alicia's arrest. While this solution had made logical sense, Keila had refused it. Keila had a vendetta against Alicia, as the freak had slaughtered her hometown with biological weapons and murdered her friend, Josh, to mock her.

They approached the Moreno outpost where Alicia was hiding. *"Be ready for anything!"* Keila told her troops as they docked with the outpost.

Chapter 49: The Showdown Between Keila and Alicia.

Keila stepped out of her shuttle and she realised that the artificial gravity on the Moreno outpost was very limited. This worried her as her troops had never trained for low gravity combat. While the gravity was still enough to prevent her from flying off when she walked there, the recoil of the weapons could prove challenging for her troops. She instructed her men to activate their Zetan ballistic energy absorbers but hold off with the Zetan bionic chip disruptors. Handheld devices had limited battery capacity, and she did not want to waste it before combat.

Keila entered the main lobby of the Moreno outpost and was greeted by a blood-soaked floor and Josh's head on a pike. Under Josh's head hung a sign: *"Welcome Keila, you are next".* Keila looked up, and Alicia swept in with a plasma sword and decapitated the soldier next to her. Before anyone had time to react, Alicia grabbed the head and jumped away to the cover of darkness. *"Hey! Your friend lost something!"* she mocked and threw back the head.

As Alicia screamed, some of Keila's troops lost their cool and started shooting randomly towards Alicia's voice. This was the cue for Alicia's operatives to hail bullets and grenades against Keila's position. The ballistic energy absorbers absorbed most of the impact, but some of Keila's soldiers fell as they had misdirected the devices.

Keila dropped to the ground and activated her Zetan bionic chip disruptor. This turned the tide of the battle as Alicia's operatives lost all ability and started acting very erratic, once their implants were disrupted. This made them easy targets and Keila's fighters eliminated them quickly.

Alicia was unaffected by the disruptor as she, opposite to most Terrans, relied on her wild animal instincts and not on bionic microchips. She swept in another time and decapitated another one of Keila's men. On her third swoop, she got hit by multiple bullets and was unable to jump away. Instead, she crawled behind one of Keila's female troops, grabbed the woman and pointed the plasma sword to her throat. Alicia screamed to Keila.

- I have one of your soldiers as a hostage. Face me in hand to hand combat, and I'll let her go.

Keila:

- You are surrounded, injured, and all your men are dead! Surrender, Alicia!

Alicia:

- Oh, heee hee!! The mighty and brave Keila, the poster girl for the Martian Humanist Alliance, the ever so famous guerrilla-fighter girl, is too afraid to face me huh!

Keila:

- I'm not afraid of you. Challenge accepted, bitch!

Keila stood up and threw away her rifle and grabbed her knife.
Alicia pushed away her hostage, hissed and said *"Excellent"*. She stared in shock as Keila pulled up her pistol and shot the exposed Alicia right between the eyes. Things went silent. Alicia paused for a second and screamed in agony. *"I'll get you Keila, I will get my revenge! Revive me and fight with honour!"* After shouting that out she dropped dead to the ground.
Keila:

- Thanks honey, but I prefer to do things the easy way.

Keila gently blew the smoke away from her pistol, and she smirked with a sweet, bright, and intelligent look in her eyes. After killing Alicia, Keila and her remaining troops dragged all the wounded and dead friends and enemies back on the shuttle and went back to Eden. They brought back their own troops to revive them while avoid being detected, and they brought back the fallen enemies to restore them and then extract intelligence from them.

Chapter 50: Brahma Reaches His Destination

Brahma stood outside Rangda's eternal prison, and he was relieved that his long 50,000-kilometre walk was over. It had taken longer than he had planned, as the searing thirst and hunger had forced him to have many extended meditations breaks to regain his mental clarity and keeping him going. Yet, despite the delays, less than a year had passed in the outside universe.

Brahma had been without food and drink for thousands of years, and yet he was immortal in this despicable place. This forced him to live while suffering from endless thirst and hunger. He had passed most of the last few millennia in deep meditation to avoid the torment, but walking to Rangda's prison had amplified his suffering.

Brahma approached the prison, and he saw that there was a tunnel made through the impenetrable wall of the building. Had Rangda managed to get out of the jail, and how had she done it? He looked at the ground where the tunnel exited and realised the solution. There was a ring on the ground.

Rangda's prison had been built using the second hardest material in the known universe, but the ring on the ground held a replicated Zeto Crystal, the hardest substance in the world. Brahma had a flashback from when they sealed Rangda into the prison.

The last thing he had done to her was to throw their engagement ring at her. This was the ring that Rangda had used to slowly dig herself out. Brahma felt the chills. He had struggled with thirst and hunger to walk here. Rangda must have struggled a lot more digging herself out of the eternal prison. She had shown an incredible determination when all she needed to do was to enter deep meditation and live out the eternity that way. What had driven her? The question filled Brahma with terror and confusion.

Brahma's terror increased when he turned around and saw Rangda for the first time in many thousand years. Her spirit was the same, but her body was disfigured. Instead of being beautiful, she looked like a hideous monster. Brahma had seen those features before, she looked like a Xeno.

Brahma:

- Rangda? Is that you? What happened?

Rangda:

- Yes, multi-faced traitor! It is me.

- What you see is my true form. I am half Zetan and half Xeno, the only one of my kind. The ultimate species in the universe.

- For many years, I used Zetan technology to look like one of you to blend in. You were blind, and you never exposed me.

- Now I don't need to blend in anymore. This is the real me.

Brahma:

- That's a bad choice, you looked better before.

Rangda:

- Says the man who cannot keep the same face for more than a couple of minutes!

Brahma, like most of the Zetans who came to Earth to pose as deities, had adapted his appearance to that which was expected by his human followers. The background of Brahma being the multi-faced deity, was that his Zetan outer layer **external DNA modifier** malfunctioned, which led to his face changing every few minutes. At first, Brahma was terrified by this, but after a while, he had come to appreciate this unique trait in himself.

Brahma:

- At least I don't look like a Xeno monster.

- So, is that why you betrayed us and wiped out the majority of all the life in the galaxy, while you were at it?

Rangda:

- I did not wipe out most life in the galaxy. Twelve inhabited planets were annihilated when I caused that supernova explosion. This was disastrous for the Zetans, but for the total biomass in the Milky Way, it was negligible.

Brahma:

- It was disastrous for the Xenos as well. What was left of us annihilated the Xeno species, before the loss of the Zeto crystals destroyed the foundation of our civilisation.

Rangda

- That's of no consequence. The Xenos will rise again, and I will rule them as their God-Queen!

Brahma:

- To be a queen, you need subjects. The Xenos are extinct.

Rangda:

- Is that so? I suggest that you look around.

Brahma looked around and what he saw shocked him. A Xeno warrior with sharp claws stared him in the eyes. Before he had time to react, the beast had pierced straight through Brahma's body, with the claws sticking out through his back.

Responding instinctively, Brahma focused his strength to his right fist and crushed the Xeno's head with a well-aimed blow. Brahma pulled the dead Xeno's claws out of his body. Brahma coughed blood, but looked at Rangda defiantly and spoke:

- Is that all you can muster?! Your friend is dead, and you'll be next.

Rangda:

- I don't think so. He might be dead, but he served his purpose.

Brahma:

- And that was?

Rangda:

- To weaken you enough for this!

Rangda pulled out a corrupted Zeto crystal. Instead of pure clarity, it emitted energy of terror and fear, unlike the uncorrupted Zeto crystal that emitted peace and unity.

Brahma:

- A Zeto crystal? Do they still exist? What did you do to this one?

Rangda:

- Yes, it would be a waste to let these precious crystals be destroyed, when I annihilated Zetani.

- I have merely turned the crystals useful to my benefit. You'll see its real power for the first time!

Rangda lifted the dark-red and fiery corrupted Zeto crystals to the sky and Brahma felt an extreme pain, Brahma felt how his head was about to explode, but that wasn't the worst part. He could also feel how his essence and soul was absorbed by the darkness of the evil crystal. A few seconds later, Brahma's head exploded, shattered into million pieces and his headless body dropped to the ground, jerking violently before it stopped moving.

Chapter 51 Keila Experiences Tremors and Vivid Hallucinations

Keila was holding an operational meeting with the angels and some of the prominent Edenites in the boardroom of the Divine Control Centre. Contrary to her predecessor, Keila preferred to keep the sessions face to face to discuss issues, instead of sending decrees. She chose to include prominent Edenites as she planned to modernise the Edenite society and create democratic and equal society. For that to happen, it was imperative for the Edenites to learn how to run their own colony and create a sustainable economy.

Suddenly, Keila started shaking and she had vivid hallucinations. She recognised the place as the Divine Dimension, but she did not understand how her mind had been transported there, as she was not connected to the Divine Detector Machine. In front of her was a terrifying monstrous woman with luminescent purple eyes and sharp fangs. The creature appeared out of thick green and smelly gas, not unlike the odour of a prison cell or a dark sewage brick well. The smell reminded Keila of a very stale, dark empty prison cell. It was the smell of the black death. This other-worldly devious woman grabbed her shirt, dragged her closer, and stared right into her soul. Keila fell to the ground. She felt anguish and despair, and she screamed at the top of her lungs in pain. She then passed out.

When she opened her eyes, the gathered people stepped back in shock. Keila's eyes had changed colour, from green to dark purple.

Metatron:

- Keila are you okay? What happened?

Keila:

- I had a vision. But don't worry, this is something that I have experienced a lot.

- I have never felt better.

Keila gave the group a very foreboding smile, and then she left the room,
while wondering who the woman in her vision was.

Chapter 52 Rangda Satisfies Her Hunger and Plans Ahead.

Rangda was feasting of Brahma's headless body and felt satisfied for the first time in thousands of years. With her mouth and lips drenched in silver bluish Zetan blood, she stopped for a moment. She asked herself if this act of cannibalism was wrong. Rangda concluded that it wasn't. She had been kept in that prison for so long, and she felt a hunger and hatred for her enemies. She was only half Zetan so technically she was another species than Brahma, and once Rangda had become a God-Queen, she could set the rules and morals that she wanted.

One of her Xeno followers wanted a bite of the body, but Rangda pushed him away. Most likely she didn't need to eat Brahma's body to capture his essence, as she had absorbed the fragments of his soul into the tainted Zeto crystals. But it felt good to eat and share Brahma's body with her underlings, when she could savage his body alone.

Rangda:

- Step away from my prey! I killed him, and his meat is mine.
- Eat the weakling that fell to the Zetan, This Zetan is my prey.

The Xenos hesitated. Cannibalism was taboo in Xeno culture as well, and that was the reason they had stayed alive for thousands of years trapped and starving in the divine dimension without killing each other. If cannibalism hadn't been tabooed in the Xeno culture they would have consumed each other in an animalistic frenzy. The Xenos had been hiding for thousands of years, close to the very dark edge of the Divine Dimension. Having received the approval from their mistress, they devoured their fallen comrade. Rangda smiled, seeing her beastly allies getting themselves some fresh meat was a joy to her eyes.

The Xenos was a savage bunch, but their energy levels and tenacity impressed her. They had something that the Zetans never have had. They had the will to dominate the entire universe. Rangda was a hybrid species, the only one of her kind. She was a half Zetan and half Xeno, a reproductive mishap that was destined to be the Zenith of all creation.

The Xenos had existed on their home planet for millions of years before Zetan explorers had imbued their genome with elevated intelligence. Like with humanity, the Zetan explorers had left the Xenos after imbuing them with intelligence. This had proven a critical mistake, as the Xenos to almost wiped out the Zetan galactic civilisation.

Chapter 53 Xenora, Xenos and Rangda's backstory

For millions of years, the Xenos existed like primitive beasts on the Xeno home planet, Xenora. Xenora had unique features for life that set it apart from most other inhabited worlds in the Milky Way Galaxy. The most unique feature was Xenora's close orbit to a blue giant star, and its' very slow rotational speed. One Xenora day was 3 months long. These circumstances led to days with a maximum temperature over 300 degrees and nights that could reach a minimum of -150 degrees. Despite these extreme circumstances, Xenora had life forms that could survive extreme conditions. This happened the following way:

All larger life forms followed Xenora's orbital rotation to always be on the side that had liveable conditions, the morning side of the planet. This forced all the animals to continually move along with the orbit, as a place would be too hot and kill them if they stayed long for the scorching midday sun to arrive.

Depending on the species, they preferred different locations in the Xenora morning. The early morning was freezing as the ice from the night had not melted yet, and this suited animals that liked ice. The late morning was very hot, albeit still bearable, and suited animals that loved the heat.

Animals were able to keep up with Xenora's rotation as the planet's rotation was very slow. As animals were forced to be moving on Xenora, life and survival evolved differently, than on Earth. To survive on Xenora, an animal species could only rely on speed, strength, and ruthlessness, as there was no time for prey animals to hide or for predators to utilise stealth.

All the plants that existed were types of fast-growing grass and other weeds, which had extremely short life cycles. These plants had lifecycles of only a few weeks between the time when the icicles and permafrost of the night had defrosted in the early morning, until the heat of the midday arrived which would cause widespread fires that killed all plant life. Having evolved to the conditions, plants on Xenora had fireproof seeds.

The water on Xenora came down as snow and ice during the night and evaporated to steam during the day. Xenora had no tilt to its star and as such had no seasons. The lack of angle meant that Xenora's North and South Pole always exist in twilight, and it was in the Polar Regions that life had originated as they were more survivable than the rest of the planet.

All animals on Xenora had very thick and sturdy skin to be able to cope with the tremendous amounts of UV radiation the planet received from its nearby blue star.

The Xenos had lived in the equatorial regions of Xenora, which were the most inhospitable regions of the planets. They had been very fearsome predators to survive under these circumstances. When the Zetans altered the Xeno's DNA, the Xenos started spreading over the planet until they reached the Polar Regions. Once the Xenos arrived at the Polar Regions, they built permanent settlements, as the North and South Pole, with its eternal twilight, were the only places where it was safe to erect buildings without the need to worry about extreme heat, or extreme cold.

The dwellers of the two Xeno cities had to be wary and on alert as the only sites suitable for permanent settlement were highly sought after by all the Xeno tribes that roamed the planet. Every time a tribe thought they would be strong enough to conquer the city, they would fight to the last individual to do so, as was the custom in the Xeno culture.

Because of their constant warring and lack of advanced technology, the Xeno tribes remained on a Stone Age technology level for over 50,000 years. The lack of technological progress had convinced the Zetan researchers that the Xenos was inferior to them. The Zetans regarded the Xenos a primitive race that would never pose a threat to the Zetan civilisation.

On the last Zetan research trips to Xenora, something happened that altered the fate of both the Xenos and the Zetans. A female Zetan scientist, Kalianka, was left behind on Xenora. This scientist was Rangda's mother.

Kalianka fell victim to a cruel ploy. One of her colleagues, a mean-spirited Zetan researcher, had tried to win her heart in courtship, but she rejected him. Feeling hurt, he beat her up and left her to die on Xenora as he decided that if he could not have her, no one else would have her either.

The cruel irony of fate was that, she had considered her assailant's proposal. Kalianka's assailant lied to the other Zetan researchers and told them that Kalianka was attacked and eaten by an animal. The other researchers did not go back to look for her because their location was getting hotter as the sun rose over the sky, and they needed to move on.

When Kalianka woke up, she felt weak and the surface temperature had risen to 80 degrees Celsius. Kalianka had no water and no means to get to a colder location. This was lethal conditions to a Zetan, as her home planet Zetani had a similar climate as Earth, and the Zetans were not adapted to the extreme heat on Xenora. She looked up and save a Xeno scout in front of her. Unable to fight due to her condition she closed her eyes and prepared herself to meet the True Maker, but the attack never came. Instead, the Xeno scout lifted her up over his shoulder and started running towards cooler conditions and a water source to keep Kalianka alive.

Kalianka woke up when someone poured icy water over her. It turned out that the scout had outrun the planets rotation speed and they were now earlier in the Xenora day cycle when it was cooler. The air was still warm, but the water was ice cold as the water had kept a lot of coldness from the long night.

Kalianka later understood that the Xeno tribe that had taken her in, saw her as a goddess and worshipped her. Eventually, she learned their language and could understand their culture. This was the best time in her life as a scientist as she could appreciate the Xenos from their own words and not just observe them via miniature drones. Her biggest regret was that she couldn't share her revelations and discoveries with her fellow Zetans. Her telepathic abilities didn't work as there was no other Zetan in the star system as the rest of the expedition had returned to Zetani.

Kalianka got a unique insight into the harsh life the Xenos were living, and she understood them better than any Zetan had ever done. Her tribe was living at the equator and they had to move the furthest distance every day to remain in the liveable zone on Xenora. As Xenora was the size of Earth, that meant that they had to move over 200 kilometres a day to the west, to avoid getting scorched by the sun.

This put a lot of pressure and forced a non-empathic approach to the members of the tribe. If someone got sick or injured, the tribe had to leave that individual to die as they couldn't travel fast enough with weak members of the tribe.

The only exception to this rule was for Kalianka. Being a Zetan, she could not move 200 kilometres a day on foot. As her Xeno tribe considered her a goddess, they did not mind sharing the burden of carrying her around.

Eventually, her tribe decided that her presence was a sign that it was time to move to the top of Xeno hierarchy. To do this, they needed to invade the Xeno city on Xenora's North Pole. They passed all the other tribes' territories on the way to the North Pole without any confrontation. The Xeno culture was very direct, and as the tribe had declared that they were after taking over the North Pole, the other tribes did not see them as a threat.

Once they had reached the North Pole, Kalianka's tribe did not stand a chance. This was because the defenders had both the numerical advantage as well as fortified city walls. As the Xeno culture required that they fought to the last individual, they all died, except for Kalianka who was taken prisoner by the North Pole inhabitants.

Being a prisoner of the North Pole city was the end of Kalianka's luck, as the city dwellers had experienced contact with Zetans in the past, they understood that Kalianka was not a goddess. They realised that Kalianka was a Zetan, a species they had previous disagreements and altercations with. They tortured and raped her to extract scientific knowledge from her.

The torture ended when Kalianka surprisingly fell pregnant. This shouldn't have been possible as they were different species, but it happened due to an unlikely mutation that took place in Kalianka's body.

To the Xenos, this was an act of the True Maker and Kalianka's misfortune turned around and she was now the wife of the Xeno high priest and the mother of their future queen, Rangda. Unfortunately, the amount of UV radiation Kalianka's skin had soaked up during her years with equator tribe caught up with her a few years later. She contracted skin cancer and died at the age of 220 years. This was a very young age to die for a Zetan, as they usually reached lifespans of longer than 1000 years.

Losing her mother at a young age, caused a permanent psychological scar within Rangda, and she blamed the Zetans for her mother's suffering and unfair treatment.

Rangda swore to get revenge for her mother with the destruction of the Zetan galactic civilisation. As it turned out, she had plenty of time to get her revenge. Her unlikely DNA that was a combination of Zetan and Xeno DNA stopped her from aging once she reached adulthood and granted her immortality. As she was a hybrid species, she was also infertile, and she looked insane.

Rangda began the long journey to turn the Xenos into a species that could contest with the Zetan for dominance of the galaxy. Her first step was to make the North Pole city an impregnable fortress so that her tribe would remain in power. This was the easy as her late mother had provided the tribe with Zetan technological knowledge. This knowledge could be used to make superior weaponry, capable of repelling any invader with ease.

The next step was to build tunnels across the planet for underground settlements, where the extreme variations in temperature did not exist. Xenora was ideal for building underground societies as the planet had limited geological activity. This meant that the heat didn't increase as they dug deeper, and they didn't need to worry about earthquakes. They kept digging for thousands of years until the tunnels spanned across Xenora, with a multitude of large subterranean settlements controlled by Rangda.

The basis for Rangda's control was that she had found out that there were Zeto crystals underground on Xenora. The unaltered Zeto crystals did not affect the minds of the Xeno species as the Zeto crystals promoted values such as the pursuit of knowledge, unity, passiveness, and the love for all life. Rangda, however, found a way to corrupt the gemstones to promote values such as lust, greed, violence, and domination. These values were more aligned to the Xeno minds, and by controlling the crystals, Rangda could control her ever-increasing number of subjects.

The Xeno underground settlements were fed in two ways. Most of the nutrition came from mould-based artificial meats. The Xenos were carnivores, but they were able to eat plant or algae-based proteins if they had to. The second way to feed her settlements was to catch the animals on the surface by climbing up tunnels through to the surface. By utilising tunnels to the surface, her tribe didn't need to move to avoid getting burnt. Instead they surfaced when outside temperatures were suitable and then dragged their prey back to the deep tunnels where they were protected against the outside temperatures.

Once Rangda's tribe controlled Xenora, they eradicated all the other tribes and set sight on their next goal, to start the war of conquest against the Zetans. The Xenos conquered their first planets easily. These planets were scarcely populated, and the Zetans living there didn't expect any threats and were mostly unarmed. The Xenos moved in, and due to their short life cycle and quick reproduction rate, they quickly got a foothold on the conquered planets. As the conquered planets were better for Xeno settlements than Xenora, they spread and created an economic base on the planets, aided by the confiscated Zetan infrastructure. After a century, the Xenos had consolidated their hold and set out to capture more worlds. This time the Zetan were better prepared, but the planets were still too far away from their homeworld to be adequately defended, and even these planets fell.

Chapter 54 The Multi-Millennial War Revisited.

Having lost several star systems, the Zetans realised the threat that the Xenos posed to their existence. But they could not mount a counter-attack. The Zetan civilisation was not based around military conquest, it was based on peace and unity, and besides, there had never been many of the Zetans. The average lifespan of a Zetan was 1000 years and the maximum number of children they could have during this millennium was five. This meant an average Zetan had a child every 200 years. The Xenos, on the other hand, had an average lifespan of 30 years, and during that time they could have up to 40 children. This meant that the Xenos could replenish their losses quickly.

The third attempted conquest by the Xenos was the Zetans second most important planet, Zetani Nova. This planet was well defended and time the Xenos were butchered with hardly any losses for the Zetans. This led to a stalemate in the conflict; every 30 years the Xenos sent a large force that ended up being nullified by the Zetan defences without reaching any progress. The Zetans, in turn, could not muster enough enthusiasm for a counterattack due to their peaceful nature. Instead, the Zetans fortified their borders and pursued peace. But even though the Zetans were able to nullify the Xenos invasions, it brought no peace. The Xenos wanted the Zetans dead, and, thus the two species always clashed.

The pointless attacks on the Zetans were a diversion by Rangda, to keep the Zetans unaware of the Xenos expansion. The Xenos settled uninhabited planets far away from the Zetans, and built up a massive invasion fleet.

After hundreds of years of skirmishes, the Xenos took the Zetans by surprise one day when they showed up in the Zetani Nova system with a 1000 times bigger fleet than they usually attacked with. Instead of the regular fleet of 300 Xeno ships, there were now 300,000 ships. Despite their inferior technology, they swarmed the Zetans and annihilated the Zetan defenders as well as all the Zetan civilians on Zetani Nova.

The loss of Zetani Nova alerted the Zetan civilisation to the existential threat that Xenos posed to them, and they rallied their forces from their other planets and mustered a counterattack that liberated Zetani Nova a decade later. Much to their dismay, Zetani Nova was destroyed beyond recognition. What was once the most beautiful planet in the Zetan civilisation was now a toxic wasteland. The Zeto crystals, which was the source of all the beauty and harmony on Zetani Nova, were gone. The Zetans also found a map that revealed the terrifying truth; that the Xenos had colonised and conquered a lot of neutral planets while distracting the Zetans with small-scale battles to distract them.

The Zetans gathered their leaders on Zetani for an emergency meeting. Their future seemed bleak and in a couple of centuries, they would be overrun by the Xeno hordes, no matter what they did to stop it. That was when Yahweh, one of the Zetan leaders, rediscovered the long-lost technology to enter and travel through the Divine Dimension, to the normal dimension.

The technology was crucial for two reasons: Firstly, going through the Divine Dimension was quicker. Moving between star systems only took days instead of years. Secondly, their discovery of the Divine Dimension meant that they could manipulate other sentient beings to fight for them against the Xenos. This was the reason for Zetans to come to Earth, posing as gods and recruiting humans to fight their wars.

With their newfound allies and considerably faster travel times the Zetans turned the tide in the war and they repelled the Xenos on every planet. The Zetans recruited the humans on Earth by infiltrating their minds and souls, and they liberated and restored the planets that had fallen to the Xeno scourge.

Rangda came up with a new plan, to use her half-Zetan intelligence and abilities. She altered her own genetics to infiltrate the Zetan leadership. Using the Zetan external DNA modifier, Rangda changed her appearance from the monstrous appearance of Xeno beast to that of a beautiful Zetan woman. Using a captured Zetan ship, Rangda travelled to Zetani. Since she had Zetan telepathic abilities, Rangda convinced the Zetans that she was one of them. Rangda seduced Brahma and gained access to the Zetan leadership as well as finding out about the Divine Dimension.

Despite Rangda's infiltration and deceit the Zetans were winning the war, and as a last spiteful effort, Rangda used her position within Zetan leadership to cause a supernova explosion that destroyed Zetani, which caused the collapse of the Zetan civilisation.

Having blown her cover, Rangda was locked up by Brahma in her eternal prison in the Divine Dimension until she escaped and killed Brahma, millennia later.

Chapter 55 Keila Has a Vision and Sets Up a Strategy for the War to Come

Keila was looking at herself in the mirror. She was pouring sweat and was determined to get back into peak fitness, something she had missed out on being the spoiled queen of Eden. The Edenite food was delicious, and she had enjoyed eating and drinking, with all the godly pleasures provided to her as offerings. This had started showing on her body, and Keila needed a super fit body to promote her ideal image, as Martian fighter.

Keila was not an armchair general that sent people to do things she didn't dare to deal with herself. Keila had led the mission to eliminate Alicia White. The mission had ended in a bloodbath, but Keila had survived it, and now she had one trump on hand. Having the bodies of Alicia and her operatives, Keila could use the Zetan outer layer external DNA modifier to pretend to be Alicia White, as this technology allows the user to change appearances. This could have great advantages if she were to infiltrate House White.

Keila looked at her eyes in the mirror. She used to have a pair of lively green eyes as a child, and eyes glowing with determination and positive energy as she got older. Her eyes had changed colour. Her current eyes were shining in a strange luminescent purple colour and they had a peculiar shape like those of predatory animal.

Keila felt a severe migraine, got dizzy, fell forward, and knocked her head on the mirror. The mirror broke, shattered into pieces and she started bleeding as she tasted the blood running down her cheeks.

The blood caused her to have a vision and she felt clarity on how to go ahead to reach her goal. She saw images of the Terran Council falling apart to fighting among themselves, and of how the Martians were attacking and destroying the Phobos Base, which had been oppressors main base for the last centuries.

Keila heard a voice speak in her head. At first, she was terrified. It wasn't the usual voice; instead, it was the voice who had told her to kill Jeshua, a year ago. But then she listened in to the voice and it made sense. They voice said that she shouldn't take on the Terran Council directly as an external threat would unite them. Instead, she should aim to infiltrate and divide them, to cause them to fight among themselves. If she could turn House Cheng against House Muller and House Rashid against House White, the Terran Council would collapse, and her Martian brethren could have their freedom from oppression.

Seeing this vision, she forgot that she was bleeding from the broken mirror shards, and instead she was smiling with her face soaked in blood. Metatron came in to examine the noise from the incident. Keila told him that she was okay, but he insisted and brought her straight to the medical ward. Thanks to stem cell technology her wounds healed without a scar in just a few days.

Chapter 56 A Cold Father's Day Meeting

Bjorn Muller was looking at the calendar. It was Father's Day, in the year 2873. Bjorn thought about his father, whom he hadn't seen for over six months the day when his father had put him under Alicia White's command.

Bjorn's father had set him to work for a monster that ate people alive and ended up sodomising him. He didn't know what the worst part was, the psychological scarring or the total humiliation he had faced, but Bjorn had refused to talk to his father after the incident.

Since the incident, Bjorn had been transferred back to Max Wellington's command and he was stationed on the Phobos Base. It had been a few quiet months, and Bjorn's biggest struggle was that he no received good food, drinks, and female companionship since he refused to speak to his father, who was the one who provided these things for him.

The door to Bjorn's suite opened. Bjorn turned around. *"Who would be insolent enough to enter his room without asking first?"* he thought. Bjorn turned around, and there was his father, Joachim Muller.

Joachim:

- You forgot to honour me on Father's Day.

Bjorn:

- What on Earth are you doing here?
- Besides, it's not past midnight yet.

Joachim:

- It is past midnight in Europe, but I'll give you the benefit of the doubt.

Bjorn:

- Happy Father's Day, Joachim...
- Why have you come here unannounced?

Joachim:

- To be honest, I am not here because of Father's Day!

- I am coming because this week the distance between Earth and Mars is the shortest. This means I must only endure three days in transit to get from Earth to Phobos instead of the 21 days when the distance is the longest.

- While the trip was less inconvenient than it could have been, I would still have preferred if you picked up the fucking phone.

Bjorn:

- We don't have that much to talk about, father?

Joachim slapped Bjorn. For a moment Bjorn thought about unleashing the fury on his father, but he kept his cool.
Joachim:

- We do have things to talk about. I won't have spent three days in fucking space getting here and three days going back for no reason. So, you better improve your attitude, Bjorn.

- You need to withdraw your allegations against Alicia White. I cannot afford a conflict with House White. John White has been my closest ally on the Terran Council for the last decades.

Bjorn Muller:

- I have nothing against John White, but his crazy mutant daughter ate a man alive and then raped me. Convince him to put down that animal and focus on his more well-adjusted children.

Joachim Muller:

- It would be unwise to give unsolicited advice to John White on how to deal with his family matters, considering my abject failure with my own children.

- I have three sons who all bring disgrace to the family.

- Michael is a lazy man without any aspirations, who like to spend our money on leisure activities for him and his family

- Benjamin is a man who engages in bedroom activities with men.

- You are my eldest son, an abject failure in the armed forces with a drug and sex addiction. I have turned a blind eye to your shortcomings as I hoped that you would have the drive to take over the company from me when I retire.

- However, your latest embarrassment is too much. You are driving away our allies and humiliating your own masculinity at the same time... Just stop.

Bjorn Muller was going to say something when Admiral Max Wellington stormed into his office. Short of breath, he looked at Joachim Muller in surprise before catching his breath.
Max Wellington:

- Sorry to interrupt your conversation Chairman Muller, but I have urgent news.

- There has been another mysterious attack. This time the attack is on House Rashid's Aljadid Salam Outpost.

Chapter 57 The Attack on the Aljadid Salam Outpost

The Aljadid Salam outpost was a House Rashid outpost that had been built to protect the shipping lanes between Earth and the nearby House Rashid asteroid mining stations. The mining stations had run dry a long time ago, but House Rashid kept a small skeleton staff on the outpost to be able to claim that part of space for future use. Sometimes gravity pulled asteroids from the fringes of the solar system to a more central location, and for occasions like that, it was useful to claim vast swaths of empty space for what could host the goldmine of tomorrow. Another reason for House Rashid to keep a multitude of space outpost guarding empty space was to keep their large army busy, far away from Earth, to avoid them interfering in internal faction matters.

The attack took place in a similar manner to the Proxima Thule attack six months earlier. Keila's vessel approached the outpost with Zetan stealth technology to avoid detection. Then they blocked all communication to and from the outpost. Then they stormed the outpost with their kinetic energy absorbers and bionic chip disruptors activated. The unprepared and disrupted House Rashid defenders never stood a chance. Keila set explosives to blow up the station but intentionally used too little explosives to destroy the outpost. This was a ploy as Keila wanted it to seem like a failed attempt by House White to destroy the outpost.

The timing for the attack had come to Keila in a vision. On the day of the shooting, one of the Chairman Ibrahim Rashid's many sons, Akram Rashid, was on-board the station. Akram was killed beyond resurrection just like the rest of the defenders.

To make it evident that House White was behind the attack, Keila and her group had used the weapons and ammunition that they seized from the battle with Alicia White. They also left some of the corpses of soldiers from

Alicia's group at the scene. These corpses, had no identity tags in their brains, but it would not be challenging for House Rashid investigators to figure out who they were, from looking at their uniforms and weaponry.

Chapter 58 A Diplomatic Crisis

Keila was drinking a protein fruit smoothie, recovering from a hard fitness session with her Edenite troops. While her female physique made her weaker than some of the men under her command, her total fitness level was well above that of her average soldier. It was vital for her to show her fittest self and the extra kilos she had added when she first became the queen of Eden were now gone, and she was in her prime.

Unfortunately, she couldn't convince Metatron or the angels to take part in the sessions as they were confident that genetic optimisation, nutrition, and selective electrical stimulation were superior to something as archaic as physical exercise.

Keila's Edenite troops were a mixture of men and women. This was the opposite of what Abraham had been preaching during his reign, but Keila believed in equality. Besides, few things were reliant on strength when it came to 29th century low gravity warfare so women could be equally suited to combat as men were.

Keila connected to the closest Spacenet node to watch the news. Her attack on the Aljadid Salam station had worked out exactly as she planned. Furious over the death of one of his sons, Ibrahim Rashid had demanded that House White released a public apology and compensated him.

House White had refused and had claimed to be innocent despite the damning amount of evidence against them. House Rashid had lost their patience and their forces had captured a House White luxury cruise spaceship, taking over 1000 passengers and crew as hostages. While no prominent House White family members were on the cruise, it was filled with other prominent American plutocrats and tensions were growing. Tensions weren't easing when rumours spread about Rashid troops slitting the throats of their hostages.

Keila reflected that this could be the powder keg that drove House Rashid and House White to war and Terran Council into disarray. Keila would not sit around and wait, as she had a new objective. A group of House Muller spies had infiltrated a nearby independent trading post. These spies were there to sabotage the non-affiliated trader to drive them to bankruptcy and incorporate the trading post into the House Muller conglomerate.

While Keila didn't mind helping independent commerce in the solar system, she was after the House Muller operatives for another reason. Keila planned for the House Muller operatives to fall unconscious and then wake up on an attacked outpost belonging to House Cheng. This would convince House Cheng that the attack was House Muller's doing.

Having made up her plan, Keila disconnected from Space Net and entered a sleep pod. While she preferred natural sleep, sleep pods were useful when time was of the essence, and she needed to be rested.

Chapter 59 Bjorn Muller Studies a Report About a Missing Espionage Team

Bjorn logged out from the computer terminal, picked it up, and threw it into a wall. The last week had been a shit storm. His father had refused to leave until he withdrew his allegations against Alicia White and cancel the arrest order against her.

Later that day, he had studied the hologram images of the attack on the Aljadid Salam outpost and recognised some of the dead perpetrators to be part of Alicia White's group. He had not shared this information as House White was House Muller's ally and he did not want to escalate the situation. Besides he could smell the rat. There was no way a battle could have taken place in the way that the House Rashid report stated.

The attack shared many similarities with the attack on the Proxima Thule station six months earlier. The Aljadid Salam Outpost defenders seemed to have been unprepared for battle, their communications had ended abruptly, and there was the mystery with a lot of undamaged bullets in the middle of the corridors, that hadn't impacted with anything.

Perhaps, Alicia had attacked both installations, but if it was true, why did she leave her casualties behind on the Aljadid Salam outpost? Bjorn Muller knew that Alicia's group consisted of 15 operatives plus Alicia. She would not leave three dead agents on the battlefield exposing their identity. The purpose of a black operations team was to conduct operations without leading back to their employer. Leaving their dead would do the opposite.

Another strange fact was that there was no sign of Alicia anywhere, despite Bjorn cancelling the arrest order. He understood that Alicia and her team could have holed up somewhere while there was a warrant for their arrest, but why would they hide now? Why would they attack an insignificant outpost? Bjorn could only come up with two explanations:

1. Either Alicia had gone rogue and worked against the interest of her family by attacking outposts and leaving her dead troops as a trace back to them.
2. An unknown group had eliminated Alicia's group and were dumping their bodies on the scene to indict House White for the attacks.

Bjorn did not share his ideas in the report as some of the information was confidential, and he did not want to share with all the members of the Terran Council.

Another thing that bothered Bjorn, was the disappearance of his espionage team on the Freedom Markets trading post. The team had been there posing as asteroid mining surveyors between jobs, while they had come to sabotage the station to make it go bankrupt. Unknown assailants had kidnapped them in the middle of the night and then dragged them onto a stolen space shuttle. The worst part was that the assailants had been caught on camera and yet they were impossible to identify. They didn't match any personal identity records in the solar system and Bjorn could not pinpoint where they were from. He stared at one of the female attackers. He could swear that she was Keila, but she looked completely different.

Bjorn closed his eyes. He needed to get over Keila. He had been obsessed with her for too long. Bjorn had spent endless nights studying hologram videos of her. Officially he had needed to learn about the enemy, but he knew that that was only a made-up reason. Since Bjorn first met her, he had been obsessed, filled with dark twisted unrequited love. Things could have been different if he had acted differently on their first encounter. If he had been kind to her, instead of opting to dominate and rape her, she could have become his wife and the mother of his children. Instead, he had made her an enemy and caused her to start the insurrection by killing his grandfather Hans Muller.

Nothing of this mattered now. Keila was dead, and she had been dead for a year. Bjorn had seen the body himself, and he had been the one to proclaim her dead. Bjorn had to let her go from his mind. Bjorn wanted to cry over how he had fucked up his life, but he didn't. Bjorn, a high-ranking member of House Muller and one of the most influential persons in Europe wasn't going to cry. He was the epitome of success, and that was how he should live his life, portraying success through a hedonistic and carefree approach. Bjorn opened a bottle of expensive champagne and lined up a significant amount of cocaine. He summoned the female companions that his father had sent from Earth. Obeying his father certainly had its perks.

Unbeknownst to Bjorn, it was Keila he saw on the hologram videos from the abduction of his espionage team. She had used the Zetan External DNA changing technology to take the appearance of an Edenite woman who was of similar stature and body type as herself. Since the Edenites were not recorded in the official population registries of the solar system, this was the perfect way to confuse her enemies.

Chapter 60 Conflict Between House Cheng and House Muller.

Joachim Muller finished the conference call with the House Cheng leadership. There had been an armed robbery against one of House Cheng's storage facilities for valuable minerals, located halfway between the asteroid belt and Jupiter. The facility had been unguarded but full of security measures in place, to incapacitate intruders and keep them locked up until House Cheng security forces arrived.

When the Cheng forces had arrived, they had found that the vaults had been emptied and that several House Muller spies had been captured in the base's non-lethal traps. While the situation was not as dire as it was between House Rashid and House White, it was humiliating for Joachim to find his operatives caught in a bank robbery. Joachim had discussed the matter with Bjorn, who had confirmed that the men were the operatives who were abducted a couple of weeks earlier.

Joachim had seen the hologram videos of the operatives' abduction and believed that they were not stupid enough to rob a House Cheng vault. The problem was to convince House Cheng his faction's innocence. Joachim showed the video of his men being abducted, but how would he make the House Cheng leaders believe him? If the roles were reversed, he would not trust the House Cheng leaders if they showed him a similar video.

On the other hand, if Joachim apologised for the incident and offered to pay repatriations, he would admit guilt for what happened or at least admit that he couldn't control his operatives.

The situation was critical because of the current tensions between House Rashid and House White. Following the hostage situation, House White had sent their troops to free the hostages. This attempt had gone wrong and had caused the cruise spaceship to explode, killing every hostage as they were choked by the freezing cold vacuum of space. As the chairman of the Terran

Council, Joachim had worked around the clock for over a week to prevent a full-scale war between House Rashid and House White. Having his credibility destroyed by his agents participating in a bank robbery was the last thing that he needed.

Joachim decided to apologise and compensate House Cheng, claiming that his operatives had worked outside of his knowledge. His incompetent son Bjorn would then have to sort out this mess and find the ones responsible for the robbery. As Joachim was heading to the vacuum tube station to travel to the House Cheng headquarters in China, he was stuck in a fearsome mindset.

Who was the real force behind all the trouble and what was their end goal? Fear was growing within him, but he did not want to speak about it with anyone, not even his closest advisors. He was the chairman of the most powerful faction on Earth and the chairman of the Terran Council, an organisation that had ruled the solar system for over 600 years. As such he could not fear anyone!

Chapter 61: A Frozen Embryo and a Succession Plan.

Keila looked at the pregnancy test, and it confirmed what she had been suspecting; that her bout of morning sickness and declining fitness was a natural effect of a parasite infection that was crucial for the survival of the species.

But how had this happened? Metatron was over a hundred years old despite his younger looks and he shouldn't be fertile anymore. Thinking back, she had lost her memory due to intoxication a few months earlier, on an Edenite celebration, and she could have had a moment of indiscretion without remembering it. It was unlikely as she occasionally checked the minds of her Edenite subjects to check current talking points, and if she had sex with anyone on Eden it would have been one the most significant talking points. Fortunately, it was easy to find out the answer as she had access to everyone's DNA on Eden in the mainframe. She entered a full-body scanner, and it revealed that the 52-day old embryo she had in the womb was of Metatron's seed.

But this created another issue. Keila had other priorities than family life. If she were to tell him about the pregnancy, he would make another attempt at dissuading her from her insurrection plans to stay on Eden with him. While she could understand where he was coming from, she did not want to give up her rebellion to please him. The gods had led Keila this far, and there were so many people suffering from the injustices of the world. She had to follow through with what she had started.

Keila closed her eyes and she had a vision. The vision was of herself, Metatron and a girl that looked like her future daughter holding an adulthood ceremony on Eden. Keila opened her eyes and felt confused. Had she come this far to give up her plans and become a mother instead? It didn't make any sense but then again, who was Keila to understand the divine plan?

To be sure she closed her eyes and studied the vision again. It was the same vision still, but she noticed a crucial detail. The date and year on the cake. The date and year were 14 years and 7 months in the future, which didn't make sense since Edenite adulthood ceremonies was when the girl turned 13 years old. Hence the child in the vision would not be born for another year and seven months. Thus it could not be the child she was carrying in her belly.

Keila made up her mind. She would not kill the embryo, but she would not carry it either. Instead, Keila would suck out the embryo and keep the future baby in suspended animation for one year. If she were still alive in a year, she would quit the rebellion and focus on her motherhood. If not... She would have the child born in a synthetic womb. She wrote a message to Metatron with instructions that were encrypted with her safety signature that would open in one year. After finishing the letter, she ordered the full-body scanner to do the procedure for her. She woke up an hour later and she was met by Metatron.

Metatron:

- What were you doing in there for so long? Is there any problem with your health?

Keila:

- No, Metatron I am fine.
- I just can't tell you what I did in there.

Metatron said nothing and walked away. Keila looked at him as he left the room and felt guilty. He knew what she had done and she felt guilty for not consulting him. Now she didn't know how to bring it up. Dealing with emotional problems like she often did, Keila went to the shooting range to let the adrenaline clear her mind.

Chapter 62 Keila's Unique Genetics.

The human genome consists of a lot of genetic information that normally doesn't activate or fill any function in the human body. The residual DNA from ancient Zetan human hybrids was an example of this kind of DNA. Every human had traces of Zetan DNA in them and yet most of them had no telepathic ability, visions, or premonitions.

The Zetan DNA had been integrated into the human genome during two periods of history. The first round of Zetan DNA was induced into humanity 100,000 years ago when Zetan scientists travelled around the Milky Way Galaxy and produced a variety of species with intelligence and a soul. That program was cancelled when Zetan experts argued that increasing the intelligence of other species across the galaxy could lead to one of these species rising and destroying the Zetans. After cancelling the program, nothing happened for 90,000 years, and the Zetans forgot about it.

10,000 years ago, the Xenos started their attacks on the Zetans which started the multi-millennial war between the two species. The Zetans realised they did not have the numbers to take on the Xenos and they needed allies. That was where humanity came in. As humanity's deities, the Zetans commanded human fighters to fight the Xenos with advanced Zetan technology.

To have enough human fighters they needed humans to multiply faster. This was why the Zetans gave humanity the concept of civilisation based around agriculture. They did this by creating hybrids between humans and Zetans. These hybrids became prominent leaders and kings for humanity that advanced human technology and civilisation. As the Zetan/human hybrids, the Zetan DNA spread among humanity and in the generations that followed, everyone had a piece of Zetan DNA in themselves. This did not affect their abilities, as an individual needed to have the complete Zetan

DNA sequence to have the unique Zetan skills of telepathy, premonition, and heightened intelligence.

Yahweh was the last Zetan to procreate with humans before the portal between Earth and the Divine Dimension was destroyed. Due to the aphrodisiac he ingested before going to Earth; Yahweh had a lot of offspring. While many of them became prominent but forgotten only one of them stood out, Jesus. Jesus, in turn, had a lot of children with various women before meeting his end, a detail that was left out as his disciples came from a monotheistic and monogamous background and did not want to promote polytheistic and polygamous teachings.

After the fall of Jesus, there would emerge a human with a full Zetan DNA sequence every few hundred years, and this individual would be incredibly gifted and special. The Zetans directed these persons towards scientific pursuits as they needed to progress humanities' science level if they ever were to activate the dormant portals between Earth and the Divine Dimension.

The last person before Keila who had an unusual Zetan DNA sequence was Jack Brown. Jack Brown was the scientist who had helped to build the Divine Detector Machine that transported Abraham's mind to the Divine Dimension 80 years earlier.

While this had been an amazing achievement, it had been a dead end as the technology to transport physical objects was different from the technology that Jack had developed. Jack's telepathic link with the Zetans was also too weak to enable them to communicate with him through the dimensions, so his only Zetan ability was his exceptionally high intelligence. As Jack Brown was so ahead of his time, the Divine Detection technology was still undiscovered by the rest of the Terran Houses 80 year later, as he and his group had been loyal to their words and had not disclosed the technology to mindwarp to another dimension.

With Keila, the Zetans had a slight problem. Despite her strong telepathic connection with the Zetans, she lacked the scientific mind to create a portal for physical movement between the dimensions from scratch. They did believe, however, that they could use her to activate the ancient Zetan portals that were hidden within pyramids on Earth.

The Zetans had intended for Keila to go back to Earth and use her heritage as the exiled Mahmoud Rashid's daughter to gain Terran citizenship, freedom, and resources to explore the pyramids and find the secret to activating the portals. This had failed when Bjorn Muller had not acted as Brahma had foreseen.

Brahma had set the plan in motion to have Keila crave for Earth so much so she would join a people smuggler that took her from Mars to Earth. Brahma had planned for this ship to be intercepted by Bjorn's spaceship, but then things fell apart. Instead of pursuing Keila with his good looks, wealth and Terran citizenship, Bjorn had gone feral and kidnapped and raped her instead, thus destroying Brahma's plan of peaceful love. For Brahma, this came as a shock. Brahma was the many-faced, all-seeing god, how could he have missed this? Another reason that Brahma had intended for Keila and Bjorn to fall for each other was that Bjorn had a high amount of residual Zetan DNA. That combined with Keila's complete Zetan DNA sequence would lead to very gifted and useful children.

The potential child of Keila and Bjorn could have become the ultimate human/ Zetan hybrid. Keila had 2 out of 3 complete Zetan DNA sequences for premonition and telepathy which gave her these abilities. She did not, however, have the full Zetan DNA sequence for intelligence, so she did not have superhuman intelligence. Bjorn, on the other hand, had high amounts of recessive Zetan DNA for high intelligence. Unfortunately, the lack of parental love had caused him to only care about hedonistic values. Bjorn's excessive drug use had destroyed his innate intelligence and talent. Regardless, Keila and Bjorn together could have given birth to a child with all the complete Zetan DNA sequences, creating a demi-god.

All of this had come to naught. Rangda was the villain behind Bjorn's terrible behaviour towards Keila. Rangda had used the fact that Bjorn had plenty of recessive Zetan DNA to subconsciously manipulate him into becoming a sadistic rapist. This had thwarted Brahma's original plan of genuine love and peaceful mannerisms.

After the unfortunate incident between Keila and Bjorn, Brahma had lost his direction and believed that he was meant to have Keila start an insurrection against the Terran Council. He had kept her alive, but he had not got closer to returning to the regular dimension. Brahma had not realised, until the very end, what a threat Rangda posed to the Zetans and how she had played him.

Rangda studied Keila from her location in the Divine Dimension. It was fortunate that she had stalled the opening of the portals when the Zetans almost got there. At that time, Rangda had not been powerful enough to fight the Zetans, but now with Brahma's soul absorbed by the corrupted Zeto Crystals, her power had grown.

The war that Keila was involved in was a complication for Rangda's plans to get Keila to Earth, to activate the portals. But she would have to do it the hard way.

Chapter 63 The Zetans Are Fearful After Brahma's Death

Zeus, Ra and Odin were looking at the Zetans that had assembled for an urgent meeting. There was 300 of them which was a smaller number than the previous year. That was to be expected. Stuck in the timelessness of the Divine Dimension hungry, thirsty, and yet immortal, their numbers had thinned out throughout the years as many of them had committed suicide as the only way out. It had been over 2000 years since the portal to Earth was destroyed, hopelessness drove many of them over the edge. There was still a lot more than 300 Zetans left in the Divine Dimension, but many of them were in deep meditation to avoid suffering, and thus they ignored the summon. Zeus didn't blame them.

Zeus thought of Brahma, and he shivered with fear. Brahma had walked off and killed himself like many others before him. But there was something with Brahma's death that did not make sense. Unlike the others, Brahma had no reason to kill himself, at least not now. Brahma had been convinced that Keila was the one they had been waiting for. That Keila was the one to open the portals and set them free. Even if something had happened that made Brahma re-evaluate Keila's usefulness, there was no reason for suicide. Keila was still alive, and even if she was not the chosen one, human life was very short, so Brahma might as well have waited.

The way that Brahma had died terrified Zeus. Most Zetans who walked away and killed themselves just faded away. It was a peaceful transition from life to death so that the soul could move on. Brahma's death was different. He had moved on in a state of fear, and it seemed like his soul had shattered into fragments. This prospect terrified Zeus. Not wanting for fear to spread among the assembly, Zeus started the meeting with an issue of practical character.

Zeus:

- I am sad to inform you about Brahma's death. He walked off and killed himself, like so many before him.

Upset chatter was spreading among the crowd after this announcement and eventually a lesser Zetan, Altjira called out.
Altjira:

- Stop lying Zeus. We all know Brahma didn't kill himself. Something terrible caught up with him and devoured his soul.

Zeus was going to speak, but Ra beat him to it:

- Don't speculate about things you don't know, Altjira. While the circumstances regarding Brahma's death are suspicious, we can't do anything about it. All we know is that he was very far away when he died, but without knowing the details, we cannot find him.

- Besides, if there is something evil and powerful out to get us, we should not split up and look for Brahma separately.

Zeus added in. He said:

- I agree with Ra, and besides, we have another issue. When Brahma died, we lost our connection to Keila. Without that connection, we cannot guide her to open the portals. We must utilise our collective psionic power to bind her to me.

Murmuring broke out among the Zetans, but no one rejected the proposal. While Zeus was not famed for having as much foresight as Brahma, there was no one else who wanted the responsibility for the future of their species. The Zetans gathered in a circle to initiate the ritual that would bind Keila's mind to Zeus. The ritual failed, and Zeus fell to the ground screaming in pain with his face burnt.
Zeus:

- I could not connect with her. I was blocked by the tormented fragments of Brahma's soul. I saw Rangda; she must be behind this!!

Zeus vomited up a lot of blood and died. Odin and Ra ran up to his lifeless body, but there was nothing they could do for him. Filled with rage and grief, Odin shouted out:

- To arms, fellow Zetans. We march to Rangda's prison at once; the witch must pay for what she has done!!

Determined, they got up, gathered their equipment, and set out for their very long walk to Rangda's prison. They left a dozen of them to form a vanguard in case the portal was opened, but the remaining 280 Zetans marched to Rangda's jail.

Chapter 64 Markus Bauer's Dilemma.

Markus Bauer was preparing his presentation for Keila and her leadership team. He had reverse-engineered the Zetan technologies so that they could be mass-produced with current technologies. Although the reverse-engineered products were inferior to their Zetan counterparts, they had the advantage of being inexpensive and fast to make. As they needed many gadgets to give to their allies, they could not use the particle replicator machine as every unit made that way was energy demanding and costly to produce. To make exact copies on the molecular level was also slower than other methods of manufacturing.

Markus Bauer refused to reverse engineer the Divine Technology, for mass production. While the other Zetan technologies were gadgets that were used for warfare they did not change anything. Humans had always developed better weapons to outwit and destroy each other. If Keila and her rebels wanted to kill her enemies, it was natural that she wanted the best weapons at her disposal, and Markus had no ethical problems with providing them to her.

The Divine Technology microchips were different. They gave the ruling classes complete control over the enslaved masses below them. This transformed the essence of humanity from individuals to slaves under a hive mind. Markus would not release this evil to the world.

Markus Bauer entered the boardroom where Keila, Metatron and the ruling council of Eden had convened. He was relieved when Keila looked at him with a smile. She raised her glass of wine and spoke.

> - Cheers to our chief scientist, Markus Bauer, for his excellent services to our cause. I already know everything that you are going to say today, but please hold your presentation to fill the others in.

Markus felt irritated. He didn't like that his boss/captor spied on his mind. However, what else could he expect? Markus drank some water and started his presentation:

- Dear delegates. It pleases me to announce that my team and I have reverse engineered Zetan technologies so that they can be mass-produced by us and our Martian allies. While the reverse-engineered versions are not as good as the originals, they are superior to the current weapons of our Martian peers.

Keila interrupted him:

- While I am happy with your breakthroughs, I am not satisfied that you haven't solved one of our most significant issues. How are we going to communicate with our Martians friends uninterrupted and secure from Terran spies?

Markus:

- I don't know how to answer that question, Ms Eisenstein. My team and I have not been working on our communications technologies. You are not letting us communicate with the outside world, out of fear that we would betray you to the Terran Council.

Keila:

- Your refusal to reverse-engineer the divine technology chips has set us back on the communications front. I intend to use the technology as a way of secure communication. I am not intending to use it to control and dominate.

Markus:

- And yet you spied on me. Whatever you intend to do; you are never going to resist the urge to use the technology to spy on the followers.

Keila found herself lost for words. She had spoken herself into a corner and Markus had been brave enough to expose her hypocrisy. She swore to herself and drank some water to moisten her dry throat. Metatron joined in on the discussion:

- Markus is right. While the Divine Technology is a tool and not inherently evil, it can be used for evil. I saw it myself when I served under Abraham.

Keila spat out her water and scorned Metatron:

- So, you are siding with Markus now? I am very disappointed with you, Metatron.

Metatron:

- Quite the opposite Keila. I am siding with humanity and the real you. The Keila I know, values individual freedoms. Yet you propose that we mass-produce technology that could enslave them. It doesn't make sense, does it?

Keila:

- So how the fuck, do I coordinate a rebellion without a reliable means of communication? I can't use Space Net because it's so insecure I might as well publish my every move on the morning news. And I don't have hundreds of secure communication satellites, unlike the Terrans.

Metatron:

- There must be a better way to beat the Terran Council than installing a worse tyranny than theirs. If there isn't a better way, we better leave the things the way they are.

Keila realised that Metatron and Markus were right. She felt ashamed over what she had become. Keila had come to Eden to stop Abraham's tyranny, and now a year later, she was proposing to spread the menace all over the solar system. Keila knew that she hadn't been thinking clearly. Just because SHE would never use divine technology to tyrannise the population, it didn't mean that it was a good idea to spread the technology. If she was to die there was a risk that someone would take her place and use it to instate tyranny, like Abraham did before.

Keila:

- You are right, Metatron. We are not going to develop something that can be used for tyranny. We'll find another way.

- I declare this meeting concluded. Return to work, ladies and gentlemen.

As everyone left, Keila stared out at the vastness of space. She felt at a loss what to do and decided to do nothing for a while.

Chapter 65 Keila Has a Nightmare and Reconciles with Metatron.

Keila was restless and had very vivid dreams. *"He's holding you back,"* a voice said. It followed up with *"Kill him, and mankind will succumb to your will."* Keila saw images of Metatron lying in a pool of blood. The perspective changed, and she could see herself looking out from a penthouse at Earth. She recognised the location and knew where it was. The view was from the penthouse level of Europeum towers in Hansstadt in the European Alps.

Keila saw herself together with Bjorn Muller and several children. That didn't make any sense. That creep had kept her as a sex slave, and he had been responsible for killing her after she had killed Hans Muller.

Finally, Keila saw a blueprint for a divine technology. It was modified, but she was unsure on how it had happened. *"This is the chip that you need. It is the human chip that you can mass-produce with your technology,"* the voice said. *"Show yourself!"* Keila screamed at the voice, but it didn't answer. Keila felt that the owner of the voice tried to disconnect from her mind, but she wouldn't let it. Using all her mental strength Keila got a very short glimpse of Rangda.

The source of the voice didn't look at all like the benevolent old man she had seen in her visions before. Instead, she saw a terrifying female witch. Did the voice belong to an evil monster? But Keila knew that appearances could be deceiving. All the leaders of the Terran council were picture perfect and looked friendly and charming on television. And yet most of them were sadistic sociopaths who couldn't care less about how the poor people got hurt, as long as they could live in luxury.

Keila needed to talk. She missed Metatron and she knew that her actions had made him feel betrayed. Metatron wanted to focus on Eden and the Edenites. He wanted to look after and improve the lives of Eden's inhabitants. Keila was focused on how to fight the Terran Council and free her Martians brethren from its oppression.

Their goals were not compatible, and yet Keila needed Metatron. She hadn't told him about her vision, as a matter of fact, she hadn't discussed the foetus with him at all. Yet he knew, and things had changed. He was not sleeping with her anymore, and Keila wondered if he slept at all. Keila decided to stop overthinking and talk to Metatron. She visited him in the command centre where he was overlooking a process.

Keila:

- You don't sleep much these days.

Metatron:

- I only need to sleep two hours a day using the accelerated sleeping pod.

Keila:

- But you used to sleep eight hours a day next to me. Getting natural sleep is good for you.

Metatron:

- I can't afford to waste that much time. My people need me, and there are lots of things I need to do.

Keila:

- You can't afford to, or you don't want to?

Metatron didn't answer; instead, he turned to the computer terminal. Keila:

- The visions that used to guide me don't make any sense to me. They have changed, and their source has changed. Please help me find my way.

Metatron:

- Why do you ask me now? You didn't ask before you killed our baby.

Keila:

- I didn't kill her! I put her in suspended animation. My vision told me that she would have her adulthood ceremony in 15 years, but the adulthood ceremony is at the age of 13. Hence she is supposed to be born in two years.

Metatron:

- And it never crossed your mind that your vision was bullshit?

Keila:

- Oh Jack, don't say that. You know that my visions are real.

Metatron:

- Don't call me Jack. That is my Terran name, and I haven't been to Earth for 80 years.

- When I lived on Earth, I was carrying out assassinations for Abraham Goldstein.

- Eden is my destiny. This is where I can redeem myself and find peace.

Keila:

- Oh yes, I keep forgetting how old you are.

Metatron:

- Yes, it's easy to forget my age when admiring my baby face.

For the first in a while, Keila saw Metatron smile. It was a tired, resigned smile but still a smile. Despite Metatron being over 100 years old, he looked young. This was because he spent most of his life cryogenically frozen between missions and had also exposed himself to a significant amount of DNA regeneration to keep him in peak condition.

Keila:

- Don't worry about your age, you got another good 100 years in the tank.

Metatron:

- I'll probably outlive you, my young lady.

He winked at her to take away the seriousness of the joke.

Keila:

- So, are we back on good terms?

Metatron:

- Sure. If you tell me why you approached me today, after a month of silence.

Keila:

- I had the strangest dream. You were dead, I was raising a family with Bjorn Muller, and I saw the human chip in its reverse-engineered form.

Metatron:

- That's good.

Keila:

- Pardon me?

Metatron:

- You wouldn't have told me about the dream if you intended it to come true. Thus, you are no longer slavishly following your visions making them become self-fulfilling prophecies.

Keila:

- I guess. So, what do you suggest I do?

Metatron:

- Well, let's free Mars, shall we? No point beating around the bush.

Keila:

- Okay, handsome, but first come with me to bed. The Edenites can wait.

After this Metatron joined Keila to bed and the two of them were reconciled for now.

Chapter 66 Keila Finalises the Reverse-Engineered Human Chip Blueprint.

Keila was watching the news. The conflict between House Rashid and House White had erupted into a series of full-on proxy wars throughout the solar system. Although the news report did not mention the affiliations between Rashid, White, and the warring factions, Keila knew that these unrelated regional conflicts were, part of something bigger, a full-on battle between House White and House Rashid. So far, she had not achieved what she wanted though, although Rashid and White were fighting it was her fellow Martians that died and her home planet that was affected. Infighting alone would not crush the Terran Council; she needed to mount a full-scale attack to beat them.

Keila studied the blueprint of the reverse-engineered human chip that she had drawn from memory with a blueprint drawing software. Keila was amazed at her engineering ability. Despite having no knowledge of engineering, she had drawn it exactly as she had remembered it.

Keila was hesitant on how to proceed. She knew that she had promised Metatron and Markus Bauer to not mass-produce the human chip and spread the technology. However, if she spread the technology, she could accomplish two things

1. She would have a secure communications channel. The divine technology microchips operated on unique wavelengths, and no-one knew how they worked. Thus, it would be impossible for the Terran Council to intercept and interpret her signals.
2. Introducing a new religion could unite Mars against their oppressors. The Martians were divided and the Terrans could turn them against each other. If she introduced a new religion with enough followers that could unite the Martians against their Terran

overlords. What better way to launch a new religion than to mass-produce human chips and spread them among the population? While other religions required faith, she could transport the messages straight to her followers.

If the Terrans got their hands on a human chip, it would be useless for them. Without the angel chip and god chip, the human chip didn't do anything. Keila would not spread the angel chips and god chips on Mars, and she would not reverse-engineer them for mass production.

Keila made up her mind. She would travel to the Olympus Republic on Mars and arrange a secret meeting with President Hellas Petrakis. Using the outer layer external DNA modifier, Keila changed her face to that of a female Edenite, but not the same looks she had used when kidnapping the House Muller operatives. She left a message to Metatron that she would be gone for a while but she did not further reveal her intentions. She asked one of her Edenite aides to fly her to one of the transport hubs that ran transports between the asteroid mining stations and Mars

A day later, Keila boarded a transport bound for the Olympus Republic. Keila leaned back and expected a few quiet weeks in space. Things would not turn out that way as the notorious space pirate Morgan Henry had the ship in his sight.

Chapter 67 Rangda Fills Keila With Enough Power to Take Out an Entire Pirate Crew.

Morgan Henry prepared to board the passenger ship that took Keila from the asteroid belt to Mars. He and his crew were looking forward to another round of violence against innocent defenceless people. This was the third time he was attacking the passenger ships this month.

Morgan Henry's attacks on passenger ships were not a random occurrence. Although the vessel did not contain anything of value and their passengers were poor Martian workers, attacking them served a purpose.

Morgan Henry was secretly working for House Cheng, and they paid him to attack passenger ships that transported workers to House Muller territory. This was payback for the robbery, where Keila had robbed a House Cheng rare elements vault and made it look like House Muller operatives were behind the theft. While House Cheng had accepted House Muller's apology and compensation payments, this was their unofficial response. By targeting and killing House Muller workers, they weakened their enemy.

Morgan Henry prepared to board the ship, it would have been easier to just blow it up from a distance, but that would have caused suspicion. Pirate attacks were to steal and rob. Blowing up ships from afar wouldn't generate any loot and wouldn't make any sense. He and his 20-man pirate crew drank a concoction that would make them violent and merciless. They attached grappling hooks and an airlock to the passenger ship, before blowing up its doors and storming the ship.

Keila woke up with a twitch when she heard the explosion. She realised that something was amiss, and she was thankful that she had opted for a private cabin instead of cryogenically sleeping the duration of the trip to Mars. Keila opened the door and released a few automatic miniature drones to get an overview of the situation. What she saw on her monitor frightened her. The ship was under attack by a large group of pirates led by the infamous mass-murderer Morgan Henry. They were busy killing and robbing passengers on the lower level, and it was only a matter of time until they moved up to her level.

Keila felt fear engulfing her. She had experienced many desperate battles in the past, but she had never been this outnumbered before. Despite her Zetan gadgets, she did not think she would be able to take on that many pirates on her own. She tried to figure out where to hide and she swore at herself for not learning the floor plan.

Keila heard the voice. It was the voice of the witchlike monster who had been guiding her visions for the last few months. It said, *"I can make you powerful enough to kill them all"*.

Keila:

  - Kill them all? Are you kidding me?

Rangda:

  - No. I can give you the power to get you out of this mess. Let go off control for a while.

Keila was tentative to the offer. She didn't trust the voice, and she had seen the being that it originated from. It looked like the manifestation of evil. Keila woke up from her thoughts when she heard tormented screams of pain from the cabin next to hers. She realised that she had to trust the voice in her head.

Keila:

  - Okay. I'll give up control for the next five minutes.

Rangda:

  - Excellent. Hee Hee Heeeeeeee!!!!

Keila felt how she lost control of her body. Her first impulse was to fight back for control, but she realised the deal she had made with the voice. Her sight changed to infrared, and her vision became narrower but broader. She could feel how the adrenaline was pumping through her veins maximising her blood pressure and heart rate. The door opened, and the amazed pirate didn't have time to react before Keila jumped and cut him in half with her plasma knife. She pulled out his beating heart and have a big bite before throwing it away. Keila was shocked by what she saw, but she let the voice remain in control.

Moving with superhuman speed, she moved to the end of the corridor, hitting the pirate around the corner with a knife to the throat. She then rushed through the lobby where four pirates where standing. She dropped a proximity mine among them and getting away before the mine blew up the four pirates who had the time to react. The sound of the explosion alerted the other pirates that something was amiss.

With haste Keila booby-trapped all the doors to the lobby with the fallen pirates' guns, she then quickly made her way over to the pirate ship and set an explosive device in its engine room before heading back to the passenger ship where an additional two pirates had fallen to her traps. She then hid in an air vent and watched all the pirate running back to their ship in panic, until Morgan Henry was the only one left on the passenger ship.

Keila jumped down and knocked Morgan to the ground. She disconnected the airlock between the ships. Baffled Morgan Henry asked:

- Who are you?

Keila hissed:

- Rangda, remember my name, pitiful human.

Morgan got to his feet and reached for his pistol, but he wasn't fast enough. Keila punched him, with a punch strong enough to penetrate his body and pulled out his heart. She then held it over her head and crushed it with her hand, licking the blood that dropped on her mouth. Seconds later the explosive device at the pirate ship went off, destroyed the pirate ship, and killed the pirates on it.

Keila regained control of her body. *"Trust in Rangda, and you'll be fine,"* the voice said before disconnecting with her.

Keila went down on her knees and vomited from the shock of having her body possessed by another being. She screamed in pain, and some of the survivors came to her assistance.

Survivor:

- Oh my god! Are you hurt?

- We need to call the Terran Council forces for immediate assistance and backup.

Keila:

- No, don't. I repeat DO NOT involve the Terran Council.

- Look after my wounds and take me straight to the Olympus Republic on Mars.

The survivors on the ship did not dare to do anything else than comply with Keila's request. A few days later, she arrived on Mars in a stable condition as her wounds were only superficial.

Chapter 68: A Cold Welcome at the Olympus republic.

The Olympus Republic was a nation on Mars that consisted of a group of underground settlements. It was one of the safer and more prosperous regions on Mars and was technically a democracy, although in reality it was controlled by House Muller. Built on the high volcanic plains around Olympus Mons, it was safe from the raiders and warlords on the ground level. Olympus Mons was over 20 kilometres up, so it was impossible to get there except via air transport and the Olympus Republic had excellent air defences that would deter any raiders from even trying. The drawback of living on the high-altitude volcanic plains was that it was always freezing cold outside and the outside air was too thin to be breathable without breathing aids.

Keila had arrived at The Olympus Republic to meet with President Hellas Petrakis whom she knew was sympathetic to Martian independence and self-determination. Although his nation was a vassal of House Muller, Hellas Petrakis was not fond of them. He had merely aligned with the faction he hated the least. It was almost impossible to survive as an independent nation on Mars, so most countries and regions aligned with a Terran Council member for "protection".

Keila stepped out of the shuttle that had taken her from the interplanetary passenger terminal in orbit to her preferred location in the Olympus Republic. As she landed Olympic Republic police arrested her. Having seen security footage of Keila butchering Morgan Henry's crew, they put her in heavy chains and kept her in place with an invisible nanotechnology force field. They transported her to a secure holding facility awaiting further instructions.

The Olympus police tried to interrogate Keila, but she requested to speak to President Hellas and refused to talk to anyone else. This was a risky move, but it worked because the Olympus police commissioner was grateful that she had killed Morgan Henry, who had killed hundreds of Olympus Republic citizens in the last month. The police commissioner contacted Hellas, who agreed to meet with the mysterious female prisoner.

Together with the police commissioner Hellas walked into the interrogation room where Keila was chained to the wall.

Hellas Petrakis:

- I am president Petrakis.
- You requested to meet me.
- Why?
- Who are you?

Keila:

- That depends. Is that man a friend or a House Muller spy?

Hellas:

- He is Andrew Bello, the commissioner of police and a true patriot to the Olympus Republic.

Keila:

- Excellent. Deactivate all cameras and microphones in the room, and I will talk.

Hellas:

- I am the president here; I decide what happens.

Keila:

- Yet I was the one who ended Morgan Henry's terror. You should hear me out.

Hellas:

- AI, deactivate cameras and microphones in sector B5

- Okay, it's done. Now talk.

Keila:

- It's me, Keila. I have found a way to defeat the Terran Council and bring freedom to our people.

Hellas:

- That is absurd! Keila Eisenstein is dead, and besides, you don't look like her. Furthermore, you don't match her DNA sequence.

Keila:

- That's because I used Alien technology to change the DNA of the outer layers of my body to give me a new appearance.

Hellas:

- Is this a joke? You are wasting my valuable time with these fairy tales.
- If it's that easy just change back.

Keila:

- I am not going to do that now. You see once I revert to my usual face, I cannot change my face again without the Zetan outer layer external DNA modifier. Walking around as Keila Eisenstein is going to attract unwanted attention.

- Take a blood sample if you want. That is going to confirm my story.

Hellas took a blood sample from Keila and analysed it. He stared at her in disbelief. How was it possible to have one set of DNAs on the outside and a different genome on the inside?
Hellas:

- Who are you?
- What is going on?

Keila:

- I told you already. I am Keila.

- I came across technology created by an ancient alien race called the Zetans. They were the species that created mankind. With their technology, I will lead us to freedom.

- Unchain me, and I will show you something.

Hellas exchanged a look with Andrew, who shook his head. Despite this Hellas released Keila from her chains.
Keila:

- Now tell your police commissioner to shoot me.

The police commissioner had no problem following that order and fired a burst of four shots towards Keila. The bullets were stopped by the Zetan Ballistic Energy Absorber and dropped to the ground. The police commissioner was going to shoot again, but Keila kicked the pistol out his hand before he had the chance.
Keila:

- The device is battery operated; don't waste my battery.

After this Hellas was convinced that Keila was the real deal and they set up a secret meeting with his cabinet to develop their war strategy.

Chapter 69: Bjorn Muller Investigates the Pirate Attacks and Confirms His Fears.

Bjorn was putting down his tablet. These bloody pirate attacks were putting a strain on the House Muller mining operations in the asteroid belt. Although no mining station had been attacked since Proxima Thule, enterprises were still struggling. The reason was that pirates had started attacking passenger ships with workers for no apparent reason. House Muller had lost hundreds of skilled workers in these attacks, and thousands of workers had refused to come back to work due to fear of the pirate attacks.

What frustrated Bjorn the most was that he couldn't do a lot about the pirate attacks as he was low on ships and manpower. Because of the damn conflict between House White and House Rashid, they had withdrawn their support from the Terran Council's security forces as they refused to work together. House Bolivar had never been interested in Space Colonization and focused on developing their territories in South America. Finally, House Cheng did not seem interested in dealing with the pirate scourge, which had left the job to House Muller themselves. While House Muller was dominant, they were not influential or wealthy enough to fund peacekeeping of the entire solar system themselves. Hence Bjorn had been forced to attend several press conferences the last month explaining why they hadn't been able to deal with the pirate scourge. Bjorn's intercom rang, and Captain Adal Schneider entered Bjorn's office.

Adal:

- There has been another pirate attack.

Bjorn:

- More bad news every fucking day. Tell me some good news for once!

Adal:

- I was just getting to that. The pirate attack failed, and the infamous pirate Morgan Henry is dead.

Bjorn:

- Music to my ears!
- How did this happen?

Adal:

- Watch for yourself.

Adal transmitted the video footage of an unknown woman assassinating Morgan Henry and his men. Bjorn stared at the footage. This woman reminded him of Keila, and yet he said nothing about it to Adal. It was a silly thought; the woman was not Keila, so why did his mind bring it up?
Bjorn:

- Impressive. I don't know if we shall reward this woman for killing a wanted mass-murderer and his pirate group or if we should kill her as she could pose a threat to us with superhuman abilities like that.

- Who is she?

Adal:

- We don't know her identity. Her DNA is not in our database, and our facial recognition system doesn't recognise her.

Bjorn:

- Was this woman involved in the disappearance of our espionage team on the Freedom Markets trading post?

Adal:

- I thought the same thing, but as it turns out. No.

Bjorn:

- I see. Where is the attacked ship? I would like to study the scene myself.

Adal:

- It's docked at Mars 4th interplanetary passenger terminal. We will pass its orbit in one hour.

Bjorn:

- Very well. Let's go there ourselves and "assist" our Martian colleagues. Gather a platoon and meet me at the shuttle.

Adal:

- Yes, sir.

An hour later Bjorn, Adal and their 30 bodyguards took a shuttle from the Phobos base to the passenger terminal to investigate the attacked ship. It was essential to come in force to show the Martian investigators who were in charge.

Mars had 24 interplanetary passenger terminals each in geostationary orbit over a specific place, each covering one timezone. Every planet had a similar setup of orbiting interplanetary passenger terminals, as the spaceship that travelled between worlds were large and difficult to land on the planets. Thus, smaller shuttle ships took interplanetary passengers between the surface and the passenger terminals.

Bjorn and his group arrived at the scene, and they spoke with the Olympus Republic officer in charge, before sending him back to Mars. Bjorn then spoke to the captain of the attacked ship, Jonas Newton.

Bjorn:

- Captain. Tell me what happened.

Jonas Newton:

- Pirates attacked us, four days ago. They threatened to blow up our ship with their laser cannons if we didn't let them board.

- We had to let them board, as our ship is unarmed.

- I thought they were going to rob us, but instead, they stormed the ship and killed anyone they could find.

- Suddenly, this mysterious woman emerged from her cabin and killed all the pirates. She had superhuman speed and strength.

Bjorn:

- Yes, I have seen the footage, captain.
- Why didn't you alert the Terran Council of what happened?

Jonas:

- We were going to, but our mysterious friend insisted that we took her to Mars before alerting the authorities.

Bjorn:

- Mysterious?! Didn't you check her identification before allowing her on your vessel?

Jonas:

- We must have slipped up along the way.

Bjorn:

- No, this wasn't a slip-up. You looked the other way and allowed this unregistered passenger to travel on your vessel. As you know, all interplanetary travellers have to be registered with the Terran

Council. Non-compliance is a severe offence. Is there any way we can identify this woman?

Jonas:

- I...

- The woman was treated for minor wounds at the medical bay. There are some of her bloody bandages in the bins there.

Bjorn:

- Excellent. Your helpfulness will be considered during your trial.
- Adal!

Adal:

- Yes, Rear Admiral.

Bjorn:

- Arrest Jonas and his whole crew.

While Adal and his men were rounding Jonas' crew, Bjorn walked up to the medical bay and examined the bloody rags and bandages with a DNA scanner. Most of the blood was from foreign sources, but eventually, a name came that petrified Bjorn Muller. The name was Keila Eisenstein.

While Bjorn couldn't be certain that Keila was the mystery woman he instinctively knew it. Burdened by the realisation, he said nothing and returned to the base on Phobos.

Chapter 70: Bjorn Muller Meets with Hellas Petrakis.

Bjorn was unsure of how to approach the fact that Keila was alive and that she had changed her appearance. If he announced that Keila was alive, he would look like an idiot for declaring her dead in the first place. But if he didn't announce that Keila was alive, she would cause more trouble.

What baffled Bjorn was not that she could change her looks. Plastic surgery was plentiful and readily available in the 29th century, but that she could change her DNA signature to make her unrecognisable for security cameras. Security cameras had DNA detection capabilities, as a safeguard against plastic surgery.

Bjorn was certain that House Muller didn't have any technologies that could mask an agent's DNA signature. It was unlikely that the primitive savages on Mars would have access to advanced technology. So where had Keila accessed this technology? Eden was her last known location and, but all the intelligence reports about Eden indicated that Eden was home to a group of cultists, that pretended to live during the Bronze Age.

Bjorn took a breath. His main priority was to stop Keila before rumours of his humiliating failure would spread. Bjorn contacted Hellas Petrakis via the hologram machine. After a while, Hellas showed up on the platform in front of him.

Hellas:

- Greetings, Rear Admiral Muller. How may I be of assistance?

Bjorn:

- We need to meet today at 3PM. I'll come by your office, don't be late.

Bjorn then hung up on Hellas. Hellas was House Muller's puppet. As such there was no reason to organise meetings when it was convenient for him. Instead, Bjorn Muller disrespected Hellas to keep him in place.

A few hours later, Bjorn landed and he was greeted by Hellas in the Presidential Palace reception area. While the lobby was luxurious by Martian standards, it looked destitute compared to Europeum Towers in Hansstadt. Bjorn ignored Hellas and walked straight into Hellas office. Hellas came after him subserviently.

Hellas:

- Rear Admiral Muller, you are missing out on the great food and refreshments that we organised for you in the reception area.

Bjorn:

- How thoughtful of you to look after my bodyguards, but I prefer to eat real food.

Hellas:

- Objection noted. We will try to satisfy your tastes better next time.

Bjorn:

- Don't bother; I wouldn't come here to socialise.

Hellas:

- So, Bjorn, why are you here?

Bjorn:

- I need to meet with the extraordinary woman that dealt with Morgan Henry. I heard she was detained here.

Hellas:

- Yes. She was detained here for questioning. I spoke with her myself.

Bjorn:

- So, where is she?

Hellas:

- She was cleared of any wrongdoing and she was free to go. She left earlier today.

Bjorn:

- Cleared of any wrongdoing? She stopped the attack from being reported to the authorities! She travelled between planets without proper identification!

Hellas:

- Those are not Olympic Republic laws, nor did it happen within our jurisdiction.

- If you wanted her arrested, you could have sent a request. We cannot detain people without a reason.

Bjorn felt angry and frustrated. Was Hellas Petrakis playing him for a fool? Bjorn realised that he hadn't been the friendly to Hellas and that he could expect the Puppet president to be obstinate. Bjorn was doubtful whether he should escalate the issue with Hellas or not.

Bjorn knew through his forensic examination that the mystery woman, was the infamous terrorist Keila Eisenstein, who he had declared dead a year earlier. But no one else knew that Keila was alive, and the last thing Bjorn did not want people to find out that she was alive. Rumours about Keila's resurgence would embarrass him and act as a beacon for the Martian resistance.

Hellas:

- So why did you come, Bjorn? What is this woman to you? High ranking officials don't come down here for migration matters.

Bjorn:

- That is correct. I am here to investigate her because of her immense capabilities.

Hellas:

- I see.

- Well, being talented and capable of looking after oneself, is not a crime in the Olympus Republic, so I am afraid I cannot do more to assist you.

Bjorn:

- Well, that's unfortunate.

- I might as well join you for the food and refreshments. I am sure the food and beverage cost a lot by your standards.

Hellas:

- We would be honoured to have you and your men dining with us.

Bjorn:

- Excellent. If you provide us with some female entertainment, I can put in a good word for you with my father.

Hellas:

- That is very gracious of you. I am sure we can have it organised.

After that Bjorn and Hellas left the office to enjoy dinner at the reception area of the Olympus Republic presidential palace.

Chapter 71: Rangda Kills Off Isolated Zetans and Increases Her Power.

Rangda was riding a Xeno leading her group of other Xenos. Being a Zetan and Xeno hybrid, she was smaller than the big and bulky Xenos and could use them as riding animals. Although she could keep up with them, there was no reason to do so. She needed to conserve her energy for more important tasks.

When Rangda killed Zeus with a psionic shock, she learned something valuable. She learned the location of a bunch of Zetans hibernating in deep meditation throughout the Divine Dimension. She would find them and kill them off for two reasons.

Firstly, she wanted to stop them from waking up and joining the Zetans that would try to stop her. More importantly, she wanted to shatter and absorb their souls using the corrupted dark Zeto crystals. This was imperative to her plan; without her corrupted Zeto crystals her psionic powers were not impressive as she was only half Zetan. With the crystals fully charged, she was stronger than anyone else.

Rangda saw a group of three Zetans a couple of kilometres away. They were awake and had detected her troops. While this was not optimal as she had preferred to kill them off when they were asleep, she had to attack.

Rangda would have to sit this fight out and let her Xeno soldiers do the fighting for her. When Rangda killed Zeus, he had counter blasted her which had caused massive internal bleeding in her brain, but not enough to kill her. The migraine caused by the blast was excruciating. Zeus had stronger psionic powers than Rangda but she had killed him when he was weak and unprepared. When Zeus tried to bind himself to Keila, he had lowered his defences and Rangda could get a lethal surprise attack in.

Rangda hissed out to her troops in the Xeno language:

- Attack them, but don't kill them. I'll finish them off.

20 minutes later Rangda arrived at the battlefield. There laid dozens of slain Xenos, but on the flipside, the three Zetans were drawing their dying breaths. She killed them off using the corrupted Zeto crystals, shattering and absorbing the dead Zetans' souls. She then feasted on their dead bodies while her Xeno army had to settle for eating their own fallen brethren. After finished eating, Rangda felt her power increasing. She roared and followed up with a sinister laugh.

Chapter 72: Strategy Meeting Between Keila and Hellas Petrakis

Keila was reading a report in her room and felt relieved. She had been holed up in this room for a week as the face she was using was too well-recognised after the news has spread about how she killed Morgan Henry. She couldn't change to another appearance as she had left the External DNA Modifier back on Eden, and reverting back to her real face, was not suitable as the Terran Council had lots of spies on Mars and they would find out if she was to re-emerge.

The report stated that the Olympus Republic scientists and engineers were able to produce the reverse-engineered Zetan technologies that she had brought for them. With access to an external DNA modifier, she would be able to change her face and DNA to that of another person. Preferably she would be a law-abiding Martian citizen to avoid attracting any suspicions. That person would have to switch places with her at this secure secret facility as it didn't make sense for the same person to be seen at two different locations at once. Keila requested an audience with Hellas Petrakis, and a couple of hours later he came down to talk with her.

Hellas:

- Hi Keila.

- Good news, our research team have made the prototypes of the reverse-engineered plans you gave us.

Keila:

- Yes, I know, Hella. I saw the report that you sent me.
- This is excellent news, are you willing to commit to the revolution?

Hellas Petrakis:

- Yes, I am willing. It is not because I enjoy the prospects of war and bloodshed but because defeating the Terran Council is the only way for me to lead my people out of poverty and oppression.

- I spoke to Joachim Muller on the hologram generator the other day. He requested 20 billion Terran Credits worth of rare elements for the "maintenance" of the magnetic field generators on the North and South Poles.

- How am I ever going to create an economy when all our resources just disappear to blackmailing plutocrats?

The magnetic field generators on the Mars' North and South Poles were imperative for life on Mars. They were put in place 600 years earlier when the Terran leaders wanted mass migration from Earth to Mars to get rid of all the undesirables from Earth. The magnetic field generators worked by sending an electric current through the planet to activate and electrify its core to create a magnetic field. With a magnetic field in place, Mars could maintain a breathable atmosphere, as its gravity was strong enough to keep an atmosphere once the magnetic field repelled the toxic solar wind. The Terran Council owned both of the magnetic field generators and guarded them with massive armies, which meant that they could blackmail Martian nations to pay them enormous sums that would keep the Martian's poor.

Keila:

- 20 billion Terran Credits? Does the Hellas Republic have that much money?

Hellas:

- Oh yes... Joachim Muller showed us that we did... If we just cut down "unnecessary" expenses such as universal healthcare and universal education.

Keila:

- Yeah, what are the lives of suffering Martians worth when profit must increase for the dividends?

Hellas Petrakis:

- Exactly. Besides, House Muller, profits won't go up this year. With the conflict between Rashid and White, House Muller must provide more funding to the Terran Council to compensate. Joachim is desperate to cover his costs.

- Unfortunately, the citizens of the Hellas Republic are the ones who will suffer unless we strike back.

Keila:

- So, do we have a deal then?
- Whose identity will I take.

Hellas Petrakis:

- You'll become Rose Menakis. A woman who unfortunately died in an accident, but her death hasn't been made public yet.

Keila:

- Excellent.

- Just one more thing; The microchips for untraceable communications. I brought you a high grade one from Eden. Mass-produce the cheaper ones to give to our troops. We don't want the Terrans to intercept our communications.

Hellas Petrakis:

- Alright, hand one over and I'll plug it in.

Keila handed Hellas a Divine Technology Angel chip. He screamed in pain as it merged with his brain as he pushed it into his ear.

Hellas Petrakis:

- Fucking hell. What kind of communications equipment is this?

Keila:

- The chip merged with your brain stem. It's the only way to make the signal secure.

Hellas:

- Just great. So how do I take it out?

Keila:

- You would have to surgically remove it.

- But don't worry about that. It works, and it will help us. Now get the basic chip mass-produced.

Hellas:

- Sure, whatever. I don't like how you talk to me like you are my boss.

Keila:

- You'll get used to it.
- Now let's get my face changed.

After that, they went to the room where the outer layer external DNA modifier was assembled so that Keila could assume the identity of Rose Menakis, an unremarkable Olympus Republic citizen.

After changing her appearance, Keila used her new identity to take a passenger ship back to the station in the asteroid belt where she had departed to Mars a few weeks earlier. This was an uneventful journey, and she made her way back to Eden where she stored Rose's DNA for future use and reverted to her regular appearance.

Keila felt how more and more Martians were connected to the Divine Technology chip. She felt a bit guilty. Keila hadn't told Hellas about the real powers of the Divine Technology chips. Instead, she had stated that they were secure communications devices.

Keila was unsure whether Hellas had exposed her lie when he inserted the human chips in his followers, as that allowed him to read their thoughts. Hellas hadn't mentioned it, and she was unsure whether he was playing ignorant or hadn't noticed the powers that angel chip gave him over his followers. In the end, it didn't matter, as Keila would still have more power than Hellas.

Once Keila came back to Eden, she was in for a hostile reception as Metatron, and Markus Bauer were furious with her actions.

Chapter 73 End of Romance

Keila was back in the gym, hitting the boxing bag. It felt good to be back exercising, as she hadn't been very physically active for the last few months. Besides, she needed to let off some steam. Keila's lies and broken promises had destroyed her romantic relationship with Metatron. Keila was upset over the breakup.

When they broke up, they had agreed to not get into each other's way. They divided power and responsibilities between each other. Keila was commanding her Martian revolution plans and her strike force of Edenite volunteers. Metatron was left in charge of Eden and transforming it into a modern and peaceful utopia.

Keila ignored demands from Rangda, to kill Metatron. Although Rangda's possession had saved Keila's life when Morgan Henry's crew attacked her ship, she was wary of the evil creature, and she would not heed Rangda's counsel unless it was desperate times. Not only had Rangda made her kill the innocent Jeshua one and a half years earlier, but Rangda had also made Keila eat her fallen enemies' hearts and drink their blood, during her possession of Keila's body. Keila almost vomited every time she thought about the carnage, she had caused that day.

Keila received a message from Hellas Petrakis. Her equipment had been mass-produced on Mars, and the Olympus Republic forces were ready to strike. Keila decided to avoid taking public transportation to Mars. Instead, she gathered her troops and used a shuttle equipped with Zetan stealth technology to get to Mars undetected.

Chapter 74: Joachim Muller Becomes Furious with Bjorn and the Olympus Republic.

Joachim Muller arrived on the Phobos Base for the second time in a couple of months. He was not happy. He was unhappy with the travel time, the Olympus Republics refusal to pay tribute and the fact that he had received video evidence of Bjorn having sex with Martian prostitutes in the presidential palace of Olympus Republic.

The travel time between Earth and Mars was seven days for this trip, compared to three days on Joachim's latest trip to Mars. This was because Earth had moved further away from Mars as part of its orbit around the sun.

Joachim didn't like being in space. What he disliked more, was handing over control. In Joachim's absence, his third son, Benjamin was left in charge of the faction. While Joachim had faith in Benjamin's abilities, he did not like the fact that Benjamin would not provide him with an heir. Joachim also disapproved of Benjamin's sexual deviation towards men, which was an embarrassment for House Muller's reputation.

What was worse than Benjamin's homosexuality, was the Olympus Republic's refusal to pay for the maintenance of Electromagnetic field generators on Mars. Instead of contributing with the 20 billion Terran Credits, they had responded with the footage of Bjorn engaging in coitus with Martian prostitutes. This was embarrassing to Joachim and was blackmail against him. Having sex with Martians was illegal for Earth humans according to Terran law. Although the law was often ignored, it was pathetic for the son of a faction leader to sink so deep.

Joachim and his bodyguards approached Bjorn's quarter at the Phobos base. Joachim didn't bother announcing his presence at his door. Instead, he used his position as Terran Council Chairman to override the electronic locks on the door and he sent his bodyguards in to beat up Bjorn and drag Bjorn to him.

Bjorn, who was bloodied and bruised, stared at his father in surprise:
Bjorn:

- Dad?
- What's happening?

Joachim:

- Two weeks...

- I am spending two weeks going back and forth to this rotten planet.

- I DO NOT like going to Mars, yet you force me to come here to clean up after your mistakes!

Bjorn:

- What did I do now?

Joachim:

- I spoke to Hellas Petrakis last week. He refused to pay us tribute for the magnetic field generators...

Bjorn Muller:

- And instead pressuring him to pay, you show up here with your goons to beat me up? Great leadership dad, I am sure that will solve the issue.

Joachim punched Bjorn on the nose causing a massive nosebleed.
Joachim:

- I am here to resolve the issue by discussing the matter with Hellas.

- Punishing you is a side-business. If you haven't figured out why you are punished yet, have a look at this screen.

Bjorn looked at the video of him having sex with the Martian prostitutes. He said nothing, and Joachim continued his tirade.

- I have had enough, Bjorn. One more fuckup and I will renounce you as my son and expel you from House Muller. After that, I will instruct Max Wellington to dump you off alone and unprotected on Mars. Do we have an understanding?

Bjorn nodded. He didn't dare to say anything against his strict and angered father. Blood and tears were running down his cheeks. Joachim's anger faded. He was ashamed of what he had become. He had used to be humane and idealistic, but his father Hans Muller had extinguished that part of his personality. So, all that remained of Joachim was bitterness, anger, and lust for power. Joachim had been relieved when Hans was murdered so he could step out of his tyrannical father's shadow. Yet here he stood, treating his own children as bad as his father had treated him.
Joachim:

- Guards take Bjorn to the medical ward and make sure that he gets the best possible treatment.

- We are all heading to the Olympus Republic tomorrow.

Chapter 75: So Close but Not Yet.

Keila and her Edenite strike force landed close to the presidential palace of Olympus Republic. Due to the altitude, it was freezing, and the air was very thin as well. To survive the outdoor conditions Keila and her troops were dressed in cold-weather suites with built-in heating and were using mountaineering rebreathers to be able to breathe the thin air at this altitude.

Suddenly, the sky became a lot brighter, and the temperature rose. Keila looked up and she noticed that several orbital satellites were reflecting sunlight down to the surface. Keila was unsure why this was the case and she hesitated on how to proceed.

Keila saw a multitude of spaceships land close to her. The ships were carrying the emblem of the Terran Council. Once they had landed, they sprayed out concentrated oxygen eliminating the need for a rebreather. But why was the Terran Council here? Had Hellas Petrakis betrayed her and if so, what was she going to do about it? If the Terran Council had come after her with this overwhelming force, she was doomed. She was stuck on the surface of a flat, featureless plain, and there was no way she could outgun them or run away from them.

Keila connected to Hellas' mind and she realised that he was unaware of the Terran Council forces arrival. This was a relief as it meant that he hadn't betrayed her, but it didn't answer why they were there. Captain Adal Schneider shouted at her:

- Terran Council Security Forces: Drop your weapons and identify yourselves!

Keila realised that she could not fight herself out of this situation and she told her troops to give up their weapons.
Keila:

- I am Rose Menakis. I am a citizen of the Hellas Republic, and the people with me are citizens of the independent Eden colony, known as Asteroid B528A.

Adal:

- I can confirm your identity, but not the identities of your followers. Explain yourselves.

Keila:

- These people are from the independent colony, Eden. They have isolated themselves from the rest of the solar system for the last 70 years and are as such not included in public records. They are here to sign a trade agreement.

Adal:

- Merchants don't usually trade armed to the teeth ready for war.

Keila:

- These are dangerous times, and as unaffiliated traders. the Edenites don't come under the gracious protection of the Terran Council. Thus, they need to defend themselves.

Adal:

- Whatever. Stand back and let us confiscate your weapons. You'll get them back at the end of the summit.

Keila:

- Summit? There is not supposed to be any summit here today. Who is meeting?

Adal:

- That's none of your concern, Martian peasant.

Keila:

- How lovely. Guys, just lend your guns to our benevolent guests, the peacekeepers from the Terran Council.

Adal:

- Smart move.

Keila and her group dropped their weapons, and they were surrounded by a group of armed Terran Council forces aiming their guns at them. Adal walk off to a luxurious shuttle speaking to someone. She froze when she realised who it was: Adal was speaking to Bjorn and Joachim. Two of her greatest enemies were within striking distance from her.

Keila closed her eyes to get inspiration and see possible potential outcomes. In some of the aggressive scenarios, she killed Bjorn and Joachim. But in none of these scenarios did she survive herself and killing either of them would not change Mars for the better. She needed to unite the Martians and crush the Terran Council for real change to happen. Joachim and Bjorn approached her.

Joachim:

- My apologies for our intrusion, Rose. You must feel terrified, being surrounded by all these armed men.

- Don't fear as my men are not here to punish you, but to keep the peace and make sure the meeting between Hellas and I can take place without incident.

- Tell me who is the leader for your Edenite friends.?

Keila:

- Eden is governed by Metatron, and the leader for this delegation is Melchior.

Joachim:

- Very well.

- Melchior, let your master know that he is better off trading with House Muller, as all other trade is subject to heavy taxation and potential penalties.

Bjorn joined in the conversation and shouted:

- Filthy liars! Give me Keila's location now. I know you are working with them.

Joachim gave Bjorn a stern look. Keila hid her fear, while considering to strike. If she was to go down, she would bring her tormentor and rapist Bjorn with her.
Keila:

- I don't understand, Sir. Didn't you announce Keila's death over a year ago?

Bjorn:

- Shut your mouth, peasant. I did not address you; I spoke to the delegation from Eden.

Joachim:

- That's enough Bjorn. There is no reason for you to abuse the local citizens.

- I apologise for my son's behaviour, Miss Menakis.

- Unfortunately, we will have to detain you and your delegation for the duration of our meeting with Hellas Petrakis. Do not worry. You are not our prisoners, only our guests and you will be served a delicious meal for your troubles.

Keila played it cool and not resist. It was evident that Muller believed in her fake identity and her backstory. Keila and her Edenite militia were led on board a Terran Council shuttle, where they were served food and drinks. A few hours later, they were released and given back their weapons and equipment. Keila was very thankful that the Terrans hadn't inspected their equipment closely, as it would have been a critical problem if her enemies had realised that she was in possession of advanced alien technology!

Chapter 76: Attacks are Coordinated with Hellas Petrakis.

After being released from Terran Council detention, Keila and her militia went to Hellas Petrakis's office in the presidential palace of the Olympus Republic. The palace had been ransacked of everything of value. Hellas commented on what she saw:

- Impressed by my new Spartan-looking office?

Keila:

- Not really. What happened?

Hellas:

- Joachim came by. He was upset at our refusal to pay him 20 billion Terran Credits. Joachim reckoned that if I was too destitute to pay him, I was too poor to afford a beautiful office. Hence, he ordered his men to take everything of value.

Keila:

- Yeah, I know. I spoke with him outside.

Hellas:

- So, your cover held then? I am impressed that you didn't attack him, causing the death of all of us.

Keila:

- I already tried that once, when I killed Hans Muller. The Terran Council is a many-headed hydra, chop off one head, and another head will just pop up.

- No, we need to unite the Martian population and destroy the Terrans main base, the Phobos Moon Base.

Hellas:

- Agreed. But how would we attack the Phobos Base? Even with the technology you provided, we have no chance for an attack.

Keila:

- Not yet, but we'll get there. I have brought some plans for us to discuss.

Hellas:

- Very well. Let's discuss these plans.

After saying this, they studied and discussed the plans until they had come up with their first objectives. Keila was to lead the covert attacks, while Hellas was to pursue diplomatic contacts with other Martian countries and factions.

Chapter 77 The Attack on House White's Gadolinium Mines.

Colonel Douglas White was overlooking the desolate wasteland that had once been the Tengil Dominion from a Terran base on Mars. He hated this placement. While it was crucial to maintain a military presence to protect the mines, Douglas did not appreciate living within an abandoned wasteland.

The Tengil Dominion had been an independent Martian society, controlling most Mars' gadolinium supplies which had made them wealthy and powerful despite their small population (3 million) and territory (10,000 square kilometres). The region had been assigned to House White when the Terran Council divided the areas of Mars to the different Houses of Earth. This was to ensure that every Martian territory had only one trading partner and that this faction controlled all their trade to bleed the territory dry.

The leaders of the Tengil Dominion ignored that they belonged to House White's sphere of influence and kept trading with other Martian nations by using smugglers and unofficial channels.

Eventually, House White leadership had enough of the obstinate people of Tengil Dominion and had destroyed the nation so that they could run the gadolinium mines themselves. They had done this by navigating a medium-sized asteroid to collide with The Tengil Dominion, destroying most of the buildings and killing most of the population at the same time, with the survivors seeking refuge elsewhere. While using asteroids instead of nuclear weapons had been costlier path of action, it had the advantage of not leaving any radioactive fallout in its wake. This meant that House White could move in and operate the mines themselves.

Managing the mines themselves had an apparent drawback; that they needed to guard the mines from desperate and needy Martians that tried to steal their valuable gadolinium. That was why Douglas White, who was half-brother of Alicia White, was assigned to lead the House White garrison in the Tengil Dominion.

Douglas hated his life. Like Bjorn, he was a too important member of his family to not be in a leadership role. However, his father found him to be lazy and too much of an embarrassment to work at the House White head-quarters on Earth. Douglas White hated his father John White, who was the chairman of House White. The bastard had left him here to rot. He made shitloads of money for his family, yet he saw very little of it himself. What angered Douglas the most was that his father held him in lower regard than his half-sister, the failed genetic experiment Alicia White.

Douglas studied the perimeter of the base. It was an hour before sunset and Douglas felt the chill as the temperature was dropping below zero. Worse than the cold was the spell of disappearances that had occurred lately. Dozens of soldiers had disappeared the last few days, and fear was spreading among his men. Douglas had begged his father to use orbital satellites to direct more sunlight down to the base to extend the days, as all the disappearances had happened at night. His father had rejected the proposal claiming that Douglas should toughen up and stop complaining about the Martian. Despite Douglas insisting that the weather was not the issue, his father had ignored his pleas.

Douglas watched the sunset. There was no movement at the perimeter, and everything seemed fine. Douglas decided that there was no point stand-ing out here in the cold staring at the empty horizon. He had soldiers and cameras to do that job, so he headed back to his private quarters. He tapped up a hot bath, made himself a cup of herbal tea and tried to warm up.

Since he got stationed on Douglas, he had turned from being a heavy drug user to be a clean-living individual. He had changed, as he reckoned that the only way to get back to Earth was to show his father that he changed for the better and would not embarrass him anymore. Unfortunately, his lifestyle change did not help, as his improved behaviour showed his father that keeping Douglas on Mars was good for him.

Suddenly, Douglas started feeling very dizzy and disoriented, and he heard gunfire. Douglas was surprised by how close the shooting seemed to be. The perimeter was three kilometres away, so the sounds should be very faint, since the thinner Martian atmosphere didn't transport sound as well as Earth's atmosphere. Someone was banging on the door, and he heard one of his bodyguards calling his name. Struggling to find his balance in his disoriented state, Mark fell over several times on his way to the door. Once he opened the door, he saw several of his bodyguards collapsing and vomiting.

Bodyguard:

- Sir, we are under attack by unknown assailants.

Douglas:

- How did this happen? Why wasn't I contacted until now?

Bodyguard:

- Our communications went down. We are unable to communicate with the different units within the base, and we are unable to contact the Phobos Base.

- Everyone is feeling nauseous.

Douglas:

- We cannot fight if we cannot communicate and coordinate our efforts. Sound the evacuation alarm.

Bodyguard:

- Are you sure sir? If we abandon the most essential gadolinium mine in the solar system, your father won't be happy.

Douglas:

- That old bastard is never happy. If you want to stay here and die for his wealth, be my guest. I am getting out of here, and I am urging everyone to do the same.

Bodyguard:

- As you wish, sir.

Douglas activated the evacuation alarm and the House White troops rushed towards the space shuttles to evacuate the base. Keila and her soldiers were surprised that this battle was a lot easier than she had imagined. Keila had never anticipated that her enemies would be this cowardly.

The reasons for her enemies' retreat did not matter, and the attack had achieved its target. Keila and her troops loaded the gadolinium metal bars onto their transports, and then they activated the explosives that blew up the facility. After that, they enabled Zetan stealth technology on their vehicles and took off.

Chapter 78: Humiliating Defeat for House White.

N ewspaper article: Olympus Republic Tribunal, 5th July 2874

Forces from House White that controlled the Tengil Dominion showed a humiliating level of cowardice when a strike force from The Mars Humanist Alliance, attacked their base. The attack by a small group of individuals prompted the 1000 men, strong military force to take off, running for their lives and leaving all their equipment behind to be commandeered by the Martian resistance. The video below shows how the Colonel Douglas White is running for his life while wearing a bathrobe.

Anonymous writer, The Olympus Republic Tribunal

Chapter 79: Meeting with Joachim Muller, Bjorn Muller, and Max Wellington.

Joachim Muller was annoyed. Due to the incompetence of Douglas White, he had to postpone his return to Earth to sort out the mess on. Terran Council troops had returned to the site the day after, but the attackers were gone when they got there. The facilities in the Tengil Dominion were looted and damaged, and it would take months to get production up and running again. Yet the biggest issue for Joachim was not the lost production, that would be House White's problem, but the absolute embarrassment in the defeat.

Images of the half-naked Douglas White running for his life had spread all over the planet, and the Terran Council Security Forces were the laughingstock of the Martians. They needed to attack and kill a lot of Martians to spread fear and erase this embarrassment from peoples' memories. But who would they attack? All Martian factions and significant population centres had sworn loyalty to the Terran Council and were controlled by their assigned overlords. To bomb and kill loyal people would spread fear, but it would spread even more dissent, and in no time, they would have another uprising on their hands.

Joachim was looking at the intelligence on hand about the Martian Humanist Alliance. This terrorist group was destroyed 1.5 years ago when their base on the asteroid Sylvia was eviscerated. Since the death of the group's figurehead Keila Eisenstein, nothing had been heard from the group. Yet, now they were strong enough to attack a stronghold on Mars and rout the defenders. Something did not add up. Joachim summoned Max and Bjorn to discuss the matter. They arrived at his suite a while later.

Joachim:

- Okay, gentlemen. Can you please update me on your latest debacle?

Max:

- Excuse me Chairman Muller, but Douglas White belongs to the army defence force. Bjorn and I belong to the space navy.

Joachim:

- That's a distinction without a difference. You are armed and funded by my company with the sole purpose of enabling profitable ventures throughout the solar system.

Max:

- Apologies, Sir. You are right.

- The survivors tell a similar scenario. Their communications went out, they were all afflicted with severe nausea, and their bullets stopped mid-air instead of hitting the attackers.

Joachim:

- This is absurd. People say anything to defend their actions these days.

Bjorn:

- Well, their claims match what we found when we reconstructed the attacks on Proxima Thule and the Aljadid Salam outpost.

Joachim:

- What are you talking about, Bjorn? Proxima Thule and Aljadid Salaam were small outposts with a few defenders and no survivors. The Tengil Dominion was large and well-defended with a lot of survivors.

Bjorn:

- Yes, but they used similar technology at every attack. They used advanced cloaking technology to get close undetected, something that blocked communications, something that made our troops nauseous and unable to fight back and something that stopped bullets in mid-air.

Joachim:

- Bjorn. This is your drugs talking. Do you have any proof for the existence of these technologies or any plausible explanation on how the Martians, can muster these superweapons out of nowhere?

Bjorn:

- It must be Keila that has ganged up with the people of Eden to undermine us.

Joachim:

- How many times do I need to hear that woman's name?!

- She is a nobody. She killed your grandfather by coming to his bed posing as a whore. Hans died from his own carelessness and nothing else.

- Besides, considering how obsessed you are with her, what disproves that you are conspiring with her?

Max:

- Gentlemen, stop arguing, please! I can assure you that Eden has nothing to with this. We have conducted a many surveillance missions over the years on Eden with nanotechnology drones, and they had all proven the same thing. That Eden, the most expensive terraforming project in the history of mankind is used for housing a strange cult, emulating living in the Bronze Age. Nothing indicates that these people have any combat military skills, and they have limited contact with the rest of the solar system.

Bjorn:

- We met an armed delegation from Eden that was meeting up with Olympus Republic officials. Explain that!

Max:

- Well, they have new leadership on Eden. The new leader has realised the foolishness in their strange ideology and is focusing on making Eden a civilised and metropolitan regime.

- I spoke to the guy over the hologram transmitter once. He calls himself Metatron, but his real name is Jack Silver. He is a former Terran citizen and seems like a decent guy.

Bjorn:

- I have met him twice. I am not a big fan.

Joachim:

- Regardless. How do we deal with this problem and how do we find out which faction is conspiring to create instability in the Terran Council?

Max:

- Well, House Goldstein and House Bolivar are the only significant factions that haven't been attacked in the last year.

Joachim:

- That is true, but that doesn't exclude the other notable players. Anyone could have ordered false flag attacks as a diversion to direct attention elsewhere. Trust no one.

- Gentlemen, I'll leave this task to you.

- I need to contact John White to stop the fool from attacking our allies on Mars. It would be helpful if he sends his own troops to defend his mining stations, so I don't have to spend money guarding them.

Joachim left the room. Bjorn and Max sat silent for a while until Bjorn came up with a new idea:

- Hey Max. The report stated that The Martian Humanist Alliance left most of the weapons and equipment to focus on stealing gadolinium. Why would they do that?

Max:

- Yeah, I thought about that too. Gadolinium is neither super expensive nor does it have any military applications.

Bjorn:

- Let's ask the AI.
- AI. What is the primary usage for gadolinium on Mars?

AI:

- Gadolinium is hardly used on Mars due to the House White monopoly making it expensive. Gadolinium's primary use on Mars is for the planet's magnetic field generators on the North Pole and South Pole of Mars.

Bjorn:

- This must mean something!
- I better discuss this with my father.

Bjorn rushed off, and Max Wellington stayed back in the meeting room. What a strange mess they were in!

Chapter 80 Widespread orbital bombings by House White

N ewspaper article: Olympus Republic Tribunal, 8*th* July 2874

In the last few days, the regions neighbouring the recently attacked House White gadolinium mine has been bombarded from orbit by a fleet of House White warships. This is a response from House White to the humiliating defeat they faced last week. House White required the leaders of the neighbouring regions to round up all members of the Martian Humanist Alliance and send them to House White for punishment. When they failed to deliver the required number of prisoners in the short time frame given to them by House White, the villainous tyrants from Earth unleashed hell upon the region, exposing them to relentless bombing from orbit. The final death toll of these atrocities is still to be determined, but it is expected to rise over 100,000.

Because of House White's barbaric behaviour, many Martian nations and autonomous regions have renounced their affiliations with their assigned Terran Council member, and the peace that has lasted for 1.5 years since the destruction of The Martian Humanist Alliance headquarters on the asteroid Sylvia, is over.

The President of the Olympus Republic, Hellas Petrakis, condemned the barbaric actions of House White and promised an extensive amount of humanitarian aid to the affected region during a press conference earlier today. He reaffirmed that House Muller is still an ally of Olympus Republic and said that he will work hard to maintain a productive affiliation with them.

Anonymous Writer, The Olympus Republic Tribunal

Chapter 81: Keila is Sent to Arm the Rebels.

Keila was watching the news reports from the bombarded areas. She felt feeling miserable. There were endless pictures of dead and wounded, many of them children from the relentless bombardment in the last few days. She was feeling guilty over what had happened. Casualties were a necessity of war, but this indiscriminate butchery was not.

Keila should have seen it coming. House White was infamous for their hatred towards Martians who they saw as an inferior race. They needed to be stopped, but the price to achieve victory was terrible suffering for the common people.

Keila turned off the news report. She wanted to talk to Metatron. She was unable to do so via the Divine Technology chip as Mars and Eden were too far apart at the moment. Keila considered calling Metatron via Space Net. It was a risky move as Spacenet was supervised by Terran Council AI, so she wouldn't be able to expose any secrets or plan. But she needed to see him. Despite their separation, he was still her closest friend and confidant.

Keila called Metatron via the holographic television. Half an hour later he responded. Keila hated that it was impossible to get a live connection, but it was a matter of the distance between the worlds being so vast that it took at least 15 minutes for a message to go between the planets, and then the same time back. She received the response from Metatron. He responded in text form without transmitting himself visually as a hologram, which was a disappointment for Keila

Metatron:

- Hi. Who are you?

Keila:

- It is me. I just wanted to see you. I am feeling sad, and I miss you a lot.

Keila thought of transmitting herself in the hologram transmitter in her lingerie. She decided not to. It felt a bit awkward to communicate with her ex that way, but also because the outer layer of her body had the DNA and appearance of another woman. To her relief, Metatron realised what she was after and sent a moderately hot hologram of himself in a tight gym outfit.

Metatron:

- Okay, we'll be in range in a couple of weeks, I'll contact you then.

Metatron disconnected, and Keila kept the hologram of him running for a while. It looked like he was in the room and it smelled like him as well. The only thing she couldn't do was to feel the presence of him, as the hologram generator just recreated a visually perfect copy by utilising a nanotechnology layer powered by an electric field. If she touched the hologram, she wouldn't feel him. Instead, she would get an electric shock, and the hologram would turn off as a failsafe. Keila felt very aroused. She hadn't had sex for many months since the breakup with Metatron. She got interrupted when Hellas Petrakis knocked on the door. She let him in, and he started to speak.

Hellas:

- Your plans are coming along nicely.

Keila:

- Pardon me?

Hellas:

- House White's brutal attacks on civilians are driving a wedge between our Martian brethren and their Terran overlords.

Keila:

- I never intended for 100,000 dead and injured civilians.

Hellas:

- Really? You are not very well versed in the politics of the solar system, are you?

- On the bright side, there are massive evidence for their atrocities, evidence that wasn't around when they butchered your hometown Pamshal with biological weapons last year.

Keila:

- Yes, you are right. It's a relief that they got caught out this time.

Hellas:

- Which brings us to the next step: I am sending you to arm the people in the bombarded areas. Officially, you'll be Rose Menakis, in charge of the humanitarian efforts. Unofficially, you'll be Keila Eisenstein from the Martian Humanist Alliance arming the population and preparing for the next phase.

Keila:

- Good plan. We'll need massive popular support if we are to win this fight. Our lack of unity has always been our biggest weakness.

Hellas:

- Good. You'll leave in the morning.

Keila:

- Yes, sir.
- I better prepare for tomorrow.
- Until we meet again, President Petrakis.

Hellas left Keila's room. She felt revitalised and optimistic. While Keila was annoyed that Hellas was treating her as a subordinate, she had played along. Keila knew that she could control him through sheer dominance via the Angel chip that he had implanted in his brain, although Keila would avoid that option if she could. Keila wanted to improve things on Mars, not become a tyrant to replace the Terran Councils' tyranny.

Keila packed prepared her Edenite militia for the days to come before going to sleep.

Chapter 82 Keila is Ambushed and Becomes a Martian Symbol of Hope.

A few weeks later, Keila was driving a hovercraft in the wasteland between two settlements. Her efforts as a rebel recruiter had gone well, and she had gained a lot of support for her revived movement.

Suddenly, Keila heard an explosion and she found herself flying out through the windshield with a trajectory for a fatal collision with the ground. Subconsciously, she activated the Zetan ballistic energy absorber that absorbed most of her kinetic energy, so she landed safely on the ground instead of colliding headfirst at 500 kilometres an hour for certain death.

Keila got up on her knees and she saw her hovercraft fly straight into a cliff and explode. She heard explosions and gunfire and took a quick look at her battery indicator. Absorbing the kinetic energy to save herself had drained her battery, which was now empty, so she could not rely on her Zetan technologies. Keila took cover behind a cliff, and she had an overview. She was surrounded by enemies that seemed to be a House White strike team. She was wounded, and blood was pouring down her head from deep cuts that came when she flew headfirst through the windshield. She was only armed with a pistol as the rest of her equipment had been on her hovercraft. Was this her end? Keila closed her eyes and hoped for a miracle.

Rangda spoke to her, offering her powers for temporary control. Keila was tentative towards the proposition. Although Rangda's powers had saved her life when Morgan Henry attacked, Keila had qualms regarding utilising the abilities of a being that she felt was pure evil. Then again, trusting in Rangda was really her only way out of this.

Keila:

> - Okay. If I give you control, can you promise me to no do any sick
> things like eating people and drinking blood.

Rangda *hissing*:

- Yes, Rangda can promise that. Rangda has been eating plenty of delicious Zetan flesh recently.

- But to help you win this battle, I need your true form.

Keila:

- My true form? I am not a monster.

Rangda:

- Your true human form. Deactivate your external Zetan DNA modifier.

Keila reverted to her real appearance, and to her relief, this healed her superficial flesh wounds. She released control of her body to Rangda and felt a massive surge in power, way stronger than what she had felt the first time around. She got out of her cover and in a fired off two shots towards one of the armed flying drones that the strike team had brought with them. The first shot wedged the trigger mechanism into shooting continuously, and the second shot destroyed the steering mechanism on the drone making it spin around shooting everywhere and killing four attackers before crashing into the ground.

This forced the other attackers to take cover and Keila got to the closest attacker and stab him in the head with her plasma knife and stole his rifle. She then booby-trapped him with two hand grenades and called on his radio, *"I am wounded, require medic!",* imitating his voice. Keila got out of sight and watched as she blew up two other attackers when they set off the booby trap. She then sprinted in a semi-circle and shot another two attackers in the back.

One of the fallen attackers had a jetpack and Keila proceeded to use the jetpack to fly up in front of the windscreen of an air support hovercraft and shoot the two pilots, before they had time to react and fire the hovercrafts weapon at her. She then shot the windshield to pieces and used her jetpack to make her way to the driver seat of the hovercraft, to take control of the vehicles before it hit the ground.

Keila flew past the other attackers and carpet-bombed them to disrupt them and stop them from chasing her. Then she set off as quickly as she could from the battlefield. Once she was out of the combat zone, she deactivated the tracking device on the hovercraft and connected the Zetan stealth technology to its battery, to make the hovercraft invisible to Terran Council satellites.

She then made her way to an unoccupied bomb shelter, got the hovercraft out of sight, and fell asleep. Keila slept for over 24 hours straight to recover from her wounds as well as the strain that being possessed had on her body. When she woke up and scanned her phone, she realised that she had gained overnight fame.

The reason for Keila's overnight fame was that House White had followed up on their spies' suggestion that Keila had assumed the identity of Rose Menakis.

Following up on their spies' information House White had opted to make the killing of Keila a live television spectacle. They had small drones filming the attack and broadcast it live. This backfired for House White, and instead of triumphant victory, they saw their elite strike team obliterated by a single woman on live television. Keila's incredible feat increased the hopes and the fighting spirit among the suppressed Martians.

Chapter 83: Open Conflict in the Terran Council.

The August 2874 Terran Council meeting was held a few weeks later in the America First Tower, which was built on the top of Mount Massive in the Rocky Mountains in the centre of the American continent. America First Tower was the headquarters of House White, and it was inspired by House Muller's headquarter Europeum Tower. It was built along a mountain peak to support its weight and give it extra height. To stroke John White's ego, the building was 10 metres higher than Europeum Tower so that House White could claim to have the tallest man-made structure on Earth.

The 2874 Annual General Meeting was filled with conflict and was the hardest meeting to organise in many years. Although Joachim Muller was still the chairman of the Terran Council, he had let House White arrange the meeting this year as he was sick of paying for the spectacle every year. The top executives made their way up to the meeting room on the penthouse level that had a 360-degree view over the Rocky Mountains and a large part of the American continent.

Joachim:

- Welcome to the AGM of 2874. We have several questions to discuss, but let's move to the most crucial issue. The instability and potential uprisings on Mars are reaching a critical melting point, and we need to take concerted actions to re-establish our dominion over the red planet.

Ibrahim Rashid who was old and frail but filled with anger, burst out:

- Our problems are due to that heretic, John White. He let his men kill my favourite son Akram, and then he conducted massbombings of the Martians turning them to against us. I request

256

an apology at once, or I will abandon these proceedings and take my delegation with me. I will break the cease-fire between House Rashid and House White.

John White turned red in his face and screamed at Ibrahim:

- I will not apologise to that filthy paedophile. We had nothing to do with the attack on the Aljadid Salam outpost, and he knows it. His men high-jacked one of our space cruise liners. When we sent our men to save the hostages from this illegal extortion, the fighting claimed the lives of many innocent Terran citizens.

- Ibrahim! You are in my territory. I require you to apologise.

Ibrahim Rashid stood up and screamed at John White:

- Fuck you pig. We are leaving.

He then picked up a jug of water and splashed the water over John White, who in turn called in security to arrest Ibrahim Rashid. Joachim felt that he had to intervene:

- Back down guards. As the chairman of the Terran council, I am giving you an executive order to escort Ibrahim Rashid and his delegation unharmed to the vacuum tubes for safe transit back to Egypt.

John said nothing and the guards did as Joachim instructed them to. Ibrahim and his men were escorted out of the building to the vacuum tubes for transport home. The meeting was paused, and the room was cleaned, and John went to change to dry clothes. Half an hour later the meeting recommenced.
Joachim:

- Now, this is an unprecedented embarrassment and a blemish on our reputation. I hope the rest of the meeting can proceed without any more incidents.

Santiago Bolivar, CEO of House Bolivar joined in on the conversation:

- Speaking of incidents. What is the story with Keila Eisenstein?

- She is the great-granddaughter of Ibrahim Rashid. She showed up six years ago and killed Hans Muller. Then she was the figure-head for a rebellion against us for four years, until your son Bjorn Muller claimed to have killed her two years ago. Conveniently he lost the body, and nothing is heard about her for years until she shows up on live television killing a House White strike team while displaying superhuman powers.

Joachim:

- I don't see what you are trying to say.

Santiago:

- What I am saying is: Does this woman even exist, or is she an ar-tificial plot device, whenever you need something done Joachim?

Joachim:

- Excuse me? Are you accusing me of using Keila to elevate my own power?

Santiago:

- I would not accuse you without concrete evidence, Chairman Muller. I am asking you.

Joachim:

- Very well. Keila exists, and if she is alive, that is unfortunate. My explanation is that someone found her corpse and either revived her or cloned her.

Chi Ping Cheng, the CEO of House Cheng joined in on the conversation:

- We have had access to Keila's *"corpse"* for the last two years. It turned out to be a non-functional clone. This indicates that Bjorn Muller and his father is conspiring against the rest of us, and Keila is their operative!

Joachim sat silent. He did not know what to do with this new information, but he could not disregard Chi Ping's claims. Was Bjorn conspiring against him? Or, had Bjorn been duped by the Edenites? Joachim was unsettled by Bjorn's obsession with Keila, but if he was conspiring with her to overthrow Joachim, why hadn't he made a move yet? Joachim turned to his other son Benjamin Muller who was the CEO of House Muller.

Benjamin:

- Thank you for providing us with this new information. It is unfortunate that you did not choose to share the information as soon as you got it. I am invoking clause 5.2 that gives us a break to review and interpret the new information.

The meeting had a second break for the day, and Benjamin and Joachim retreated to a room where they met with other high-level House Muller executives. They were dumbfounded by the new intelligence. House Cheng had offered to immediately ship the body of Keila Eisenstein together with their lead scientist Tzi Chen Cheng to give a talk about why the body was a fake. They would arrive within a couple of hours. Joachim and Benjamin had no idea on how to react to the new information, but they knew the meeting had gone terribly wrong. On top of all their troubles their attempts to bring House White and House Rashid closer had blown up, and they needed to contain the damage.

They spent the next few hours communicating with representatives for the two factions trying to contain the damage and maintaining the peace on Earth.

Chapter 84 An Autopsy and an Action Plan

T he faction leaders met a few hours later in an unusual meeting spot: The morgue. Tzi Chen Cheng gave them a demonstration on the body proving that it was a fake, in the form of a non-functional clone. After this, they agreed to skip lunch as the visit in the morgue had dulled their appetites and they instead went back to the boardroom for further discussions.

As they gathered in the meeting room again, Joachim Muller resumed the proceedings.

Joachim:

> - As you can see there is a lot of division among us. It seems that
> our enemies have learnt that the best way to control the enemy is
> to make them fight among themselves. We are not going to fall for
> this ploy though.

> - I have written an action plan for how to get us out of this crisis.
> We need to A: stop fighting among ourselves B: Stop random-
> ly bombing Martian Settlements as that just unites them against
> us. C: All start contributing to the Terran Council Forces and D:
> Share intelligence among us so that we can anticipate the enemies'
> next move and see through her deceits. Do you all agree on this,
> gentlemen?

Santiago Bolivar:

> - I agree with what you say, but I have a question:

> - Why are we bothering with Mars? We at House Bolivar are not
> very involved in the Martian business, but it seems that you are

losing billions on Mars every year. Why not just leave the damn dustbowl to govern itself?

Joachim Muller:

- A good question Santiago and I'll give you the historic pretext.

- In the 23rd century, the population of Earth was a staggering 25 billion individuals. It was hell for rich and poor alike. The planet was polluted, and there were constant strife and public unrest. Like on Mars today, but worse. That was when my ancestors in House Muller came up with the solution. To reduce the population by mass-sterilisation and deportations to Mars. There were a lot of fights but due to their iron wills they achieved their dream.

- Since the 24th century, Earth has had a stable population of 1 billion individuals where everyone can have a fulfilling life. We achieved this by enforcing strict population control and adherence to genetic pre-selection in the community. This way we have almost entirely got rid of all crime and undesirable behaviours.

- Now in the 29th century, Earth is a paradise where everything is clean and the population can thrive.

- We gave most of the population paradise to the low cost of limited freedom.

- Now, what would happen if we left the Martians to fend for themselves?

- They would reach our technological level, and on top of this, there would be a lot more of them as they still are driven by their short-sighted, selfish individual needs to procreate. They would expand their territory, starting off with attacking our asteroid mining stations that are essential in bringing wealth and abundance to Earth without the destruction of our environment. Eventually, they would invade Earth, and we would fall, leaving Earth at the mercy of these ravaging hordes. They would mass migrate here, and within a couple of centuries, the planet would be the overpopulated hellhole of the 23rd century.

- So, to sum things up: To contain the Martian hordes and keeping them in place is not for today's profits but for the future of our planet and our people.

John White added in:

- Thank you for the history lesson, Joachim. I agree that it's crucial for the future of our children to contain the Martian threat. I will try my best to not escalate my conflict with Ibrahim Rashid any further.

The remaining faction leaders also agreed, and they ratified the document with Joachim's action plans.

Afterwards, Joachim and Benjamin spoke in the vacuum tube transport pod on their way back to Europe.

Benjamin:

- That went better than expected. We saved the day in the end.

Joachim:

- No, this is a disaster. They were all playing lip service. They are never going to follow this document.

Benjamin:

- You might be right, but I hope you are wrong, father.

Joachim:

- Only future will tell.

Benjamin:

- What do we do about Bjorn?

Joachim:

- It is difficult. We can't leave him in as an officer in the armed forces after this debacle, and we can't take him back to Earth. There is only one solution, but it is hard. He is my son and your brother.

Benjamin:

- I see. It would be better if I dealt with the issue?

Joachim:

- Yes, that would be better.

They nodded in acknowledgement and then drank their drinks in silence for the remainder of the trip.

Chapter 85 Keila Recuperate Her Body and Prepares Her War Strategy.

Keila was recuperating in a secret hideout in the Olympus Republic presidential palace. She wanted to make a live public announcement declaring that all Martian territory was now free from Terran Council overlordship, but she realised how foolish that would be. The Terran Council had a lot of weapons in orbit around Mars, and if she were to show up publicly, it wouldn't be long until they bombed that area to dust.

Keila was looking at her reflection. She had her real appearance as it was no point pretending to be someone else within her inner circle at the Olympus Republic. Keila saw a few grey hairs. This worried her as she was only 24 years old. Since she let Rangda possess her body for the second time, she had felt weak, out of shape with her body aching. Had Rangda when giving her superpowers and controlling her body, also drained her life force? It was a small price to pay as Rangda's intervention had saved her from certain death on both occasions, but it still worried Keila.

Keila stretched her aching body and got up. These worries were her vanity speaking. Besides, from a vanity point of view, her purple predator eyes were a more significant concern than her aging. She got up and walked to Hellas Petrakis office. He wasn't busy, something Keila knew from spying on him via the Divine Technology chip. While it felt a bit rude to spy on her allies, it was for her safety and their own good. If someone were to betray her to the Terran Council, the Olympus Republic would be doomed in the bombardment that would follow.

Hellas Petrakis gave her a concerned look:

> - I am a bit worried about your health, Keila. The DNA regeneration serum I gave you yesterday should have reversed your aging and yet you look worse off today than you did yesterday.

Keila tried to joke it away:

- Never tell a lady she looks old Hellas, I thought you knew that?

Hellas:

- I'm just worried that the serum doesn't seem to work on you.

Keila:

- I am more worried about most Martians that cannot afford the serum, and instead die way too young.

Hellas:

- I have raised the issue with Joachim Muller on several occasions.

- His stance is that it is unwise to extend the life expectancy before we lower the birth rates. Otherwise, we'll be overpopulated in no time.

Keila:

- I thought Mars has always been overpopulated. It is the dumping ground for unwanted people in the solar system.

Hellas:

- I reckon with a balanced economy it could sustain a doubled population living in relative prosperity.

- From 4 billion living in poverty to 8 billion living in moderate prosperity.

- But let's not discuss economic theories for now. Just have faith in my ability to reform Mars economy without our Terran overlords.

Keila:

- You have believed in my ability, Hellas, so it would be rude to not reciprocate.

Hellas:

- So, how are our plans for the assaults going?

Keila:

- Both good and bad. It is difficult building up a sufficient force outside the North Pole and South Pole bases without being detected by orbital satellites. If we destroy those satellites too early, the Terrans will realise that something is amiss and send reinforcements. We must rely on a small force and the element of surprise as well our superior technology for the missions to succeed.

Hellas:

- So, all that we have is hope? I thought we had gained a strong following among the population.

Keila:

- We do. It would be challenging for the Terrans to take control of the rebelling areas on the ground. That's why they are resorting to orbital bombardment.

- The excellent support among the population is imperative for the second stage of our attack. The bases on the North Pole and the South Pole can be taken with small forces relying on superior technology and the element of surprise. The attack on the Phobos base on the other hand, requires a large fleet of small ships and it will be a bloodbath no matter what we do.

- But I have faith in our coming victory.

Hellas Petrakis:

- Faith is good, but do you have any logical reason to believe that our plans will succeed?

Keila:

- No, but logic doesn't win wars. If you look at it arithmetically, we have no chance against the might of the Terran Council armed forces. Yet we have beaten them time after time coming this far. They are fragmented and fighting among themselves. There will never be a better chance than this.

Hellas:

- You are right, Keila. Join the attack on the North Pole on the Spring Equinox just before the sun rises. I will lead the attack on the South Pole just after the sun sets. If it all works out, I will meet you here after we destroy the Phobos base.

Keila:

- Sounds good Hellas. Until we meet again.

Chapter 86: Bjorn Muller Realises Keila's Plan and is Almost Killed by an Assassin.

Bjorn Muller was looking at satellite maps, mapping the movements of the Martians. As the Terran Council were losing control over many areas, the lawlessness on the surface was increasing, and he could see that many bands of raiders had emerged on the surface. This was to be expected, and it was a problem that needed to be resolved before order could be restored. It posed no threat to the Terran Council, and it was better to let the Martians experience lawlessness for a while. That way, they would beg the Terran Council to return and protect them, and they could return to Mars as saviours instead of being the enemy.

Bjorn noticed something. There were large gatherings of raiders close to the South and North Pole of Mars. This didn't make sense as there weren't any major population centres to raid there, plus that it was freezing in the Martian Polar Regions, so how did these raiders sustain themselves? Then it occurred to him. The Martians had stolen a lot of gadolinium the previous month when they attacked House White's gadolinium mines. Gadolinium was the main component in the magnetic field generators on the North and South Pole that was imperative to give Mars a magnetic field to sustain its atmosphere. Could the bands of raiders in the Martian Polar regions be an army waiting to take control of the magnetic field generators?

There was a knock on the door. It was a waiter bringing Bjorn coffee. The man left the coffee on his desk and walked out towards the door when Bjorn noticed something. The coffee on his desk wasn't the one he ordered, and the waiter was new as well. He shouted out to the waiter:

- Hey. This is not the coffee I ordered. Where is Fritz? He is the one supposed to work today.

The assassin mumbled *"Scheisse!"*, turned around and shot Bjorn with a silenced pistol. His aim was off by a bit, and he hit Bjorn in the shoulder. Bjorn dropped to the ground, and the assailant ran towards his desk to shoot him again. Bjorn anticipated this and threw a gold bar that he had under his desk and hit the robber in the head causing him to miss his shot. Bjorn jumped up and punched the assailant who dropped his pistol out of reach for both of them. Bjorn got on top of the assailant, hit him several times in the head and screamed out. *"Who are you and who sent you?!"*

The assailant didn't respond, and instead, he pulled out a knife and stabbed Bjorn in the side, puncturing his kidney. Bjorn was bleeding heavily, and the assailant pushed him away and made his way to the pistol. He aimed the pistol at Bjorn and said *"Auf wiedersehen, Bjorn"*. He did not have time to shoot, as Bjorn's bodyguards rushed in and shot the assassin in the head before he could fire the shot. Bjorn passed out and was taken to a medical bay.

A few hours later, Bjorn woke up and Captain Adal Schneider, was waiting by his side.

Adal:

- I am so relieved that you survived the attack on your life.

Bjorn:

- So am I, Adal.
- What did the attacker say?

Adal:

- Not much. The bullets from your bodyguards struck him through the brain stem. It would be impossible to revive him and question him.

- Furthermore, he had no ID chip, and his DNA was not in our database.

Bjorn:

- It is in the database, Captain. It's above your rank. I recognised the man. He is a black op operative for House Muller. One of our top men in the field. The question is: Who sent him?

Adal:

- You think your family wants you dead?

Bjorn:

- It doesn't look better. I have a dozen potential suspects. My father, my brothers, my uncles, or my cousins. I hope it wasn't my father or brothers.

Adal:

- That is terrible. Bjorn. I don't know what to say.

Bjorn Muller:

- Don't worry about it, Adal. I don't see any reason for them to come after you.

- Do you have any news about Fritz?

Adal:

- Yes, unfortunately, he was found dead in the kitchen. The assailant must have strangled him to take his place and poison you.

Bjorn:

- Is it possible to revive him?

Adal:

- Yes, but it would be expensive. As his position is a non-combat position, he is not covered by the army medical insurance, and he doesn't have enough funds to pay for the procedure once he wakes up.

Bjorn:

- Don't worry about the money. Just revive him, and I'll pay the bills. I want Fritz to make my coffee!

Adal:

- Of course, sir.

- I suggest you are resting in the medical bay for the next few days. The attacker destroyed your kidney, and it will take two days to grow a new one.

Bjorn:

- Okay. Not the best way to spend two days, but bring me enough opiates to make it worthwhile.

Adal:

- Yes, I will let the doctor know.

Bjorn:

- Good. Now go and take my place in my absence.

As Adal left, Bjorn thought whether he should do anything about the suspected troop movements near their military bases. He decided against it. After his family sent assassins to kill him, he was done serving House Muller. As soon as he had received his medical treatment, he would go back to Earth to make them pay for this bullshit. He groaned in pain but he felt a lot more comfortable after a nurse gave him a shot of morphine, and he fell into a blissful sleep.

Chapter 87: Keila Conducts Surveillance at the North Pole.

Keila was conducting surveillance from the top of a hill, 30 kilometres from the Terran Interplanetary Security Forces' North Pole base. Protecting the most important Terran Council installation on Mars, was a formidable fortress which would be a lot harder to attack than the smaller fortress that guarded House White's gadolinium mines. Keila could not expect the Terrans to be unprepared for the attack either. They were arrogant and convinced of their superiority, but they could not be stupid enough to stay unprepared, after she had defeated them several times

Keila wondered whether her idea to conceal her followers as raiders was a good plan. The advantage was that she could move around her units on the Martian surface, and it was unlikely to arise any suspicion from the Terran officers that observed the planet from orbit.

The drawback was that she could not use heavy military equipment that would have helped her when attacking fortified installations. Raiders on Mars were not using heavy military equipment as it was immobile and did not fit their raiding and pillaging operations. Raiders never bothered the Terran Council's activities on the Martian surface, and they rarely got in each other's way.

Keila took a deep breath. She really hoped that the Zetan technologies would be enough in the battle to come. Otherwise, her troops would be butchered by the fortified and heavily armed defenders.

Keila wanted to pray. But to whom would she direct her prayers? The voice that had guided her, had gone silent and instead she was evoked by the demonic creature called Rangda. Keila did not trust Rangda, despite Rangda having saved her life twice. The second time had come at a steep cost, and Keila had aged irreversibly. She aimed her prayers to the True Maker despite knowing that it was pointless.

The deistic god, The True Maker, had gained a lot of popularity in the 25th century. In the 25th century, a Zetan had inadvertently revealed the truth to a Martian that the only real God in the universe was The True Maker. The True Maker suited the Martian mind as it was a great force setting the law of nature and creating everything. However, the True Maker that it had neither the desire nor the ability to change outcomes in people's daily lives.

Having finished her prayers to The True Maker, Metatron contacted her via the Divine Technology chip. Keila was happy to see him as she hadn't been able to communicate with him since she left Eden.

Metatron studied Keila. He was worried about what he saw. She looked at least a decade older than she had been the last time he saw her, half a year ago. While her old looks didn't bother him, he worried that she had aged so significantly in a couple of months. While Metatron was a very young-looking 122-year-old, due to his extended periods of cryogenic sleeping and usage of DNA regeneration, Keila was a mature looking 24-year-old, and they both looked like they were in their late 30s.

Metatron:

- Keila! You have aged a lot in six months. What happened?

Keila:

- I let her possess me again. I had no choice. They would have killed me.

Metatron:

- You let Rangda possess you? Why on Earth would you do that?

Keila:

- I was scared. I was intercepted by a House White strike force. There was no way out, and they would have killed me... or worse.

- I did what I had to do. And Rangda helped me. I am sure you have seen the television footage as everyone else.

Metatron:

- Yes, I saw it. Didn't know if it was real or not until now.
- So, what is new, except for your aging?

Keila:

- I am at Martian North Pole. Tomorrow, we'll perform coordinated attacks on the Terran Council outposts. If all goes well, we will proceed to storm the Phobos base.

Metatron:

- Sounds risky. How did you get enough heavy weaponry within range of the bases? The Terran Council is mapping the Martian surface.

Keila:

- I didn't. All our troops are posing as raiders and they are using light equipment. I am gambling that the Zetan technology, and the element of surprise is enough to beat them.

Metatron:

- That sounds incredibly risky.

Keila:

- Change always is.

Metatron:

- Yes, about that. I was visiting a female adulthood ceremony yesterday, and I came to think of our child. If your vision were correct, I would need to insert the embryo in a synthetic womb next week to fit the right birthday.

Keila:

- I don't know, Metatron. After all that has happened, I am not too sure that I can trust my visions. Can we talk about it next week?

Metatron:

- You might not want to be around next week. You have some dangerous days ahead for you. I want to know your will; in case you perish.

Keila:

- I want you to do what makes you happy if I am no longer around. Besides, I am not going anywhere.

Metatron:

- Very well. I'll talk to you in a couple of days, Keila.

Keila:

- Yes, talk to you later.

Keila leaned back and sighed. She didn't know what she should have told Metatron. Her vision had shown her, her daughter and Metatron. She had no idea what would happen if she died before her daughter reached 13 years of age. It was all confusing, and it made her restless.

But then she felt optimism. The visions would be correct, and she would settle down on Eden with Metatron and live a happy life. The fact that he still thought about her proved that it would happen. Keila went to sleep, and she slept peacefully despite the anticipation for the decisive battle.

Chapter 88: An Empty Prison.

After many months of marching, Odin and his Zetan host reached Rangda's prison in the Divine Dimension. Odin was terrified by what he saw. The prison was empty. On the ground, laid the bones of Brahma and the remains of a Xeno. This had terrifying implications for the future. How had Rangda got out? How had she killed Brahma? How had the Xenos made their way into the Divine Dimension?

Odin made a terrible realisation. The tormented screams that he had heard psionically lately, were not Zetans who killed themselves, but Zetans that had been killed and eaten by Rangda and her Xeno army. For every Zetan that fell to the beasts, the Xenos would get stronger as they would fill up, while the starving Zetans would remain weak.

So, what should he do? Odin spoke to Thor and Ra.

Odin:

- Rangda tricked us! We should never have listened to Brahma's pleas to spare her and imprison her instead of killing her outright.

Ra:

- Yes. That was a fatal mistake. But we must not dwell in the past. Instead, we must look forward.

Odin:

- Yes.
- My son, what do you suggest that we do?

Thor:

- We must return to the Divine Palace and summon every Zetan. We cannot be divided. Only by standing together can we hope to survive the onslaught of our eternal enemies.

Odin:

- Excellent plan my son. Let's start the summons at once.

Thor:

- Yes, but first, there is another thing. To be able to face the coming Xeno onslaught we must eat, and there is only one food source left for us here.

Ra:

- What you are suggesting is blasphemous and forbidden.

- If we eat the Xenos, we are no better than the beasts we are fighting against.

Thor:

- But if we don't, we will all succumb to the enemy.

Odin:

- This is not a choice for the three of us to make. Let's summon all the Zetans to the Divine Palace and let the assembly decide our future.

Having said this, they gathered the Zetans that were with them into a ring to increase their collective psionic capabilities and commence with the summoning.

Chapter 89: The Assault on the North Pole Base.

Keila looked at her watch. The time to strike was now. She ordered her troops, masked as raiders, to start moving. While it would have been better to equip them with proper Martian military armour, the element of surprise was imperative for success. She gave the command to the Olympus Republic army to send missiles to knock out the Terran Council satellites that covered the targeted areas. This would expose her, but it would stop the Terrans from orbital bombardment of the battle zones until they had replaced their broken satellites. She ordered her troops to move towards the fortress. They were moving behind a large number of light trucks and hovercrafts that were equipped with large high capacity batteries attached to reverse-engineered Zetan technologies.

The limited functionality of the reverse-engineered Zetan technologies was a hurdle that could hinder for the success of the operation. While the handheld technologies worked, they were limited by the battery capacity of each individual machines. To breach massive fortresses like the one on the North Pole, Keila needed something that was scaled up, both in range and battery capacity. While her scaled up Zetan technologies should work, there had been no way to field test them as that would have risked that the Terran Council found out about the technology. Keila's troops moved towards the fortress in a circular formation, aiming to encircle the stronghold. She had 500 trucks and 10,000 infantry which were more than the number of defenders, but the defenders had automated defences and heavy weaponry, so she would not stand a chance if their Zetan technology did not work.

As Keila moved closer, she could hear the Terran Council commanders shouting out warnings on the megaphone. She ignored them, and her troops kept advancing towards the fortress. Eventually, she stopped 200 meters away from the 300 metres high, impenetrable metal walls of the fort.

A Terran officer came out in a helicopter to parley with Keila's group.
Terran Officer:

- You are intruding on Terran Council Security Forces territory.
State your business.

Keila:

- We request that you surrender immediately, and lay down your
weapons. Martians should manage the North Pole magnetic field
generator.

Terran Officer:

- Is this a joke? The most massive fortified facility in the solar system with a ragtag band of raiders, requesting that we surrender?
Your pathetic forces wouldn't even make your way through our
automated outer defences.

Keila took off her helmet and revealed her identity to the Terran Officer.
She then spoke again.

- I am Keila Eisenstein of the Martian Humanist Alliance. The
Terran Council's reign of terror ends today. I declare Martian In-
dependence. From this day on, no Terran shall ever set foot on
Mars armed and unwelcome.

Terran Officer:

- Looks like I am up for a promotion.
- Activate Automated Defences, fire at will!

The Terran Officer flew back in his helicopter to the relative safety of the
fortress, Keila said a prayer to the True Maker before facing the automated
defences of the fortress.

The fortress' defences rained down a barrage of artillery and machine-
gun fire on her troops. To her great relief most of her Zetan technology held

up and absorbed and stopped the barrage but at a few places the technology failed, and she saw those sections obliterated and the soldiers occupying them dead beyond resurrection. Eventually, the barrage ended as the Terran weapons overheated and needed to be reloaded.

"Charge!" Keila yelled, and her troops equipped their jetpacks setting the direction for the top of the walls. The desperate defenders tried to shoot them with the automated defences but to no avail, as the computerised defences were still overheated and reloading. Keila and her troops landed on the top of the battlements and in the courtyard of the fortress. Keila and her soldiers dropped off a few crates with amplified Zetan bionic chip disruptors in various areas of the courtyard. This disrupted and confused the defenders, who got very nauseous, when their bionic chips were interrupted. Keila and her troops charged the defenders. They charged this with activated personal ballistic energy absorbers and equipped with plasma swords.

They were equipped with plasma swords as they wanted to charge the enemy quicker. Plasma swords were also better than as Terran armour was designed to withstand a lot of shots while it was not intended against the blasting slices of plasma swords.

The confused, nauseous, and panicking defenders stood no chance against Keila's powerful army. Although some of her troops ran out of battery and were killed by the defenders, the majority of Keila's troops reached their target and chopped their foes to pieces with their plasma swords. They were helped by the fact that the Terran troops were nauseous from the bionic chip disrupters and untrained in melee combat.

They reached the gate of the main building that held the magnetic field generator within. It had impenetrable walls, and Keila ordered some of her troops to find a way to blow up the front gate.

Keila led a group of soldiers to scale the walls of the fortress, trying to find a suitable entrance. They found a ventilation tunnel that led them to the main hall of the fort, where the defenders were waiting for them.

Keila entered the complex and she felt a sharp pain in her shoulder. She fell backwards over a ledge, dropped several levels, hit the floor and fell unconscious.

Chapter 90 Saved by the Bell

Douglas White was looking at the unconscious Keila Eisenstein. Since the debacle in the Tengil Dominion, where he was humiliated when he escaped while wearing his bathroom robe, Douglas had been stripped of his rank. For the last few months, he was forced to serve on the edge of Mars in the cold and darkness as a regular soldier.

Douglas panicked about his oncoming death. The North Pole fortress had been breached, its defenders slaughtered, and by pure luck, he had been among the ones in the inner military camp when the hell broke loose. All communications with high command were blocked, and if they choose to respond, they would respond by bombing the military camp to avoid it falling into enemy hands. Douglas heard how the attackers tried to blow up the front gate, and with every explosion, the citadel was shaking.

From the bright side, if he could film himself killing the terrorist Keila Eisenstein. This way, he would redeem himself, and with a bit of luck, his family would bring him back from the dead. He bound Keila to a chair and woke her up by throwing a bucket of ice-cold water over her.

Douglas:

- Miss Eisenstein. We meet again.

Keila:

- Yes. And this time you even got your clothes on... Although I suspect you don't like your a "private grade" uniform.

Douglas:

- Yet, I rather stand where I am standing, than sit where you are sitting.

Keila:

- What difference does it make? My troops will breach that gate any minute. When they do, you'll be dead. Your only chance is to give up, and I'll spare you.

Douglas:

- Yes, but I will not disgrace myself again. I will not be paraded as your prisoner. This is how I redeem myself.

Douglas lifted his pistol to shoot Keila. She stared him into his eyes to make him hesitate. It worked well enough to stall him for a split second, and that was all that was needed. The next explosion that hit the building, dislodged the construction fittings of a large bell hanging a few levels up. The bell fell, and hit Douglas in the head, killing him. Thus, Keila was saved by the bell. A few minutes later, Keila's army breached the gates, and the remaining defenders surrendered. Thus, the North Pole's magnetic field generator had fallen into the hands of the Martian Humanist Alliance.

Chapter 91: Keila's Address to the Martians.

Keila was looking at the reports from the other battlefields. Her coordinated attacks had granted her total victory on the Martian surface. This was due to the introduction of advanced Zetan technology and because the Terran forces had been understaffed as the Terran factions were busy fighting each other. Unfortunately, President Hellas Petrakis had died beyond resurrection when fighting for the South Pole, so there was no unifying political force to look up to.

Keila knew that her victories would account for nothing unless she destroyed Phobos base. The Terrans would return, and she could not utilise her Zetans technologies to surprise her enemies if she gave them time to regroup. Keila needed a decisive victory today. Without the Phobos Base, it would be hard for the Terrans to stage another invasion and she could declare Martian independence.

Keila produced a television clip that showed battlefields and how the Martian Humanist Alliance's flag hang over every significant Terran Council base on Mars. The camera showed how she sat in a chair in the command room of The North Pole base. Keila spoke into the camera.

- Dear Martians. For over 500 years, the Terran Council have terrorised and dominated our people and turned us against each other. Today we achieved unprecedented success by taking every major Terran stronghold in a single day. We did this by uniting and acting like one. But the greatest challenge is ahead of us. To defeat the Terran Council, we need to destroy their Phobos base. The Phobos Base is their staging ground their centre of power in our part of the solar system. The Martian Humanist Alliance cannot fight this battle alone. That's why I am urging everyone who has weapons or ships to take to the skies at 3PM Olympus Republic time. Together we'll face our foes. Many of us will die, but remember. They can end our lives, but they can no longer steal our freedom. The True Maker bless you all!

After finishing the address, Keila fell to the ground in pain. The bullet wounds in her shoulder were not critical, but the 15-meter fall that had knocked her unconscious were. Although a 15-meter fall was not fatal on Mars due to the lower gravity, it was enough to maim her and put her out of action. Melchior, the highest-ranked member from her Edenite militia, ran up to Keila.

Melchior:

- Mistresses Keila. You are hurt.

Keila:

- Yes, but I need to stay strong. The assault on Phobos starts in three hours, and I need to lead it.

Melchior:

- No! Mistress Keila, you are too injured to be useful. You need to stay here, recover, and lead us after the enemy has been defeated.

- I will lead the attack if you let me.

Keila:

- But Melchior, you are not Martian, you are an Edenite.

Melchior:

- That is irrelevant. My ancestors came from Mars and were tormented by the Terran plutocrat Abraham. Fighting the Martians' oppressors is also my fight.

Keila:

- Okay, Melchior. You have convinced me. May the True Maker be with you, and may we meet again.

After that Keila gave Melchior a Divine Technology god chip and she inserted it into his brain. If he was to control the attack, he needed to co-ordinate their forces. Keila groaned in pain and fell unconscious. Melchior rushed her to the medical ward.

Chapter 92: Joachim Rejects Max's Request to Abandon the Phobos Base

Admiral Max Wellington studied Keila's TV statement in awe. When the Martian Humanist Alliance had conquered the Terran Council bases on Mars, they had acquired a lot of weaponry as well as shuttles and minor space attack ships to attack his position.

This would not have been a big problem if he had his full fleet at his disposal. However, Max hardly had any ships at his disposal. As four out of five factions had stopped providing the Terran Council armed forces with weaponry and personnel, a skeleton staff guarded his base. This crew was insufficient to fight the might of a unified Mars.

The Martians would be united against him. The utter defeat of the Terran Council's ground forces was an unprecedented event. In hindsight, Max regretted that he hadn't investigated the rumours of a new revolutionary technology. 100,000 Terran troops were dead or captured on the Martian surface, and there was nothing Max could do to save them.

Captain Adal Schneider entered the command room and Max spoke to him:

- Captain Schneider. Why are you here? I asked Bjorn to come. I know that Bjorn was cleared for duty yesterday.

Adal:

- That is correct Admiral. However, Rear Admiral Bjorn Muller requested that I went to talk to you while he is preparing ISS Supreme Earth.

Max:

- Very well. And what does Bjorn suggest that we do?

Adal:

- He agrees that we should abandon Phobos, regroup with a large fleet, and retake it in a couple of days.

Max:

- Yet he refuses to come here and say this to his father.

- No matter. Step up on the hologram machine together with me Adal; we must convince Joachim Muller that retreat is our only option.

The two officers stepped up on the hologram machine to Joachim, ten minutes later they received a response from Joachim:

- You are not to surrender or leave the Phobos Base. If you do, you'll be tried for treason. If the base is lost, set Phobos on a collision course with Mars. If we cannot have it, no one else should.

Adal:

- But a collision between Phobos and Mars would be a cataclysmic event that would wipe out all life on the surface.

Max:

- Yes, I think that is Joachim Muller's intention.

Adal

- So, we are dead unless we repel a massive invasion force or wipe out most life on the most populous planet in the solar system.

Max:

- Yes, more or less.

Adal:

- Boss. I must admit. I hate my job.

Max:

- So, do I.

Max took up a photograph of his daughter Magda who died in a rare form of incurable brain cancer and whispered for himself *"Magda, we'll soon meet again."*

Chapter 93 Bjorn Muller Tries to Destroy Mars to Save Himself.

Bjorn was standing at the command bridge of ISS Supreme Earth. He looked at the massive swarm of small spaceships and shuttles heading in the direction of the Phobos base. It was an awe-inspiring sight, watching the masses rise together as one to break the chains of tyranny and free themselves. Many of them were in dingy shuttles that were not flightworthy, but it did not matter. There was too many of them, and they were too determined

Bjorn estimated that there would be over a million Martian attackers in thousands of ships while his defenders constituted of a hundred ships and a total of 15,000 defenders. Against a swarm like that, it did not matter what he commanded. He and the vessels he commanded would run out of ammunition before the enemy ran out of ships and then they were doomed.

Bjorn sat in silence. He was impressed by the people rebelling against their allocated lot in life, trying to improve their destiny. Bjorn realised something. He was Terran and superior to the vermin race that was trying to end his life. He would destroy them all when they were on the verge of achieving their freedom.

He called captain Adal to his side:

Bjorn:

- Captain. I am relieving of command, and I hand it over to you. I have one final mission to do before the end of this war.

Adal:

- I know that you want to run, Bjorn, but there is no point. Your father has forbidden retreat and besides, how far can you go in a small fighter ship?

Bjorn:

- You are mistaken. I am not running. I do what is needed to preserve our future.

Adal looked down in the ground. Was Bjorn going to perform the atrocity that his father had ordered? Was there not any better way?
Adal:

- Okay, Citizen Muller. I grant your request to resign from the Terran Council Security Forces. Feel free to acquire a small ship for your transport off this command ship.

Bjorn:

- Thank you, Adal. See you on the other side.

Bjorn headed for the docks. He got on a small ship and travelled to the thrusters that governed Phobos' artificial gravity.

Chapter 94 Keila Wakes up With a Vision to Stop Bjorn Muller.

Keila woke up with a twitch. She had a vision showing what was about to happen. She needed to stop Bjorn Muller at once. Keila limped towards the exit of the medical ward. An Edenite medics approached her.

- Mistress Keila. You should not move. You are injured.

Keila:

- If I don't move, we'll all die. I have seen it. I need a shuttle to take me to Phobos at once.

Medic:

- What are you talking about?

- Our troops have overrun the Phobos base; they are fighting inside the station as we speak.

Keila:

- It's a trap, The Terrans are going to use the Phobos Base itself as a weapon to destroy Mars. I need to go now.

Medic:

- Very well I'll help you to the shuttle and I'll come with you.

They reached the hangar and as it turned out the only ship that remained was a small fighter spaceship designed for one person. Keila farewelled the medic and headed off.

Chapter 95 A Divine Intervention

Keila landed at Phobos next to its artificial gravity thrusters. Bjorn Muller was already there. Keila realised a fatal flaw. In her hurry to get there as soon as possible, she had forgotten to pack her equipment, weapons, and Zetan devices. Bjorn saw her coming, screamed something, but she couldn't hear him. The gravity generating thrusters on Phobos was in the vacuum of space and there was no sound. Bjorn took up a pistol and shot Keila twice. He tried to shoot again, but his gun jammed. Keila picked up her plasma sword and tried running towards Bjorn, but she could barely walk. Bjorn waved at her and shook his head. He smirked, put his finger on a detonator, and set off an explosive charge. The blast knocked Keila to the ground. Bjorn got on his spaceship and took off.

Keila tried to get up. She was in terrible pain as her blood was boiling, freezing, and evaporating at the same in the freezing cold vacuum of space. The explosion had changed the direction of the thrusters and they were now pushing the Phobos moon on a collision course with the Martian surface. If there was a collision, that would melt the crust of the planet and kill all life, as the Phobos Moon was massive enough to make a collision with Mars devastating.

Keila tried to make her way to the thrusters' rudder to change the trajectory of Phobos to avoid a collision with Mars. The rudder was rusted shut. No matter what she did, she would never be able to change the trajectory of the moon. In a matter of hours, they would all be dead. Keila collapsed next to the rudder.

As Keila closed her eyes preparing to take her last breath, she saw her. She saw the True Maker herself. The eternal origin of the universe, the all-knowing creator that never intervened was communicating non-verbally to her.

Keila got up and realised that her wounds had sealed. She felt reinvigorated, and her hopes were surging. Summoning all her strength, Keila turned the rudder 180 degrees, changing the trajectory of Phobos from a collision with Mars, to a collision course with the Sun. Keila got into her fighter spaceship and set after Muller.

Keila intercepted Bjorn and destroyed the engines on his ship with her weapons. She then followed his ship as he crash-landed on Mars.

Chapter 96: The Fall of Bjorn Muller.

Bjorn Muller woke up from the crash-landing and got out the ship. He was in immense pain as he had broken his leg and had a metal pole penetrating the side of his body. Bjorn knew that he would bleed out and die within minutes if he tried to pull out the pole, so he left it in. He got out of the ship and noticed that he had crashed at the edge of the Olympus Mons mountain. He looked up and saw how his father's plan had failed. Phobos was moving away from Mars instead of getting closer. He heard a familiar voice and turned around.

Keila:

- Bjorn Muller! I have finally won the war for my people.

Bjorn looked at Keila in disbelief.

- How did you do that? How did survive with a punctured lung and a destroyed liver?

Keila:

- What are you talking about, I am fine?

Bjorn:

- Really? Look again.

Keila looked at her body. Bjorn was right. She was bleeding out, and she struggled to breathe.
Bjorn:

- It looks like we are dying. We might as well talk to each other and die in peace.

Keila collapsed to the ground. She was coughing blood, and for the second time in less than 20 minutes, she was dying.

Bjorn:

- You know Keila. I never intended for any of this to happen. Things could have been so different between you and me.

Keila:

- That doesn't change the fact that you tried to kill 4 billion individuals to save your own skin. You'll end up in hell for your crimes.

Bjorn:

- If there is such a thing as hell. Yes, you are right.
- But hell will be nothing new for me.
- You have made my life a living hell for the last six years.

Keila:

- What are you talking about? You were the one who kept me as a sex slave for two dark months, before I escaped. I was a young girl. Full of dreams. You destroyed my faith in people on Earth.

Bjorn:

- Yes, you are right. I did those things. But the one I hurt the most was myself.

- Before we met, I had these visions of you in my dreams. You, I, and our daughters were running the solar system for everyone's benefit.

- When we finally met, I was crippled by my fears. I realised that you were the woman from my dreams. But I also realised that you were half Martian and half Rashid, so my peers would never allow us to be together.

- I was a friend of your father, Mahmoud Rashid. He fell in love with an Edenite woman against his grandfather's wishes. This caused them to be forced into exile on Mars.

Keila felt dizzy and confused. She didn't know if it was the blood loss talking or if she was shocked by how similar her visions and Bjorn's visions had been. When Keila was a teenager, she had dreamed about going to Earth and meeting someone like Bjorn. She had seen Bjorn in a lot of her visions recently, displaying an alternate reality where she was together with him in peace and love. She had dismissed them as nightmares, but maybe this was meant to happen, until Rangda came along and changed things.

Keila:

- I had many visions of you too before we met. You turned out to be my nemesis. You were the reason I disregarded my mum's objections and tried to go to Earth.

- But instead of being my white knight, you were my tormentor and rapist.

Bjorn:

- I did not know what else to do. Keeping you as my sex slave was the only way for me to keep you near me. My father would not object if I held you as a sex slave, but he would never allow you to be my partner.

Keila:

- Bullshit. You knew what to do, but you choose to not do it because it was the challenging thing to do

- You were a spoilt brat that felt superior. You thought that you could take whatever you wanted by birthright. But you were wrong. Some things are not to be stolen; they are only to be given. Love is one such thing.

- I'll make you answer for your crimes and it won't be easy for you this time.

Bjorn:

- Keila. We are dying in the wilderness. I don't think we'll need to worry about the future anymore.

Keila:

- You are forgetting one thing. We might be on Mars, but we have access to Terran technology. If we die, we'll get revived, and you'll answer for your crimes.

Hearing this, Bjorn realised what he had to do. He pulled the metal stake out of his body to bleed out. He dragged himself to the edge.
Bjorn:

- I am the son of the Terran Council leader Joachim Muller; I will not be trialled here. Goodbye Keila.

After saying this, Bjorn threw himself off the edge of Olympus Mons freefalling for five kilometres. It took so long time for him to hit the ground that he died from the blood loss before he reached the surface. He smiled as his body was falling towards the ground. In death, Bjorn finally found peace.

Before Keila almost died, she contacted friendly troops via the Divine Technology chip, and they brought her to a facility with Terran technology where they could revive her. She thought of Metatron, she closed her eyes, and her whole world turned black.

Chapter 97 Keila's Independence Speech.

A few days later, Keila woke up. She knew that she had been dead for a while and yet she had not experienced any afterlife, just a long black dreamless sleep. It hadn't been too bad, but Keila was a bit curious if this disproved the afterlife or if she hadn't experienced it as her soul was not ready to move on.

Keila looked out through the window. There were a lot of people ignoring the cold to see the saviour of Mars. She walked to the podium and gave them a speech. It wasn't well-rehearsed as she just had woken up from the dead, but she did put some effort into it.

> - Fellow Martians. Six months ago, no one would have believed me if I said that we one day would be free the Terran Council. We have destroyed the Phobos Base, the symbol of our oppression. We mourn those who died for our freedom.

> - We have come a long way, but we need to be vigilant. We need to win peace before we can live in freedom. The only way we win peace is we are strong enough to stop any attempts from the Terrans to bully us from the sky. We must have enough weapons aimed at the heavens to deter the Terrans from ever bothering us again. With this in place, we can finally win our freedom.

Having said this, Keila returned to her bed to recover from her wounds. She looked at a report from her commanders. The Terran fleet had retreated to Earth, and a lot of fringe worlds had overthrown their Terran Masters and pledged themselves to her cause. The Terrans would have to accept Martian peace and independence now.

As it turned out Keila was mistaken. The Terran Council had united behind Joachim Muller, and they had no intentions of participating in peace talks. On the contrary, they planned to end the Martians forever.

Chapter 98: A Final Solution.

T he Terran Council member held an emergency meeting in the Europeum Towers in Hansstadt. They were looking at a report put together by Mathias Muller, Supreme Commander for the Terran Council Security Forces, and Joachim Muller's brother.

The situation was critical. Following the annihilation of their Martian expeditionary force, the reputation of their military might was in shambles. To make matters worse, the Phobos Base that hosted their base for their Martian expeditionary force had been slung out of orbit, and was heading straight for the Sun. While Phobos was too small to make an impact on the Sun, the loss of their base of operations made it almost impossible to invade Mars.

The annihilation of their Martian expeditionary force had prompted the Terran Council to withdraw their ships to Earth to regroup. This in had caused many asteroid mining colonies to rebel and either declare independence or pledge allegiance to Keila's organisation The Martian Humanist Alliance.

The loss of the asteroid mining colonies was worse for the Terran Council than the loss of Mars. While Mars served as a dumping ground for unwanted dissenting citizens, the asteroid mining colonies brought back vital supplies to keep the Terran Economy going. Keeping the economy going was imperative for the Terran Council as they based their power on economic might.

Joachim Muller:

- Thank you for your report, Mathias. I will discuss potential solutions with the members of the council and I'll get back to you.

- Welcome council members. These are desperate times, but one good thing has come from this. We have stopped fighting among ourselves. I have a suggested solution to this crisis, but first, I would like to hear how all of you want to deal with the crisis.

Santiago Bolivar:

- Let us accept peace with Mars. Let them keep their cold, polluted dustbowl of a planet but make sure to retake control of all the Asteroid mining stations.

Joachim:

- Yes, Santiago. Financially that would make sense, but like I said the last time you brought this up, it is not a viable long-term solution. If we leave the Martians unchecked, and they will want to expand in a generation or two. They don't pose a threat to us now, but in century or less they will, and they will stage an invasion of Earth.

John White:

- Yes, I agree with you, Joachim. I think we should take a full fleet with all our large ships and bombard them from orbit into submission.

Joachim:

- Yes, but that won't work this time. Without a base of operations, our ships can only carry so much ammunition and supplies before going back to Earth. The Martians can hide in their bloody tunnels for a few days before we need to go back to resupply. We'll never win a war that way. Besides, the Martians will anticipate orbital bombardment, and they'll have a lot of weapons aimed at the skies to fight back against any attempt to bombard them from orbit.

Ibrahim Rashid:

- I suggest that we bombard them with our whole fleet and stage an invasion at the same time. While they hide in their tunnels. We land with a lot of heavy troops and take back our lost fortresses on the surface. From there we can project power and force the Martians to submission.

Joachim:

- That won't work for three reasons. 1: The Martians are way more numerous than us, and they are even more numerous than our military personnel. 2: It is it impossible to supply these bases without a base of operations in orbit. 3: The Martians have discovered a technology that disrupts the bionic microchips in our soldiers' heads. Before we consider an invasion, we need to replace the implants and retrain our soldiers.

Chi-Ping Cheng:

- What about a blockade of Mars? We use our forces to regain control of the asteroid mining stations, and then we stay out of reach for the Martian surface weapons, while we blockade their interplanetary trade.

Joachim:

- That would not work against the Martians. They are already dirt poor, and they have hardly received any interplanetary imports for the last centuries, so they wouldn't be affected if the trade stopped.

Chi-Ping Cheng:

- Okay Chairman Muller. You have argued against every solution we have put forth. What kind of masterstroke do you have on your mind?

Joachim Muller:

- I suggest that obliterate Mars and mask it as a natural disaster.

- In six months', time, the asteroid B600 is passing Mars, missing it by only 500,000 kilometres. It is a 10-kilometre asteroid travelling at 80,000 kilometres an hour. If it hit Mars, it would wipe out most of the life on the planet. It would be easy to change the trajectory of the asteroid to impact Mars.

Chi-Ping:

- But wouldn't the Martians send their own expedition to divert it from hitting them?

Joachim:

- Of course, but they wouldn't get far. We would send a large fleet to escort the asteroid until it was too late to change its course.

- Since we are still at war with the Martians, we have legal rights to attack all Martian vessels that we come across.

- We are not going to admit that we are directing a large asteroid towards Mars, causing genocide.

John:

- Excellent Joachim. This is a great solution. B600 is large enough to kill off most of the population and dispersing the Martian atmosphere while leaving the planet in good enough condition for resettlement once the dust settles.

Chi-Ping:

- Yes, but I am worried about what the Terran population will think about this. While they don't love the Martians, they wouldn't condone Martian genocide either. They might even rebel against us.

Joachim:

- Don't worry. They won't find out. We own and control the media and the Space Net. We can send the dissenters that question us to resettle Mars.

Ibrahim.

- This is an excellent plan. Death to our enemy. Slay them all.

Joachim:

- Excellent. Do we have an agreement? A decision of this scale will require blood verification. I will write down the order, and then all of us will spill our blood on this panel to verify that we agree to it. To change the directive we all need to drop our blood again on the same panel.

They all did as Joachim requested. They took a small knife and spilled a drop of blood each on top of their faction's seal to verify the order. After this, they sat quiet. They had ordered a terrible atrocity even by their standards.

Eventually, they made their way back to their respective countries speaking to no one about what they had agreed on.

The official statement was that Terran Council would not discuss peace with the Martians, as the Martians needed to be punished for their surprise attack on their Terran protectors.

Chapter 99: The Redirection of The Asteroid B600.

Joachim Muller hung up the phone. He had dispatched the order to a joint Terran Council secret operations team. The Terran Council rarely performed mutual secret operations as its members were more likely to perform secret operations, against each other. But for this mission, it was imperative that they were all represented. They had agreed to the plan and no faction should be able to accuse the others if the plan failed.

The special operations team would land on B600 and install fusion rocket thrusters that redirected B600 on a collision course with Mars. They would stay on the asteroid to safeguard it from attackers and to be able to abort the mission until it was too late to change the trajectory of the asteroid. With this in place, Joachim called his brother, Supreme Commander Mathias Muller, to make sure that a fleet escorted the asteroid.

Joachim:

- Good evening, brother.

Mathias:

- Good evening Joachim. I expected to hear from you yesterday. Delays are not good for our efforts.

Joachim:

- You are correct.

- The Council trusts in your judgement on how to subdue the rebellious asteroid mining colonies and we only have one specific order for you.

Matthias:

- So, you finally trust my judgement? Tell me about your specific order.

Joachim

- You are to lead a group of ten star-cruisers and escort the asteroid B600.

Mathias:

- B600? There is nothing of value there. Besides it has an orbit that makes it to mine it.

Joachim Muller:

- We have received information that the heinous Keila Eisenstein intends to use the asteroid as a weapon against us. We want to direct it into the sun to get rid of it, but you need to guard it against Martian interference for the time being.

Mathias:

- This is terrible. That woman has no limit to her evil schemes and atrocities.

Joachim:

- Yes. So, can I count on your support to keep us safe?

Mathias:

- Yes. Of course, brother.

Joachim:

- Good, your fleet will depart tomorrow. Joachim out.

Joachim hung up the phone. He considered to involve his brother in the plan but he had decided against it. The fewer that knew about the asteroid strike, the better.

Besides, Mathias might have objections on this genocidal mission. Mathias Muller was a stern military man, but he had always tried to minimise civilian casualties. A general that tried to minimise civilian casualties would not agree to destroy the most populous planet in the solar system. But destroying Mars was imperative. Joachim knew that the Terran Council could not control and dominate Mars' downtrodden population any longer. If the Martians were not destroyed, they would grow stronger and come after the Terran Council with a vengeance.

Joachim sat down in his room and listened to classical music. He was looking at a picture of Bjorn. He mourned the loss of his son despite giving tacit approval for his assassination a few weeks earlier. Joachim looked at the images from Bjorn's childhood as well as an evaluation of Bjorn's DNA.

According to the DNA assessment, Bjorn had exceptional DNA, and yet he had ended up being a whoremongering drug addict. What had gone wrong? Joachim considered reusing Bjorn's genetic material to clone him as a baby. Joachim decided to wait. If everything went according to plan, he could do it when things had calmed down, so he had more time for the project.

Chapter 100: Emergency Meeting in the Martian Council.

Keila was sitting in an underground meeting hall in the Olympus Republic. It was the meeting hall of by the Olympus Republic parliament, and it was situated far underground, safe from orbital bombardment.

Keila had summoned all Martian leaders to decide the future of the planet. It would not be an relaxed meeting. Different regions of Mars had different cultures, goals and rivalries and they were no longer united against the common enemy, as the Terran Council hadn't been seen or heard from in the last month. The complete silence from the Terran Council was an ominous sign. Keila had hoped that they would accept her peace proposal or at least communicate in some way, but there was only silence. Thus, they were still at war with Earth.

The worst part of being at war with the Terran Council was that they were cut off from Spacenet networks. Thus, they had very little knowledge of what was happening outside of Mars. Space traffic to and from Mars had ended as the Terran Council blockaded the planet. The blockade was not a big deal for the survival of the Martians, as they were used to only delivering shipments, but rarely receiving shipments because of their previous trade arrangement with their Terran overlords.

Keila looked at the delegates from her position in the late President Hellas Petrakis chair, in the centre of the large amphitheatre building. This was a unique occasion. For the first time in the the planet's history, the planetary leaders had gathered to decide their future without Terran interference.

What was the future of the Martian people and what would Keila's role be? Keila wanted to replicate what the Terran Council had created for Earth when it came to building peace and prosperity for the planet. She also wished to implement democratic leadership that benefited the ordinary citizen on Mars.

As the de-facto leader of the Martian Humanist Alliance, Keila's voice would be important for the future of Mars, and it was vital for her to align with politicians that would follow through with their promises. But how would she know if they were honest?

If she implanted Martian politicians with Divine Technology chips, she would know their thoughts. However, this would also make her the dictator of the planet, a worse dictator than the ones she had aimed to replace.

Suddenly, a member from the Science Commission, Jasper Svensson, interrupted the meeting:

- I am sorry to interrupt. But we have an urgent crisis!

Keila studied Jasper. She didn't know him, but she had met him briefly a few times when the Olympus Republic was reverse-engineering her Zetan Technologies.

Keila:

- What is the problem, Jasper? My door is always open, but not during a planetary meeting!

Jasper:

- B600 is the problem. A 10 kilometres large asteroid travelling is on a collision course with us. It will impact us in five months. I will show a hologram model of it for you to see.

Jasper activated the 3D hologram generator in the middle of the room. It showed how the asteroid was heading towards Mars and the estimated effects of the enormous impact it would cause. The gathering studied the 3D model. If Jasper were correct, the collision would kill off the majority of Martian life and cover the planet in a thick dust cloud for the next ten years. Keila spoke:

- Why haven't you brought up this problem until now, Jasper? The flight paths and orbits of all large celestial bodies have been mapped and estimated for the coming centuries.

Jasper:

- Because the asteroid was meant to miss Mars by 500,000 kilometres. Something is changing its path.

Keila:

- Do you think the Terran Council is behind this?

Jasper Svensson:

- I don't dare to speculate, but a large fleet of Terran ships is heading towards the asteroid.

Keila:

- This is not good. Would you be able to redirect the asteroid from hitting us?

Jasper:

- Yes, as long as I am on the asteroid at least a month before the impact.

Keila:

- Very well. Gather a team and take our fastest ship with stealth capabilities to intercept the asteroid as soon as possible.

Jasper Svensson:

- Thank you, Mistress Keila. I will gather a team at once.

As Jasper Svensson left the meeting room, an upset chatter began. Most of the assembly wanted to surrender to the Terran Council to avoid total destruction of their home planet. Keila put an end to the discussion.

There was no point in yielding a month after their victory, and besides, it was impossible to communicate with the Terran Council as Mars was disconnected from Spacenet, their transmissions were jammed by the blockading fleet, and they received no answers from the Terran counterparts. They have to pray that Jasper and his team would be able to carry out the crucial task at hand.

Chapter 101 Meeting between Joachim Muller, Benjamin Muller, and Mathias Muller in Europeum Tower

Mathias Muller was presenting the last month's achievements when it came to suppressing the rebellion in the solar system. It had been an overwhelming success, as all Terran factions had united behind the Terran Council Security Forces instead of fighting among themselves.

The Terran Council had crushed the uprisings on the asteroid mining colonies as well as those on Jupiter's and Saturn's moons. This had been easy to do as they had closed down Spacenet, thus blocking the rebelling colonies from communicating, cooperating, and coordinating their plans. It also helped that the Terran Council was the only force that had a deep space fleet, i.e. a navy that could travel for months without the need to replenish their supplies.

With all the threats contained, the Terran Council could now focus on dealing with the Martian uprising.

Mathias:

- We have secured control over the solar system. The shipments from the asteroid mining stations are up and running again. So, how do you wish to deal with Mars? I have heard, that they are desperate for peace?

Joachim:

- Yes. But I will not grant them any peace. Not after what the treacherous bastards did to us.

Matthias:

- With all due respect brother, but we cannot invade Mars. We don't have a base of operations in the area anymore, and if we move our ships close enough to bombard the surface, they can respond with their ground to air weapons that would devastate our forces.

Joachim:

- Yes, I am aware of that. But like a said, I am not considering peace with those treacherous scumbags

Matthias:

- So, what would you have us do? Do you want to blockade them indefinitely?

Joachim:

- Sure, why not. Let them have their "freedom" in their dusty dirt-poor desert.

Benjamin:

- How about we resume control over Phobos, and push it back into orbit around Mars?

Joachim shook his head and gave Benjamin a disapproving look, he then spoke mockingly:

- Brother, teach my son basic science, please.

Mathias felt an uncomfortable but brushed it off and started lecturing Benjamin on why his plan wouldn't work.

- The Phobos base is bound for a collision with the Sun, which means that it is falling towards the centre of gravity in the solar system. We do not have the technology to pushing such a massive object away from the centre of gravity.

- We could save it by driving it sideways to make it orbit the Sun.

- That would, give it an orbit between Mercury and Venus, and we do not need a military base in that part of space.

Benjamin:

- I see. So, what do you suggest?

Mathias Muller:

- Well I have realised that the conflict Mars is stuck in a deadlock. We can't invade them, and they can't harm us either. I suggest that we listen to them and give them their independence.

- To stop their influence, I suggest that we transport an asteroid from the asteroid belt and put it in orbit around Mars. On that asteroid, we can build a new base to make sure that our presence is known to our enemies.

Benjamin:

- But uncle, you just said we can't move large celestial bodies?

Joachim:

- Benjamin. When pushing an asteroid from the asteroid belt towards Mars, you are driving it towards the Sun. It is a lot easier to move an object towards gravity than pushing it against gravity.

Mathias:

- Yes, Joachim, you are correct.

- Speaking of other things. What is the deal with B600? It seems to be on a collision course with Mars.

Joachim:

- Yes, that is the reason why you are meant to escort it. Our scientists have discovered that the asteroid is on a collision course with Mars, and they are working to divert it and make it crash into the Sun instead

- You are there to stop the Martians from reaching the asteroid, as we fear that they are going to redirect it to collision course with Earth.

Mathias:

- That is unlikely. The orbit of B600 is very remote from Earth.

Joachim:

- Yes, but you didn't foresee the Martian surprise attacks that wiped out our armies on Mars, did you?

- Do your job and keep B600 safe from the Martians. I will update your systems with the correct trajectory of the asteroid to keep you from worrying.

- I will see you at dinner before you leave.

Mathias:

- Thank you, brother. I will see you at dinner.

Mathias left the room. Joachim and Benjamin looked at each other in silence for a bit before Benjamin spoke:

- Do you think he fell for the falsified trajectories you uploaded into his PDA?

Joachim:

- Hopefully. If not, I have an assassin in place to kill him, should it be needed. He trusts this spy so she won't fail us, unlike the amateur you sent after Bjorn. But let's hope I can keep my brother alive, shall we?

Benjamin:

- Yes, father. You are always one step ahead. Who is this assassin?

Joachim:

- I wouldn't be one step ahead if I told you. Now freshen up and get changed. You have a farewell dinner with your uncle to attend.

Chapter 102: An Assassination and a Destroyed Ship.

A few weeks later, Supreme Commander Mathias Muller was back on his command ship escorting Asteroid B600. He studied the trajectory of the asteroid, and it didn't make sense. The asteroid was headed for the sun and yet the instruments on his command ship indicated that he was heading towards Mars. Mathias called in the captain of the vessel, as well as his secret mistress, Melissa Schiller, to talk.

Mathias:

- Melissa, can you explain this: The trajectory of B600 will direct it into the Sun. Yet our ships escorting the asteroid, are heading towards the Mars

Melissa:

- Don't worry about that Mathias. Didn't your brother tell you that he had men redirecting the asteroid to collide with the Sun instead?

Mathias:

- Yes, he did. I am not comfortable with the secretiveness of the mission. I am the Supreme Commander of the Terran Council Security Forces. I shouldn't be on this mission, and yet he withholds information from me.

Melissa:

- Don't worry about it. Why don't we have a quickie now that we are alone on the command deck?

Mathias:

- Don't be silly, the command deck is full of cameras.

Melissa:

- We have access codes to override the cameras and turn them off.

Mathias was considering Melissa's proposal. He didn't get further as he got a call on the hologram generator. The call was from a small Martian science vessel which confused Mathias as the spaceship had to be close to contact him directly, as Spacenet had been turned off for Martian vessels. Yet he wasn't aware of any Martian vessels in the vicinity.

Mathias' curiosity got the better of him, and he ignored the directive to ignore all Martian transmissions. The hologram of the Martian scientist Jasper Svensson came up on the hologram generator.

Jasper:

- Thank you for answering our transmissions. You Terrans haven't been talkative lately.

Mathias:

- I was curious about how you contacted me. Mars is far away, and you are blocked from Spacenet.

Jasper:

- I am much closer than that.
- Anyways. I have an urgent request for you.

Mathias:

- You are not in a position to make requests to me. I am the Supreme Commander of the Terran Council Security Forces, and we are at war with you.

Jasper:

- Oh, sorry about my word choice. I am pleading you to help us.

- B600 is on a direct collision course with Mars. I have arrived with a team to redirect it from hitting Mars.

Mathias:

- We already have a team on the surface of B600 that is working to redirect the asteroid into hitting the Sun instead.

Jasper:

- That is not true. B600 was meant to miss Mars by 500,000 kilometres, and now its trajectory has changed to a direct collision with Mars.

- I know we are at war Mr. Muller but please work with us in. If that rock hits Mars, most of our population will die. I know you dislike seeing innocents die.

Mathias was confused and did not know what to believe. Jasper's claim supported his own suspicions that the asteroid was heading for a collision with Mars. However, Jasper was one of his enemies. The cowardly enemy who had surprise attacked and killed his men two months earlier. Mathias would be a fool to trust the enemy. Then again, he did not trust his brother either and he did not want to become an involved in the worst genocide in mankind's history.

Mathias:

- Mr Svensson. I would like you to come by my ship and parlay under the banner of truce. I want to go to the bottom with your claims.

Jasper:

- I would be honoured to meet you, Supreme Commander.

Half an hour later, a small shuttle with Jasper Svensson docked with Mathias Muller's command ship. Mathias' troops stripped him nude to search him for weapons, scanned him for any viruses and pathogens and then gave him a crew tracksuit for his visit. He was escorted to a meeting room where Mathias was waiting for him. They shook hands and started to talk.

Meanwhile, Melissa Schiller was watching the men via the CCTV. She was feeling guilty about what she had to do, but she had no other option. Joachim Muller had warned her that it might come to this, that her lover would betray her people and befriend the enemy. She couldn't let that happen. She entered a command into her encrypted phone and activated a microscopic dormant poison ampule that she had inserted into Mathias' body when he was asleep. The hidden container released a fast-acting nerve agent that killed the victims by corroding away their brains, preventing any resurrection attempts.

Jasper looked in terror as Mathias was dying in front of him with blood pouring from his eyes. A few moments of agony later, Mathias lay dead on the floor. Melissa stormed in and shot Jasper in the head. She looked straight into the camera and spoke:

- Crew Members of ISS Terran Dominion; Our Supreme Commander Mathias Muller was just murdered during a parley with this treacherous Martian creature. This is unacceptable. Destroy his ship and the rest of his crew.

Seconds later ISS Terran Dominion opened fire at the Martian ship and destroyed the research ship with its massive firepower.

Chapter 103 The Infamous Keila Eisenstein's Operative Assassinates the Foolish Supreme commander Mathias Muller

News Broadcast in the Terran Council News Network, 25th October 2874: *After the dishonourable attacks on our military bases conducting humanitarian aid on the Martian surface two months ago, Terran Council chairman Joachim Muller has ordered a blockade of the Martians until further notice. This wise order was broken by his brother Supreme Commander Mathias Muller yesterday, and he paid dearly for his gullibility.*

Mathias Muller agreed to parlay with the assassin Jasper Svensson, who posed as a Martian scientist. The killer linked to the nefarious terrorist Keila Eisenstein wasted no time and killed Mathias, using a tiny poisoned needle that he smuggled past the ship's security. The ship's security officers then eliminated the threat before he could cause any more damage. The spaceship with Jasper's co-conspirators was also destroyed as a precaution.

Chairman Joachim Muller comments: "I am still mourning the loss of my dear son Bjorn, and now on I have lost my dear younger brother. I can assure you all that this strengthens my resolve and I urge everyone to avoid Mathias' mistake and ignore all contact with our Martian enemies." - Joachim Muller.

Joanna Lechinsky, Terran Council News Network Journalist.

Chapter 104 Desperate Times Require Desperate Measures.

Keila looked at the video that depicted the murder of Supreme Commander Mathias Muller by her lead scientist Jasper Svensson. Had Jasper assassinated the supreme commander during a parlay? What an idiotic thing to do, especially with a supermassive asteroid heading on a collision course with Mars in 4 months. Or had the Terrans turned their backs on Mathias and killed him to blame her?

Keila did not know why the Terran Council want to kill their own Supreme Commander, but the reason didn't matter to her. She needed to come up with a way to save her people, and she was running short on options.

Keila closed her eyes to think. She heard Rangda calling her. Keila had ignored Rangda and the visions she was getting for the last few months after realising that Rangda was inherently evil. Besides. using the powers that Rangda could grant her aged her a lot. She had used Rangda's abilities twice, and it had aged her over a dozen years. While Keila did not fear death, she did not fancy the idea of dying of old age in her 20's.

Realising that the situation was critical, Keila opened her mind and allowed Rangda to talk to her.

Rangda:

   - You have been avoiding me, little girl.

Keila:

   - Yes. Speaking with an evil alien is not on the top of my list.

Rangda:

- The concept of evil is in the eye of the beholder. I did what I had to do to save my people. Just as you are.

Keila:

- So how do you explain the massive aging I have experienced after letting you help me?

Rangda:

- That is not my fault. I did not intend for you to age. But your feeble human DNA cannot accept the powers that I am lending you without consequences.

- Regardless, you are talking to me now. So how can I help?

Keila:

- The Terran Council has sent a giant asteroid to crash with my home planet to kill most of its population.

Rangda:

- Yes, I know. Such a terrible waste of life. So much death and so little eating.

Keila:

- So, your objection is not the killing itself, but the wasting of the meat?

Rangda:

- Yes. Killing for eating is natural, and part of the cycle of life. Killing without consumption of the fallen is unnatural and depraved. Typical human and Zetan behaviour, done out of greed and hunger for power. Unlike like my noble Xenos, who kill to live.

- Anyways. You want help, and I can help.

Keila:

- How? Can you redirect the asteroid that is directed towards my planet?

Rangda:

- No. But I can attack the humans on Earth, making it easier for you to redirect the asteroid.

Keila:

- I see. What's in it for you?

Rangda:

- My Xenos and I are hungry, and human meat is delicious.

Keila was contemplating her options. She wasn't very fond of the idea to release a host of man-eating aliens on the surface of Earth as this would kill a lot of innocents. But the Terran Council had sent an asteroid to exterminate her people like they were low-life insects. Sending them some man-eating monsters to deal with would make them realise that Martians and Terrans shouldn't fight each other but unite as one.

Keila:

- Okay. I want your help but on one condition. That you only kill and eat the soldiers, not the citizens, and that you allow the enemy to surrender.

Rangda:

- Surrender? What a strange concept. Is that something humans really do? Abandon their honour and becoming someone's slave? Very well, I promise.

Keila:

- Good. So how do I unleash your army on my enemies?

Rangda:

- There are four pyramids spread across the Earth. They all need to be activated at noontime local time, the same day. Doing this will power up the portals between my dimension and your dimension.

- Open your mind, and I'll transfer the information you need to achieve it.

Keila opened her mind, allowing Rangda to transfer her the information. Keila was fascinated by seeing the undiscovered inner workings of pyramids across Earth. To most people, these pyramids were just ancient piles of rock. Keila:

- Got it. One more thing. How do I move around on Earth? I don't think they'll grant me an entry permit.

Rangda:

- Alicia White...

After this, Rangda disconnected but Keila knew what she had to do. She summoned Melchior, her Edenite aide and second in command to her office. Keila:

- Melchior. I need to go to Eden at once. I am leaving you in command of Mars for the time being.

Melchior:

- I see. Are you abandoning us, Mistress Keila?

Keila:

- I would never do that! After visiting Eden, I am going to Earth to fix things.

Melchior:

- Going to Earth? That's suicide.

Keila:

- No, it's not. I have a plan.
- Do you trust me, Melchior?

Melchior:

- With all my heart.

Keila:

- Then rule Mars in my stead until I am back. I'm heading back to Eden. May the True Maker be with us until we meet again.

Melchior:

- It has been an honour serving you Keila. Farewell.

After promoting Melchior to command, Keila left Mars with a small group on a stealth shuttle transport ship heading for Eden.

Chapter 105 An Emotional Visit on Eden

Keila was docked to the Divine Control Centre. She exited her shuttle and met up with Metatron. It was a touching sight. She hadn't seen him for over nine months, and despite their breakup, she had missed him a lot. Keila found it strange that she hadn't been able to get over him, as she many times during their relationship, had found him boring. Maybe a boring a partner was what she secretly yearned for, after these years of war. Keila looked at his face. Metatron seemed both sad and happy to see her. He approached her and spoke.

Metatron:

- Welcome back, Keila.

Keila:

- Thanks, Metatron. I have missed you.

Metatron:

- Then stay with me. You are the reason we are apart. I have never pushed you away.

Keila:

- I know Met. But this was something that I needed to do.

Metatron:

- Yes. I want to show you something.
- Come with me.

Keila and Metatron walked together to the medical bay. They stayed next to an artificial womb. It contained a three-month-old foetus.

Metatron:

- This is our future daughter. If everything goes to plan, she will be born on the 25th of March, the date of her adulthood ceremony in your visions.

Keila:

- That is nice.

Metatron:

- You don't seem very enthusiastic.

Keila:

- I know. There is a lot of pressure on me. 4 billion lives are at stake.

- Besides... The visions...

- I have had visions of me having a family with Bjorn Muller back on Earth. The premonitions are confusing me, considering what happened between Bjorn and me.

Metatron:

- Well. Those visions are never going to happen. No point thinking of "what ifs" in life. You got to deal with things that happens.

Keila:

- Yes, you are right.

Metatron:

- Can I ask you for a favour? How about you stay back on Eden and give birth to our daughter. I don't want her to end up being a soulless, emotionless individual like I am. I want her to be like you.

Keila:

- You don't need to worry about that. You are the best man I have ever met, and you sprung from an artificial womb. Besides, what is a soul anyway?

Metatron:

- Good question. Maybe it's only a social construct.

Keila:

- Exactly.
- Sadly, I cannot stay. I got to finish what I started.

Metatron:

- Maybe you should try inaction for once? Perhaps the Terran Council wants to scare your people with their imminent doom and then divert the asteroid from colliding with Mars in the last minute.

- I don't think they will slaughter billions of people in cold blood.

Keila:

- They do, unfortunately. Bjorn Muller tried to crash the Phobos moon onto the surface of Mars when his defeat was imminent. I stopped him in the last second.

Metatron

- That is a shocking disregard for human life!

- Very well, then I understand why you must go.

Keila:

- Good. Did you find me a suitable team of Edenites to pose as Alicia White's crew?

Metatron:

- Yes, I did.

Keila:

- Did you tell them that it was a suicide mission?

Metatron:

- No, I did not, because I have faith in your return.

Keila:

- Good.
- Show me Alicia White's corpse and all the information we have about her.

Metatron:

- Why?

Keila:

- Because I need to know about her to act like her.

Metatron downloaded all the files available on Alicia White from Space Net. As Eden officially wasn't participating in the Mars/ Earth conflict, they had full access to Space Net, and yet they didn't find much. All the information they found was that Alicia White was the daughter of John White, the Chairman of House White. Alicia White was born 25 years earlier and she was missing, presumed dead. Her picture on Spacenet was edited to make her look like a normal Terran and not like the genetic freak she was.

Keila:

- This is very little information on a woman who was one of the wealthiest on the planet.

Metatron:

- Yes. House White is trying to keep her identity a secret. No matter, this is the information that we have.

Keila:

- Yes.

- Let's not waste any more time. Use the outer layer external DNA modifier to change my looks to Alicia's.

As Keila transformed into Alicia's body, she experienced something strange. Keila felt how her physical body changed drastically. When she had disguised as Rose Menakis and Edenite women she had always felt like herself, just with a different face, but not when she was posing as Alicia White.

Keila felt an urge to consume blood, and raw meat. Another desire also increased, her sadistic sexual urge. Keila felt no need to repel this urge, and she pushed Metatron to the ground and pulled off his pants. He was surprised but did not resist her advances. She then jumped on top of him and rode him until she climaxed.

Afterwards, Keila got off and said. *"See you later, lover boy"*. She got dressed and headed for Alicia White's captured shuttle. Keila gathered her Edenite strike team that also had assumed the identities of the fallen members of Alicia White's black operations operatives. Once they were all onboard the vessel, Keila set the course for Earth.

Chapter 106 Passing Earth Immigration

Keila was looking in amazement as she got closer to Earth, The blue home planet for all of humanity. It was the first time she saw it, but she remembered dreaming about going there when she was a child. During the rebellion, Keila had been around a lot in the solar system, and yet the blue planet was the most beautiful thing she had ever seen. There was not much time to marvel at its beauty, as she needed to get through Terran customs immigration orbiting Earth.

There were a lot of Terran Council warships that defended the perimeter. But where was it best to receive her clearance for landing on Earth? The natural thing for Alicia White to do would be to obtain an entry permit from a House White ship. But if she docked with a House White ship, she risked running into someone that knew Alicia, and that could expose her. As it happened, destiny decided for her, and she was contacted by Hilda Muller, Bjorn Muller's much younger cousin.

Hilda:

> - Alicia White! Welcome back to Earth. Would you please dock with ISS Blue Haven, so we can clear you for re-entry to Earth?

Keila *hissing*:

> - Clear for re-entry? I am the daughter of John White. Let me pass.

Hilda:

> - Spare your bullshit, Alicia. I am the daughter of the late supreme Commander Mathias Muller. Comply with our rules or face the consequences.

Keila:

- Very well. Let's do it your way, but don't waste my time.

Hilda:

- Excellent. Dock with my ship ISS Blue Haven, and we will process you and your entourage for re-entry to Earth.

After speaking to Keila, who appeared to be Alicia, Hilda turned to the soldiers.

Hilda:

- I want you to be very thorough when examining this group. There is something amiss with someone disappearing for over a year and then reappearing without warning.

Hilda felt puzzled. It was likely that the *"Alicia White"* she had been talking to over the hologram generator was a Martian spy. But while a spy could use plastic surgery to change their physical appearance, they could not change their DNA so her advanced scanners would detect if *"Alicia White"* was a Martian spy and not the real deal.

Hilda wanted to detain Alicia, so she'd have plenty of time to verify her identity, but this was not a realistic solution for a high-ranking citizen. Instead, she opted to have an informal chat. Keila's ship docked with ISS Blue Haven, and Hilda lead her to a dining table set with delicious food and wines. Keila poured herself a glass of delicious red wine that tasted like paradise to her tastebuds.

Hilda:

- Welcome back to Earth. Alicia. I apologise for our need to verify the identities of yourself and your operatives.

Keila:

- Apology accepted, since you're providing me with this excellent food and wine.

Hilda:

- So, you appreciate our produce?

Keila:

- Of course. House Muller is famous for making the best food and drinks on Earth. Much better than the food I have eaten in the last year.

Hilda:

- Yes, speaking of the last year. Where have you been?

Keila:

- I have been hiding. After Bjorn's allegations against me, I felt no desire to go back to Earth. With Bjorn out of the picture, I want to return to Earth and live the kind of life I deserve.

Hilda:

- Speaking of Bjorn, was his allegations against you correct?

Keila:

- I'd rather not say. What amused me about this whole charade was how vital non-consensual sex became for Bjorn, who was known to be a rapist himself.

Hilda:

- I agree. The man was a creep. I hated how he sized me up with his eyes when I was younger.

- Whatever you did to him; I condone it.

- I just need to check a thing. I'll be right back.

Hilda went outside of the room and checked the reports on "Alicia" and her group. Both their facial features and their DNA matched the records. They couldn't have been killed and cloned as they only had been away for one year and it would take much longer to get clones aged to a mature age, even with accelerated cloning. They were also unlikely to have joined the Martian side as they were prominent Terrans and had nothing to gain from switching sides. Hilda to allow Alicia and her group re-entry to Earth. She walked back to the dining room.

Hilda:

- Alright, Alicia. You and your group have been granted re-entry to Earth.

Keila:

- Thank you, Hilda. And thanks again for the delicious food and wine.

Chapter 107 Pyramids and Estranged Fathers.

The next few weeks, Keila and her group travelled to the pyramids that Rangda had mentioned in Keila's vision. There was a total of four pyramids that needed to be activated at noontime in their respective time zones; these pyramids were spread across the globe ranging from Central America, the Pacific, Asia and Egypt. They needed to prepare themselves if they were to succeed, as they needed to find and activate all of the pyramids within one day for Rangda's plan to work.

To move quickly to the activation points in the different pyramids, they needed to excavate the sites. To be able to rush in and out from the excavation point was crucial as they only had a couple of hours between activating one pyramid until they needed to enable the next, and the pyramids were 1000's of kilometres apart. Fortunately, their spaceship had a high top-speed, so if they were able to move in and out of the pyramids quickly, there was no problem reaching the next pyramid on time.

The only issue was the last pyramid they needed to reach. The Cheops Pyramid, which lay in Rashidium, the capital of House Rashid's territory. Its activation point was not easily accessible. While they could excavate the other three pyramids using lasers, they knew that House Rashid would not allow them to excavate their gilded pyramid.

Keila decide that her only option was to activate the other three pyramids first and then blow up the walls exposing the activation switch in the Cheops Pyramid, using mono-directional explosives. Then they could enable the fourth pyramid, and open the portal of dimensions, before House Rashid soldiers had the time to stop them.

The night before the operation, Keila was finding sleeping difficult. It was hot and humid in her Central American excavation camp, and the mosquitos didn't make things better. Keila feared for her own life, and she worried about the fate of her home planet. B600 would impact in 1 month and 1 week, and she was unsure whether there would be enough time to divert the asteroid from crashing with Mars, which would lead to Martian genocide. Strangely she also felt guilt and pity towards John White, Alicia's father. While he was a monster who had caused the death and torment of countless Martians throughout the years, he was a loving father who missed his daughter.

Keila had received a lot of messages where he begged her to come home and see him. Many of these pictures also contained pictures from Alicia's childhood and different milestones of her life. Keila found the pictures moving; despite John White being a public figure he never stepped away from his freak daughter and stood by her despite public opinion. He could have hidden her apart, and yet he always stood by her side.

Keila received another email from John White, who thought that she was Alicia.

Dear Alicia.

I don't know why refuse to talk to me. Please answer, and we can work things out.

I will be in Rashidium in the next few days for a Terran Council meeting, so we can meet there, and you can tell me more about your new-found interest in pyramids.

/ Dad

Keila read the email. She was contemplating whether it would be a good idea to answer. Keila decided to use John's love for Alicia to make him do things for her. She answered his email.

Dear Father.

Thank you for wanting to be a part of my life again. I haven't answered your messages because I am upset that you didn't stand by me when Bjorn Muller ordered my arrest.

I am studying the pyramids because I am looking for an ancient forgotten technology that we can use to defeat the Martians. I am willing to share my findings if you are willing to divert B600 from impacting on Mars' surface.

/ Alicia.

A few minutes later, Keila received a response from John White.

Dear Alicia. I don't know how you know about B600, but I guess intelligence gathering is your specialty. I am unfortunately unable to help you with B600 collision diversion, as the destruction of Mars was a blood oath made during a Terran Council meeting. The only way to reverse the order is to issue another unanimous blood oath, repealing the order. This requires the mutual agreement of all Terran House leaders, not just me. I hope to see you in Egypt, nonetheless.

/ John

Keila read the message and felt hope. If she failed to initiate Rangda's portals she could try to use her Alicia White disguise to infiltrate the Terran Council meeting and "persuade" the Terran Council leadership to see things her way. Keila asked one of her Edenite operatives to pull out one of her teeth and replace it with a small container of extremely toxic nerve gas. Then she injected herself with an antidote that would grant her immunity to that poison for the next 96 hours.

Satisfied with her prospects of success Keila fell asleep.

Chapter 108: Keila Activates the Portals and is Arrested

The following day, Keila woke up, and when the time approached noon, she approached the centre of the Central American pyramid where she could perform the activation sequence. The sequence was hidden to the others, and only Keila could see the hidden switches that she needed to activate to enable the portals. Keila's ability to see the secret activation codes in the pyramids was due to her Zetan DNA sequences, and due to her psionic connection to Rangda.

After Keila had activated the Central American pyramid, she rushed to her spaceship, so she could fly to the next Pacific pyramid, in time to enable that one as well. She repeated this procedure with the Pacific and the Asian pyramids, and she reached the Cheops Pyramid in the outskirts of Rashidium. Keila and her Edenite operatives brought stun guns to knock out the guards and unidirectional explosive charges to destroy the wall that blocked their way to the activation chamber in the pyramid. She activated the last pyramid, but nothing seemed to happen.

Keila ran out from the pyramid and realised that she was surrounded by a large group of House Rashid security forces.

Security officer:

- Alicia White! You and your group are all under arrest for assaulting security guards and vandalising Rashid property. Surrender immediately!

For a second Keila thought of fighting back, but then she stood down. As long as they believed she was Alicia White, they wouldn't dare to do anything against her, so she would be better off biding her time.

Keila looked in disappointment at the pyramid from the backseat of the truck she was in. Whatever she had done hadn't worked, and no portal had opened! Keila was put under house arrest in a luxurious private suite in Rashid tower, while her associates were held in small holding cells in the basement.

Chapter 109: A Confusing Science Report.

Joachim Muller was reading a confusing science report in the vacuum tube transport that took him to Rashidium for the Terran Council meeting. According to the report, Earth's day had slowed down by 2 seconds in the last 24 hours. This did not make any sense to Joachim. If Earth's rotation had slowed down that much, this would lead to a lot of friction energy from the deceleration. This would cause earthquakes or a significant rise in the surface temperature. But there hadn't been reports of either. Furthermore, the scientist had claimed that the reason for Earth's slower rotation speed was connected to the vandalism Alicia White had performed on the Cheops pyramid the day before. These claims were absurd, and Joachim made a note to have that scientist fired when he got back from the Terran Council meeting.

Apart from that, Joachim found the meeting to be a waste of time. There wasn't much for them to discuss, but they had agreed to meet often and be more transparent, as they needed to stay united to avoid their enemies turning them against each other, as Keila Eisenstein had done before.

Chapter 110: Time for a Trial.

Keila was looking out through the window of the luxury apartment in Rashid Tower where she was under house arrest. Posing as Alicia White had perks and even as a prisoner, her life here was more luxurious than it had ever been. But Keila could not enjoy the luxury. Time was running out for her Martian comrades. Scientists on Mars had estimated that B600 needed to be deflected at least a month before colliding with Mars for it to pass on a safe distance from the planet. It was now one month and two days from a collision and time was running out. Her plan had failed, and Rangda had betrayed her. She had been staring at the damn Cheops Pyramid for the last day, and although it was beautiful, covered in gold reflecting the sunlight, it hadn't done anything, and she was stuck here unable to do anything to save her friends.

Everything changed when a few Rashid guards entered the apartment.
Guard:

- Time to freshen up and look decent, Alicia.

Keila:

- Why is that?

Guard:

- Because you are answering to the Terran Council for your crimes in an hour.

- Strip naked and have a decontaminating shower. We have provided fresh clothes for you here.

Keila thought of arguing back but decided against it. It was evident that the guards were suspicious towards her, but as long as they didn't detect the nerve gas she had hidden in a fake tooth, it did not matter. Keila showered and got dressed in her allocated clothes. It was a fancy dress, but their intention was obvious; she was their prisoner.

Keila followed the guards when they were leading her to the meeting room on the penthouse level of the tower. She was filled with a bittersweet feeling. While she could deliver justice to her enemies and save her people, she would most likely not get out of here alive.

Chapter 111: A Crucial Late Realisation.

Hilda Muller was having a relaxed afternoon as a guest in the Rashid tower. She was attending the Terran Council meeting in Rashidium. Hilda was important enough to participate, but she wasn't powerful enough to have much impact on the results. Hence, she saw these meetings as a few days to mingle, relax and have excellent food and drinks.

Hilda was enjoying the view from the Terrace of the 30th level of the Rashid Tower. It was a beautiful day, and Rashidium was as beautiful as ever. Built as an oasis in the desert of the Giza valley, the lush Residuum city shone like an emerald in the desert. It's most remarkable feature, was the great pyramids of Giza, restored to their former glory and covered in a thick layer of gold.

The three pyramids were covered in over 10,000 tons of gold, and the most remarkable feature was how the gold was acquired. A century earlier, House Rashid scientists had discovered a medium-sized rogue meteor that was made of gold. This was because it was created by a supernova explosion and it had been floating around the galaxy for eons before entering the solar system. House Rashid scientist had landed the golden rock on Earth without causing an impact, which had been a great engineering feat. Rather than putting this massive amount of gold in circulation causing the gold prices to drop, they had opted to gild the pyramids, creating one of the great wonders of the future world. Hilda turned around, and Markus White, an attractive bachelor, greeted her. He was visiting Rashidium under similar circumstances as Hilda.

Markus:

- So, this is where the party is?

Hilda:

- I guess the party just got started.
- Did you come out to marvel at the pyramids?

Markus:

- Yes... I am marvelling at the pyramids among other things.

Hilda:

- You flirt! I met your cousin Alicia, the other day.

Markus:

- Any claw marks or scratches from your encounter?

Hilda:

- No, she was acting pretty civilised. We had some beef steak and some wine.

Markus:

- You mean that you had some steak and wine, and she was eating raw meat and drinking blood?

Hilda:

- No of course not. Why would she act like that? She was quite thirsty and had several glasses. I guess that's what a long time in space do to you.

Markus:

- That's impossible. Alicia doesn't drink alcohol!

Hilda:

- Well, she did when I met her. I'll show you the security feed, so you can see for yourself.

Markus looked at the video from the security cameras and he froze for a moment. Not only did Alicia taste the wine but she drank quite a lot of it. Markus:

- Where is Alicia now?

Hilda:

- She is answering to the leadership for her vandalism of the pyramids.

Markus:

- Come with me at once and bring some guards. We need to stop her now!

Hilda:

- I don't understand?

Markus:

- We are dealing with an imposter! The real Alicia White has a condition that makes alcohol deadly to her.

- Quick, gather some guards and rush to the meeting room. We must catch her before it is too late!

Having said this, they rushed to gather a few guards and then took the lift to the Penthouse level of Rashid Tower where Keila posing as Alicia was put on trial by the Terran Council leaders.

Chapter 112: Keila kills the Terran Council Leaders and Redirects B600 to Crash into the Sun.

Keila was listening to Ibrahim Rashid, who gave a lengthy statement on how priceless the pyramids were and the gravity of her crime. She knew this was charade so that he could make more money in compensation from House White for letting her go. But all of this was irrelevant. She hadn't come here to get involved in Terran Council politics; she had come here to end them and save her home planet from destruction. Yet, she felt fear. Keila knew if she did what she had to do; she would not get out of here alive. She didn't want to die, she wanted to live on Eden with Metatron and her daughter. But if Keila didn't act, her inactivity would cause the death of 4 billion people, and she would never be able to live with that knowledge.

Keila heard the lift beeping in the lobby, and she saw Hilda Muller accompanied by several guards moving towards her. This forced her to act. She jumped up to Ibrahim Rashid and pushed his hand on a handprint scanner. She activated the blast doors and sealed off the room before the guards got in.

John White yelled out:

- Alicia! What on Earth are you doing?!

Keila pulled out the fake tooth and released the very toxic nerve gas in the room.

Keila:

- I am not Alicia.

The nerve gas paralysed the Terran Council leaders. They were filled with fear as Keila deactivated the Zetan Outer Layer external DNA modifier and her appearance reverted to her real looks. Keila pressed the broadcast button so that all of Earth would be able to see what happened this day. Keila thought of giving a speech to the camera, but there was no time for such nonsense, she needed to save Mars and time was running out. She dragged the council members one by one to the blood oath machine and dropped some of their blood on the device. Eventually, they had all had their blood dropped on the device, and the command prompt was unlocked. Keila wrote:

Redirect B600 to collide with the Sun, instead of impacting with Mars. Then destroy the steering mechanism on the fusion thrusters as this is a final, irreversible order.

Unfortunately, the crew was currently 30 light minutes away, so it would take her at least an hour before she knew if they had carried out the order or not. Keila made one last effort before the guards got through the blast doors. She needed to make sure that the Terran Council leaders were not revived. She found a massive metal sculpture and started bashing in their heads. When she was done, she was covered in blood and brain matter.

Keila tried contacting Rangda to be possessed by her as a last-ditch attempt of getting out Rashidium alive. Rangda didn't respond. Instead, Keila went to the window, found a comfortable chair, and marvelled at the sun setting behind the gilded pyramids.

Chapter 113: The Portal Opens; Rangda and the Xenos Swarm in and Capture Keila.

As the sun was about to set behind the pyramids, Keila was stunned by intense blue light as the portal to the Divine Dimension opened. Out of the portal came a swarm of Xenos lead by Rangda. The House Rashid security forces were taken by surprise when the Xenos appeared, and most of them got slaughtered when the wave of Xenos came rushing towards Rashid towers. The Xenos was unstoppable for the Rashid defenders as they had stolen ballistic energy absorbers from the Zetan armouries in the Divine Dimension and because they had a top running speed of 100 kilometres an hour which was faster than any of the Rashid defenders on foot could match. The main reason, however, was that Rashid's was caught off guard and only had police and light units patrolling the streets.

Keila heard the gunfire, sirens and screaming approaching her position and she felt hopeful. Rangda had kept her promise and had come to save her. Keila could see how the Xenos were scaling the building with immense speed. The Xenos were fearsome looking, but one of them stood out from the others. Keila figured that, the odd looking one must be Rangda.

Rangda appeared in front of her on the other side of the window. The window was made of very thick fortified glass, but Rangda destroyed it by letting out a high-pitched shriek that shattered the glass

Keila:

- Rangda! You came to save me?

Rangda:

- I came, yes. But not to save you. You are my prisoner!

Keila:

- No! I will fight you then.

Rangda:

- No, you won't.

Rangda blasted Keila with a psionic blast, and Keila fell unconscious. Rangda lifted Keila over her shoulder and made one of her Xeno Warriors jump out of the window with her on the back as it was quicker to fall down than climbing down again. Just before impacting the ground, Rangda with Keila on her back jumped off the Xeno warrior with such force that it neutralised the terminal free-fall velocity she had, and she landed safely, while the Xeno soldier was splattered and killed when he hit the ground.

Rangda handed over Keila to one of her fastest Xeno runners, and she rode another Xeno back to the portal as quickly as possible. Rangda knew that the humans would respond with aircraft and heavy weaponry and she did not want to be stuck on Earth when that happened. Rangda brought Keila to the edge of the portal and gave out a loud shriek, to command her Xeno forces to retreat. She lifted Keila over her shoulder and went back to the Divine Dimension. Shortly, afterwards Rashid security forces arrived in force, carpet bombing the Xenos, and killing the aliens who had been too preoccupied in frenzied eating to follow Rangda's retreat order.

Chapter 114 B600 directed into the sun

Captain Melissa Schiller watched as B600 changed course, and she had to change her own ship's course to avoid getting hit. She called in her second in command, Commander Michael Berndt.

Melissa:

- Michael! Why is the asteroid changing course?

Michael:

- The High Council must have ordered them to change the course. Maybe the Martians agreed to peace.

- Of course, there was going to be a solution, the council would never massacre four billion people.

Melissa:

- Then why didn't Joachim tell me?

Michael:

- Why do you think the leader of the Terran Council would run every decision with every single captain in the space navy?

- Unless the rumours are true...

Melissa:

- What rumours? I am the captain of this ship. I command you to reverse B600 to a collision course with Mars.

Michael:

- Very well this makes it easy for me.

- Captain Schiller, you are under arrest for the murder of Mathias Muller and for conspiring to mass-murder innocent civilians. Soldiers arrest her.

Melissa:

- You don't have the authority to arrest me!

Michael Berndt:

- I have the loyalty of my men. I will figure out the rest later.

Melissa was screaming as she got locked up, but it mattered little. Her involvement in the genocidal plan was foiled, and a few months later B600 crashed into the Sun, ceasing to be a threat.

Please read the ending in the Divine Finalisation!

Don't miss out!

Visit the website below and you can sign up to receive emails whenever Martin Lundqvist publishes a new book. There's no charge and no obligation.

https://books2read.com/r/B-A-QIOG-TVZT

BOOKS 2 READ

Connecting independent readers to independent writers.

Did you love *The Divine Sedition*? Then you should read *The Divine Dissimulation*[1] by Martin Lundqvist!

[2]

When God dies, A villain takes his place!

In the distant future, the wealthy villain Abraham Goldstein funds a top-secret project to travel to heaven and meet God. Upon reaching heaven, he finds out that God is dead. He also finds the technology necessary to take gods place and become a god in the eyes of men.

Many years later Abraham and his group of angels, genetically engineered super soldiers, rule Eden; an artificial world simulating the Holy Land during the Bronze Age. They rule with terror and fear following the ancient laws. One day, an accident turns Abraham's closest angel Lucifer against him, an event that plants the seed of Abraham's destruction.

Meanwhile, an ancient force is conspiring in the background to make its return to our world.

Read more at martinlundqvist.com.

---

1. https://books2read.com/u/mqZE5e

2. https://books2read.com/u/mqZE5e